D1502885

THE

A

DANA

HAIRCUTTER

NOVEL

THOMPSON

Skyhorse Publishing

Skyhorse Publishing books may be purchased in bulk at special discounts for sales promotion, corporate gifts, fund-raising, or educational purposes. Special editions can also be created to specifications. For details, contact the Special Sales Department, Skyhorse Publishing, 307 West 36th Street, 11th Floor, New York, NY 10018 or info@skyhorsepublishing.com.

Skyhorse® and Skyhorse Publishing® are registered trademarks of Skyhorse Publishing, Inc.®, a Delaware corporation.

Visit our website at www.skyhorsepublishing.com.

10 9 8 7 6 5 4 3 2 1

Library of Congress Cataloging-in-Publication Data is available on file.

Cover design by Erin Seaward-Hiatt

Print ISBN: 978-1-5107-2580-5
Ebook ISBN: 978-1-5107-2582-9

Printed in the United States of America

THE

HAIRCUTTER

For Anna-Patrick

CHAPTER ONE

THE WOLF JOB

The day after I murdered Jenny, I was standing in the kitchen crying with a jug of milk hooked around my finger—I was thinking, *Oh god, here I am just a regular human wanting a glass of milk even though I stabbed a living thing to death just yesterday!* My father, Father John, was kicked back in his La-Z-Boy in the den. I could see the tips of his cowboy boots bobbing in the doorway to the kitchen. I thought, *Shh!* I thought, *Don't let him hear you cry!* I thought, *Just pour the milk!* It landed like a virgin laughing and the glass filled like a virgin relaxing. I watched with my mouth messed up and quivering like it would slide a shit out.

Then, I flinched so hard the glass flipped off the table. Father John's face was snarling at me where his boots had been. A bubble grew from my nostril and popped—I swatted at it.

My brother Darron walked in, "Whoa, don't cry over spilled milk!"

I said, "WHAT JUST HAPPENED?!"

The virgin spread its legs on the plastic floral floor.

My father added crying to the fact that I was thirty and still living at home, and he multiplied it by the bloodstain I'd made on the welcome mat yesterday. His total was to tell me to pack my stuff. He took me to the bus station with a toothbrush in his hand and nothing else.

We got on a bus that took us three days and two nights from Ten Sleep, Wyoming, to New York City. Our seat had a spring poking out of a slash in the vinyl between us, which we picked by choice. If there had been a glass under the seat that was half-drank or half-poured, and if the driver had turned around to ask us if it was half empty or half full, I would've gotten off the bus to wait for a different driver, while Father John would've ignored the whole thing cause it didn't have anything to do with scrap metal or favors. Which is all pretty useless to poke at if it's a wolf playing poker saying, "the better to understand your father with, my dear," when this dear doesn't *do* understanding, and definitely doesn't do touching knees.

Father John read billboards the whole way, cross-armed and picking his teeth. He called my mother from a gas station pay phone, and I'll never know what he said. The miniature bus bathroom leaked a floral mist when people went in and out of it, and as a coincidence I found a magazine on gardening crumpled at my feet. We all swayed as customers on a coach not knowing the route but knowing damn well where we were getting off. A malnourished lady with a coon hat on her son talked nonstop to her aisle neighbor who was a good-listener fat lady with a grey mustache, so I was glad Father John and I could just read and pretend it was too loud for us to be able to talk as well, not that we *would've* talked if able—we'd have just found something to curse at under our breaths as if suddenly mad at it.

We rolled through seven states without so much as "check that pretty pasture" or "what state are we in." The only thing I said was "Whoa!" if I suddenly thought of Jenny while reading my flower magazine, which felt like going from standing at a kitchen window watching a bunny hop the backyard to standing at a kitchen window watching a hopping bunny get squashed by a slaughtered body falling on it. The magazine mocked me rightly, telling about how life was gladiolus before the murder and how now, after the murder, it's gladiolus for everyone but me.

The lady with a coon hat on her son talked about her old boss Larry firing her, "I've been at that diner since the last two Christmases. I says to him, *You're a son-of-a-meatball, I got a son at home.* I says, *You gonna fire me from the bowlin' team too?* I says, *Cause I quit.* And I went and I got his lucky pen outta his pocket on his shirt, and I dumped the free candy dish into my purse, and I bumped the front door with my ass and it went flyin', and I says to him, *Your lucky pen just went missin',* and I held it up. And I told the first person in the parkin' lot, *You know what? I'm free,*" and she kept her mouth in the shape of that "free" with her eyes hooked on her aisle neighbor and held it while switching from stroking her son's coon tail to scratching his mosquito bite. Her son spent the drive with food smears on his face, walking the aisle hunting for a certain-someone-interesting, and found it interesting that there was a certain someone in everyone he saw.

"What's *your* name?"

He cast spells with a wand made out of duct tape and said there's a live snake in it. "I taped eem up." He dipped it into our seat spring to "recharge eem" a couple times and I saw his teeth went so straight out of his face they could've been a shelf for Larry's lucky pen if the president ever came to their house. I don't do kids, but I would've poked his belly had I not told him to go away. In the mornings, his "mumma" woke up coughing till all the other smokers joined in and made like dogs barking that they wanna go outside to smoke. I watched him introduce his hat to a roadkilled muskrat on the side of a five-lane highway. I watched him suck his mumma's thumb instead of his own. I watched him flex his baby biceps so hard he grunted and his face shook—a trick he did for semi drivers when they coasted by the bus on their cloth, dick-scented benches, waving nicely at him like we're one happy world. His coon tail lifted high when he ran to his grandma's car in Indiana, and his mom's ponytail was the size of a string of drool as she walked casually to the car in white pumps.

The bus went silent without them. Like our senses had truly been sucked up by that wand and were now riding taped up with a snake in the back of that car to Coony's next chapter. Lady's mustachioed aisle neighbor was like a lone house left standing after a twister. She was all we had left. She sat still for a while in her XL shirt with a picture of a rock 'n' roll rooster on it, until she felt miscast as the new star of the show and got out a ball of yarn—her exit. Outside it started raining grey like a stage curtain closing the show. Her tinkering hands ticked the needles around skillfully—fine, we get it—that's a wrap, folks. I looked in my green Velcro wallet for something to do, but besides car wash tokens and a bank card, I only had paper scraps and the little pencil that fit in there. Father John was sleeping but facing me. I couldn't make my lists in front of him because he always tore them up—once he even grabbed one out of my hands and ate it. Truth was, I wanted to spend that ride asking him questions about what the hell's going on, but I couldn't ask questions because he always tore those up too and never once thought to eat one. I know my own father, thanks very much, and what's your return policy like?

We pulled up to "the city" in the late afternoon. I looked at my father and he was lolling his head snoring in a way that whispered "boo" on the exhale and got scared on the in.

"Wake up," I said, "It's your big city."

I pulled down a window and stuck my hand out. New York City was crisp in weather, the buildings were sharp in their cluster, each sharp building letting you know just how many damn buildings there were. My father hacked himself to attention and got his arms re-crossed, then let loose one last "boo" through the weave of his Wranglers.

When I was twenty, I dropped out of Parts Management training at a tire factory in Bozeman, Montana. It was a good job that I gave up because I didn't like the big city and wanted my simple life back home in the town of Ten Sleep. Father John never forgave me, and brought it up every time New York came on TV. He'd turn to me and pretend to watch my face for signs of fear. "Bozeman's not a city," he'd say. Ten years later, we were here. It was fate, or it was my punishment, or it was just what it was.

We got off the bus at Port Authority Bus Terminal and found the subway, where people were sitting so close to each other they touched. Where people ate apologetically bringing their mouths to their food instead of the food to their mouths. Where people stared at each other and then looked up at advertisements when they were caught. One man had a normal man's body, including trousers and a tie, but his head/face was the size of a boulder and it was bubbly like his brain had boiled. *And he was smiling.* I called him Planet Head like he's here observing Earth. Father John was busy relating to a pole like it was a pussy little glass of champagne he was being forced to hold. Planet Head was sitting between two people who were curving away from him like leaves on either side of a (cat-chewed) tulip. And across from him was a woman sleeping with her mouth open and there was probably a NASA hidden camera in her throat recording him. I thought, "He's gonna stab us all." After that, I just kept my eyes on Father John's toothbrush till he took it from his shirt pocket and put it in his jeans so I couldn't see. I didn't ask where we were going on the subway. I didn't say "wow" when, at one of the stops, he got out to buy a Coke from a vending machine and got back in before the doors dinged shut. That was him showing a last sample of what he wanted me to be.

He'd said at a midnight McDonald's stop in Ohio, "You ain't a man."

He said it to the orange pop coming up my straw.

I looked at my reflection in the window and snarled at all the greasy fingerprints on the glass, then realized Father John might've thought I was snarling at myself, so I switched to pretending that my hamburger was "especially good for some reason."

He said, "You killed Jenny, you fuckin' retard." He said, "What're you now, thirty-five?"

"I'm thirty."

"Well you're damned weird and we both know it," he said. "That's why we got you that little fridge for your room is so you'd stay up there is what!"

We'd never had such a father/son moment before, let alone one in a restaurant facing each other. Lady and Little Boy Coon Hat were gone, so we were bare-all. Father John kept having to lift his cowboy hat off his head so he wouldn't have to let *communicating* be the main thing he was doing, and I tried to keep it casual—nodding, whistling, pointing a finger, going, "Oh hey, what about Darron? Why's he ain't along for the trip?"

He said, "Darron's got a successful hobby. He's his own thing."

My brother Darron lived at home too, and his successful hobby was dancing at the Blue Bear Saloon. Like the moon and stars, he showed up every single night and shined for anyone who looked. He wore all black and danced hours on the rambling wooden dance floor like he got hit by a car once and never told anyone. I have no idea why he did it. There weren't even other people dancing.

At the Times Square station there was an escalator that my father and I both knew was five times longer than the puny one at the mall, but we just stepped on and were transported five times farther then we'd ever been transported before. I farted hard to show how I won't buy into being impressed.

And I'd farted too soon: when I saw Times Square, I started shaking. My brain started boiling and my head/face grew to the size of a child who's hugging its knees in fright. More like Times Scare. Or, hell: Scare Time. Where's the hidden camera? People in Japan zoomed in on a Wyo cowboy and his large, fat son.

My father shouted, "Noisiest bullfuck I ever seen!"

I shouted, "Huh?"

He walked us to a bald spot in the crowd, shoving crowd members out of his way, "I said we're throwin' you to the wolves, you heard me!"

A cop on a horse galloped past with a beat stick.

I shouted, "Whoa!"

Then it was my turn to speak more, and it paralyzed me dumb. All the colors of skin in the world rushed past my planted mass on their way to be quicker than me. All the billboards rearranged their letters to spell *Say Something!*

I chose, "It *is* noisy, you're right, and there's *horses*—hey, who *knew?*"

He shouted, "Alright, I'm goin'," and left.

I started following him but did the old Hollywood stop after two steps. You know. It was then that I understood what the whole bus ride really meant.

Times Square was a blur except for the plaid shirt on Father John's back as it walked away. I'd gotten that shirt at Salvation Army but it was too small for me, so I'd left it draped on the arm of his La-Z-Boy like whispering "you can have this" into a Dixie cup up in my room. Little did I know, that plaid would be stained on my brain one day. When I look back on watching it walk away, I always say in my head, "Movie moment alert," as a tic before switching to a better thought. Why wonder why the sky is blue if you can just not look up? Coughing on tears, I watched my father cut through the crowded crowd. My heart throbbed eight times, going, "MOvie moment alert," "MOvie moment alert," "MOvie moment alert," "MOvie moment alert," "MOvie moment alert," "MOvie moment alert," "MOvie moment alert," "MOvie moment alert," before he sunk back down into the rock veins of New York City.

That was in '93. In the following eight years I ate every single meal alone, unless you count eating near people at restaurants or at baseball games. Once, I ate on the subway next to someone who was eating chicken wings and dropping the bones on the floor, and many times I ate off snack tables at open-to-the-public events; I also ate in parks next to family picnics.

I'm cutting to the wolf job now as I should the chase.

It was the year 2000—ring-a-ding-ding. I worked alone in the basement of a law office—I ran a bunch of suction tubes—so after work I'd be happy to be back worming through the streets of the Big Apple. I'd either cut hair on my hours off, or I'd go to bookstores. I've been into "Lit" since I learned that it's something you can memorize and be good at. I do lists of who wrote what and when they wrote it. I like to get recommendations and then tell if I've already heard of the recommendation and then add what else the author wrote and when they wrote it.

So it was: a cold summer day while I walked into a south-bound wind on Broadway Street. Being like the Flatiron building, my large body divided the wind. People flicked their eyes at me when I passed them, but hey, I was flicking mine too. I strode into Biggest Browse Bookstore, fanning my jean jacket and soaking my Met's T-shirt in sweat. I wheezed and sucked in my stomach to get around the shoppers that crowd the bestseller tables. I saw one of the employees shelving books in Horror and I went to talk to him—it was the artistic boy Finn (a name you could pin without hesitation to your grandma's sweater).

Tall, thin, red-cheeked Finn said, "Do you want to drive a wolf cross-country?"

The Haircutter picked food out of a molar and flicked it.

Finn said, "I do art installing for this gallery owner who has a wolf right now because one of his artists is doing an art project with it."

"Huh? A *what?*"

"A wolf. They got it from someone's fucked-up cousin in Wyoming who trapped this wolf and had fifteen albino cats too, and a *boa constrictor*—really fucked up—I saw him and he's *cross-eyed* by the way—so they convinced him to deliver all the animals to New York for five grand cause this gallery owner loves animals and always rescues them, but anyway the other day they were like what do we do with this wolf now that the show's had its run? And I was like, I know a guy from Wyoming, I'll ask him if he wants to drive it back out there to release it where it's from."

"How do you know I'm from there?" The Haircutter said.

"What? You're H.C. from Wyoming," Finn said, then he got out a cell and said, "Oh, I just got a cell."

"Huh!" The Haircutter said, and Finn clipped it back to his belt, saying, "Even though I can't afford it."

These employees are my friends, The Haircutter realized, adjusting his stance, crossing his arms, smiling so hard that giggles slipped out like there was a giggling little girl skipping rope with his intestines.

"His pack's probably somewhere in the Bighorn Mountains—you gotta help him get back, man. Otherwise it's just some rescue center where he's fenced in," Finn said. "It's weird but it's easy. The guy's name is Mr. Christmas and he's really eccentric, but trust me I do shit for him all the time and he always pays as soon as the job's done. And he's oil money rich, right, dead parents, so don't worry about anything—trust me, he does weirder shit than this and he won't even remember it, he's got so much going on."

Finn climbed an old wooden ladder and shelved a copy of *Deadly Scares and Their Meaning*.

A woman with a long braid and a body like a gourd looked up at him and said, "Excuse me, where's the restroom?"

Finn said, "There's no drinks allowed," pointing to her coffee. "It's on the second floor in Children's."

"I just wanted to browse with a coffee," she said and walked away.

"I know," he called after her.

He came down off the ladder, "But I told him about you and he trusted you right away, so he's got you, right, he's got your back—you're in if you wanna be in. So don't fuck it up for me either, cause this guy's the best contact to have. But I trust you—I can tell you're honest no matter what you seem like. I'm a people person—I like hooking people up. I like everybody so don't worry, even though I'm twenty-one I can tell what's going on, I went to Oberlin, but you probably don't even know what that means.

From what I understand, it'd basically be about you just driving the wolf in the art haul van and then opening the hatch when you get out to the mountains—really easy, and I'm sure he'd pay you at least a grand. *I* would do it, but I'm afraid of dogs."

The Haircutter was dry heaving. He unbuckled his belt a notch.

Finn said, "He was like, does your friend wanna drive my wolf out there for cash when we're done with it? I was like, I'll ask him and let you know."

Why had it never occurred to me before?

The Haircutter said, "It just hit me I realized I could see someone there. Someone I sort of left behind," saying more about his personal life than he'd said in the past eight years.

"That's what I'm talking about. Hooking people up," Finn said.

"And plus, I'll show up in front of my father with a wolf."

"Yes, that's what I mean. He'll be like, Whoa, he totally surpassed my expectations," Finn said.

We were two scientists falling calmly into a black hole sharing a cigar as I said, "A quick wolf job. I'll tell him: I don't have much time . . . I'm just in town for a quick . . ."

In an alley on 135th and 5th, Leslie Christmas lifted his left arm and cocked a pearl-handled pistol in its hand. He fired eight holes into the haul of a moving truck. He walked around to the other side of it—repeated the act while howling. In an art gallery on 20th and 10th, Charlie Quick, Christmas's right-hand man, ran a palmful of wolf slobber through his light, European-grade hair—a cigarette in his lips, a caged wolf behind him—as he told a reporter on speaker phone, "The wolf was rescued from an *abusive domesticated* situation and will be returned to its natural habitat as soon as we're done with it!" In the basement of a law office on Broadway and Reade, The Haircutter's suction tubes were at rest as ten inanimate objects. On 37th and 6th, his fitted mattress sheet sat tinted dark where his farts go, and on Broadway and 12th Street, The Haircutter accepted the strange and prestigious offer of driving a wolf cross-country to release it in the wild, to parade the wolf in front of his father and "see someone" that he'd "left behind."

The day of the wolf job, I smiled at myself in my bachelor-dirty bathroom mirror. I had on my good outfit—my collared shirt with the ducks flying on it and my good forest green belt. I got out a frying pan for breakfast and did up everything I had left in the fridge. I ate at the table where I'd laid out the US map and the set of truck keys I'd picked up from Finn at Biggest. He'd also made me sign a legal document promising I'd drop the wolf where I said, and that I'd drive the speed limit and accept all responsibilities. I picked up a pen and put a big X on Wyoming with my chest puffed out. Then I struggled to fold the map up (which I did every time after that till I lit it on fire in a dirt lot in Ohio and it folded itself). I hooked my jean jacket around my finger and slung it over my shoulder, I picked up my suitcase of clean clothes, and left to do the wolf job! Happy as an exclamation point, innocent as a space .

On 20th and 10th, I approached a mini semi-trailer truck with a long whistle sliding out of my teeth. The cab part was sun-faded red and the haul was white with bullet holes shot into it so the wolf could breathe. I used the keys on the gigantic driver's-side door and hoisted myself in. The first thing I saw was a note on the passenger's seat. It wasn't ripped out of something; it was a clean sheet of paper with a name at the top in gold: *Leslie Christmas*. And there was a typewritten message for me:

Mr. H.C.,

I am Charlie Quick, the first assistant to Mr. Christmas. I will contact you at a later date to make his acquaintance.

There is a per diem in the glove box along with vehicle registration. There is a peephole drilled in the wall above the back bench. Remove the peg stopping it and use the funnel found in the food bag behind the passenger's seat to funnel food through to the wolf. You are not responsible for cleanup. To release the wolf, press the yellow button with the back-door symbol on it. Under this letter you'll find an issue of *Wolf Fancy*. Read it to find where best to deposit the wolf so that he might find his pact again. The truck should be returned to the neighborhood in which you found it and the keys should be discretely left under the floor mat.

Mr. Christmas wants you to know that the wolf was used in an art piece that commented on the struggle between the adult ego state and the child ego state.

Thank you for a swift delivery.

Charlie Quick

Of course I crawled right in back with the note still in my hand and unstopped the peephole and stopped it right back up again when I saw a werewolf slurp up his long phallic tongue and look at me.

—

It took me a good hour to figure out how to drive the machine and in retrospect the entire scheme was highly dangerous for everyone involved. But since I didn't know that at the time, I just enjoyed it.

I felt on top of the world. I thought, *What an easy way to feel on top of the world!*—ride in a tall truck looking through a tall windshield, bowling down the freeway on an endless lane. I rolled down the windows and turned the radio up and stopped to get road snacks. I used the per diem on postcards of the states I liked. I howled and waited to hear if the wolf howled back. I sang along to songs in the low operatic voice I hadn't used since high school choir. I heard stories on the radio at night that brought me to tears, and I cried freely cause it was dark out. I masturbated freely cause it was dark out. I slept at motels and I slept at gas stations on the back bench with the peephole over my head.

One night I took out the peg (it was a cork with a red wine stain on the bottom) and looked in on the wolf with a flashlight. He scrambled up, his claws slipping on the metal floor. His prey-stained teeth snapped at the rod of light that shone dust and wolf hairs curlicuing as he advanced. He licked the peephole and whimpered. His whimpering seemed to ask, "Why are you doing this to me?" He sounded like he had milk stuck in his throat. It was all so human—I funneled a pinch of gummy bears into the hole so he'd think it was weird, so he'd (hopefully) figure it was a sign I knew he was trying to talk. Later I used the flashlight to fart and read *Wolf Fancy* like a teenage boy. I learned that my wolf was an "Arctic Tundra Grey" according to his extra-large size, but there was no information in the mag on finding pacts, unfortunately. All the wolf did was pace by that peephole the whole trip. A pact with hunger is all he had.

Did I think about jostling the wolf? Of course I thought about jostling the wolf. I winced at every bump in the road. I wished that Mr. Christmas had given him a tranquilizer for the trip. The least he did was give him a three-sided wooden crate to sleep in, the opening of which faced the front of the truck. So through the peephole I could see him curled up pouting in there, the blanket provided ripped to shreds and pushed in frustration with, I'm guessing his snout, into a corner of the haul. It was a wolf. A live, pungent wolf.

One day I had a misfortune when I paid for gas at a Common Cents and it slipped that I had a wolf in back.

The Haircutter slid a hundred-dollar bill across the counter. "Red-and-white semi on pump four. The one with the wolf in back," he said, chuckling.

The male gas station attendant, wearing rose-colored glasses like some sort of pervert, took the bill and put it through the necessary hoops and ladders.

"This seems like a nice town, what I've seen of it," The Haircutter said, pocketing his change and keeping his hand there to jingle it.

"Got a lot of goons running through here," the attendant said, and he sat back down on his stool and looked at a small TV on the counter. It was tuned to a show in a courtroom.

The Haircutter stuck his head over the counter and looked, "Ooh! What's the verdict?"

The attendant spun his toothpick around in his mouth.

The Haircutter wiped his brow and did a long whistle. "Yeah, I'm haulin' a wolf," he said.

The attendant kept his head pointed at the TV, but his eyes flicked to H.C.

"I said I've got a wolf in back."

The attendant yanked his face in toward his neck.

The Haircutter folded his arms and scuffed his shoe and it made a high *pip!* sound. He drew some snot into his throat and swallowed it. He said, "I'm, ah. I'm drivin' it from Manhattan over in New York. It's for an art dealer over there who's got this art wolf he wanted me to release in the wild. We're doin' it all under the radar since it's not exactly legal, so."

The attendant took his toothpick out of his mouth. "Well is that right," he said. "Hell, I'd like to see it to believe it."

"You're welcome to, actually! There's a peephole."

The attendant snarled and pronounced, "A peephole?"

The Haircutter slapped the counter. "Come on. Come, I'll show you."

The attendant dazzled a grin.

I was like, "You just remove this peg here. Pardon the mess. Call it a road trip. Hey, and watch the smell. I recommend you don't put your nose up to the hole."

The attendant said, "Well I'll be fucked. That's a wolf."

"Told you!" I screamed, delighted.

I'd never had a big responsibility like that, and something so fun. I fondled the steering wheel and said to the attendant, "And see I don't know if this is Italian leather or what, but I've only seen somethin' this big used for drivin' a boat."

And he said, "What else?"

I said, "Well, he's got a food bag there if you wanna funnel some feed in and watch him wolf it down." I said, "Hell, they thought of everything." And that's when I said, "Here!" and popped the glove compartment. I waved the thousand-dollar per diem in the attendant's face like I'd just won it as a prize for being dumber than a box of rocks. I said, "Cold hard cash." He grabbed it faster than you can say *What just happened?*

"Now let me tell you something about laws," he said. "It's illegal to transport a wolf in the way you're doing. And it's cruelty to animals on top. So I'm actually gonna keep this cash and you're gonna get the hell outta my station or I'm calling the cops."

I said, "Well *fuck you!*" It was the first time I'd ever told someone that.

He got out and walked back up to his place of work, stuffing my wad in his wallet and spitting before he opened the door. Didn't look back at me once. I just sat there like, *Whoa!*

I replaced the peg in the peephole and grunted on back to the driver's seat. I drove on, my hair whipping in the wind. That wasn't the point—money. The point wasn't even that my father thought I wasn't a man and now through my very own contacts I was showing up after eight years of estrangement for a quick wolf job. The point was: the woman I'd left behind.

May I introduce: Carol Mary Mathers. I was slicing down the road towards her. I kept having to stop to sit on toilets because my stomach held that old steel butterfly that was ripping up my guts. I honked into john bowls across America. The last time I'd seen her was eight years before when I'd looked up from Jenny's twitching body and Carol was gone.

When I lived in Ten Sleep I started going every night to watch Darron dance at the Blue Bear Saloon because Carol worked there. She was a bartender, so I could sit and talk to her. I tipped her in car wash tokens and she waved at me with her fingers grouped like batting lashes. She was in college at the time studying Lit, so we discussed whatever she'd learned that week, and I liked it very much. And when I started falling in love with her, whenever I went to Blue Bear was the only time I felt calm. Otherwise when I wasn't "with" her, I'd have that steel butterfly nonstop and I'd have to go shit all the time, cursing her for the cause. I couldn't eat for the first time in my life. She probably thought I was a monster fatass since all I'd do is come in there and order up a bunch of food cause I was starving and, like I said, finally calm cause my "girl" was right there. And in case you're thinking I was delusional, she liked me back.

The Haircutter's puffy white sneaker pressed pedal-forth on the old open road. The Haircutter drank coffee and smacked his lips. Sun broke yolk on the horizon. Grassy plains bordering the black strip before him laid memories of Ten Sleep out to view.

Ten Sleep got its name because it took ten sleeps to get there from an Indian camp. Now all Ten Sleep has left of Indian culture is hunting. Everyone's got elk or deer in the freezer and everyone's got guns—even one strapped to the foyer wall in case a hoodlum rings the bell (even though a common belief in Wyoming is that the wind keeps the riffraff out). In Wyo, men leave bars and families leave restaurants walking tipped back at a slant because the wind pushed them to walk that way over time. Talk about a weather system.

I left behind a family of three: my mother, my father, and my brother Darron.

Darron's my really nice younger brother, who's only ever been good to me. The only thing he ever did wrong was keep a dead baby bird in a shoebox under his bed because he wanted to watch it decompose. He's always had the same unisex haircut and a rat-like quality to his face, which matched the rattail he's had his whole life at the nape of his straight neck. My mother used to say, "Yank his till!" all the time for me to yank his tail if she wanted to tease him but couldn't reach. Before entering nicer places, he always tucked it in his collar. It was a family member, as well as a family member's member.

My mother is "Just Plain Patty," who's got a stack of Romances on the back wall in the basement so she can lick her fat finger and trace down the line till, "Ooh *Larrisa's Crystals!* It's been a while since I've done that one," followed by her wet, barking coughs which to me is a comfort sound. She looks like her shoulder bones were just plain removed—they point to where the wall meets the floor. Her face is so stretched out from frowning and being old it ripples when she dries her hair. She's always worn a blanket as a shawl, and the fringes will dip into your Campbell's when she's bending around the kitchen and she'll say, "Gol dang it!" and suck it off. She drives a van called Fair Fare, and she's driven that van for thirty years servicing drunks from 7:00 p.m. to 4:00 a.m. who pay her whatever they think is a fair fare.

And my father, we for some forgotten reason have always called Father John even though he makes a point to litter something out of the car if he passes a church. He has a jaw that looks made by two swings of an ax, and he wears a tan cowboy hat that I've never touched. Growing up, it was the only thing in the house that was kept clean. He has a heartthrob quality that looks like he's squinting in the sun. Him and I have the same long-lashed girly eyes that my mother always couldn't shut the hell up about. ("My Baby Blue Eyeses!") She's real in love with him, even on the shy side about it. At the family dinner table he'd tell us what to fix about ourselves, and my mother would nod and say, "Father John knows. Trust eem."

I left behind my childhood home on Lardy Street, which we all lived in, pretending I wasn't thirty and Darron wasn't twenty-eight.

I left behind a job at Brother and Son's Carwash, which had a giant cowboy spinning in the lot, waving in a howdy pose. He wore a yellow suit and yellow hat and was taller than a tree. At work I'd hear his gears squeak each time he completed a circle and it felt like a little mock on his part, like, "Hey, I'm up here laughing with this great view." Which is not to say I hated my job at Brother and Son's—the opposite. I was happy with my Wyo life, it's my father who wasn't.

I left behind Jenny's dead body; I just killed her and walked away.

I left behind the only woman I'd ever loved. Now if that ain't either romantic or pathetic, I wouldn't know which one.

To get to Carol, I barely slept. I ground against the speed limit. New York to Wyoming took three days. I remember cornfields and velvet cattle. I remember the smell of manure and skunk taking turns like snickering cousins. I remember the low sexual sound of radio hosts when night wind cooled my neck, and their loud breakfast sound when I could smell dew drying. I remember the sky looking just like heaven: the clouds beading up, spreading; the sun somewhere lending light to edge the clouds in gold. The road did a design of dipping down and drawing itself up—like wings.

I thought about if I'd changed in the eight years since I'd seen her. I thought, *Well, I've got some new clothes. I don't wear cowboy boots or hats anymore. I've got my jean jacket and my collared shirts now.* I thought, *My hair's the same.* It's always been the same brown color in the shape of the hair you snap onto a plastic man. I thought, *You've probably gained a few pounds from age and you know it.* I thought, *Hey, you're The Haircutter now! You're a new man with a new name!* I said, "Haha!" out loud and the wolf finally (meaningfully) howled.

CHAPTER TWO

THE YELLOW-SUITED COWBOY SPINS

It's eleven o'clock p.m. All is quiet on the Midwest sprawl, save for a drawn-out rumble in the clouds. In the desolate parking lot of the supermarket, a lone goose's beadular eyes pucker against a wet wind blowing extravagantly in its "face." Lilacs bray on their branches, their aroma flung and wasted on the alley behind my childhood home. A rottweiler jangles by, sniffing for bitches in heat. A couch rots and a raccoon steals the stuffing, his burglar mask on. Antlers sit by back doors as tokens with the velvet half-gone. Wind licks the gutted stomach of a still-steaming buck, hung and slightly swinging in the neighbor's garage. Wind perks the black body hairs of my mother, Patty, as she smokes a Salem standing before the breast-high brittle weeds that fill the chain-linked confines of my old backyard. Little does she know, as rain collapses down upon Ten Sleep like the clouds are cumming (collapses so hard and so suddenly it hits her Salem out of her hand), that her long-lost eldest son is asleep at a gas station 150 miles out in Warner and, come tomorrow afternoon, will be at her bell with a wolf.

Doughnuts. Coffee. Make a second shit stop cause you're nervous. Nervous: these germy little spirit ladies shoot around your stomach streaking caustic stars, their throats warbling a high note so fine water ripples worldwide. That high note rattles the bowels and loosens whatever's in them. And whatever's in them then pants at the butthole like a dog wanting to go outside. You open the door in a toilet and the bowel dog rushes out, barking. The ladies unceasingly streak. It's the shit they don't show you in chick flicks. Nerves! Pull off and park the twenty-ton truck all for a thin line of poop. Rock that confused wolf again and again by pulling that damn machine over again. Wipe that red sensitive butthole again. Will it bleed? Let it. You're lovesick. But wet a clump of toilet paper and hold it back there for a quick soothe. Return to the truck and sit on the pain. Now drive. Smiling.

An Arctic Tundra Grey wolf paces in the back of a semi coursing 75 miles-an-hour, 70 miles-an-hour, 65 miles-an-hour, and slowing. The Haircutter pulls into town.

I pulled into Ten Sleep at 4:00 p.m., an hour I've always liked. It was when my mom would finally get out of bed and start making us some food.

I parked in front of the house and my truck shadowed the balding yard. When I got out and shut the door, the slap echoed down the block.

My childhood home had ivy growing up on each side of it and meeting on the roof. Like curtains that went moldy staging the acts of same-ol' same-ol' inside.

I rang the bell because I didn't feel right walking in.

Diiing-Dooong!—as if my family's rich.

My mother opened the door and put her fat hand over her mouth and shook it there. She had more grey hairs. She went in for a hug, but flinched halfway to say, "I'm sure I'm even fatter!" I hugged her by just tapping my fingertips on her back like we do and said, "Hi. Hello. Hi."

I stepped into the house and looked around to the music of her sniffles and squeals. She said, "I feel like I just got Publishers

Clearing House! It's about time! Gol dang it, I almost don't believe it!" Then she got embarrassed and turned to slowly saying, "Well, I wondered why you never called, but I knew you would at some point, but gol, what's it been that the time's added up to, five years?"

"Eight," I said.

I could tell Father John wasn't there because the house felt like a bully. He has a feel that turns the house into just a house doing its functions, groaning its floors, giving its rooms and light switches. But even if he left for a flash to go retrieve the paper, the house seemed on the brink of telling me to stop breathing so loud.

All its stuff looked exactly the same—even had the same thinning towels hanging on the hooks in the toilet cabinet next to the kitchen; it had the same ornamental china shelf on the floor of the dining room with the screws and hammer still out next to it ready to put it on the wall; it had the same smell, which blended with my breathing after one sniff but was enough for me to get a kick out of it. The velvet horses couch sat stiff in its place under the front window. Grandma's old furniture pointed at a new TV. Five remotes were on the coffee table with the same basket of dusty potpourri, a bit sun-faded now. The kitchen still had yellow tiled walls. Still had a wad of gnats over a pile in the sink. I sat in my old seat at the table and Mom said, "You still like bacon sandwiches?"

I said, "Absolutely," and getting ready to eat had always put us in a good mood, so she came and kissed my cheek.

"So weird to see you!" she said, wincing.

I touched her mushy spotted arm and said, "Same here."

I saw Father John's seat had his butt impression on his cushion and it made my stomach ladies whisper, "Ready girls?"

I looked back at Mom and saw she was staring at me harder than anyone in the eight years I'd lived in New York had. It came with a nasty feel so I farted and that shook her off. She started moving around the kitchen with the same old *tick!* sounds coming from her hips and knees. She had a new shoulder blanket on, but it had the same old fringes that swung lightly when she moved like they had no choice in the matter. She saw me watching and came over with a frying pan and pretended to smash one of my hands with it.

"Hardee-har. Look how young you make me seem," she said. "Why didn't you write at me if you weren't gonna call?"

"I called you!" I said.

"Just the once to see if you had any letters!"

Yes. The truth was, I called the once to see if Carol had contacted them asking for news from me, and I never called again out of stubbornness for my dad, of course. What kind of "man" needs to call home?

"Mom, Father John dropped me there and left me!" I scoffed and laughed it off like I hadn't thought about it in a long time.

My mother slapped the table and said, "I told eem! I told eem he shouldn'ta done that! I told eem he abandoned my boy! I spent two years not lettin' eem talk to me, Junior!"

And stuff like that.

Without saying Go, I finally looked over at the spot where I killed Jenny and it made me say, "Whoa!" out loud and Mom said, "What?" And I said, "Whoa coke-a-moe," to brush it aside. She laughed a high *hm!* sound appreciating her big son's rhyme. I was like, Alright.

She cooked the bacon while I prepped four slices of bread by putting peanut butter on them. She kept turning around to ask little questions like, "Now do you *get* snow there or not? . . . Right, see that's what I thought . . . Now, y'all do a subway over there, isn't that right? . . . and *does* that cost, or? . . . *TWO DOLLARS?!*"

All my mother's ever known is her Fair Fare van. It's the only job she's ever had—thirty years running. She works all night long, which is why she was asleep during the day my whole life. What she does is she gets drunks from bars and takes them home, or the other way around. She'll beep outside their house like she's their friend (which she is) and they'll chat happily towards the bar, and then she'll see them later throwing themselves at the door of the van and opening it with more force than necessary. I know that my mom is most comfortable at work, and I know that that's why she does it. Her blanket falls off her shoulders when she's in her driver's seat—it'll even annoy her and she'll get it out from under her and ask someone to fold it and set it on the floor. She'll chat in the most relaxed voice she has, and she only has it at work. It's her ultimate relief, her safe place—a smelly van full of her drunks.

As we were eating our sandwiches, Darron came in.

"*What?! Brother John?!*" He locked his legs and his eyes rimmed up red. "Well let me get a hug for a surprise like that! I almost just passed out!"

I stood up to hug his small, muscular body.

"Nice to see you!" he said, laughing and beating my back. He had those same bruised-looking eyes, and a few grey hairs here and there in his razor cut, and he looked a bit clammier.

"You gained a little weight in the face?" I said.

"Hey! You're one to talk!"

I smoothed my hands over my belly.

"Shit, brother!" He took out a handkerchief and blew his nose. He fed it back into his pocket, smiling. "That's not your truck out there is it?"

"Yeah, it's a mini-semi I guess. I'm just in town for the night, actually, cause I came on a hired job."

"Hey!" My mother said through a mouthful, "You didn't tell me that!"

"Well, you didn't ask why I'm here. I got hired by an art dealer in New York to transport a wolf cross-country, so that's what I'm here for. I've got a wolf in back."

"A *wolf?*" Darron said.

"Yeah, I'm set to release it tomorrow morning and head back outta town, so."

"Junior, gol! You shouldn't leave that soon. There's your old bed for as long as you want and you know you're welcome to stay. Frontier Days is comin' up. We could getcher old fringe vest out. It's up there in a box I'll bet," Mother said, trying to sell me something she didn't give a titty about. She was busy with her sandwich.

Darron said, "Now when you say wolf. Does that mean a domesticated wolf, I'm assuming?"

I said, "Nope. A wild one."

"Shit! Let's go see it!" He hit Mom's shoulder.

"Say! I'm eating my snack right now," she said to him, ticked off. When she chewed, her sparsey black mustache hairs drew circles. I took a bite of my own sandwich, then finished it in four more. I eat those on Wednesdays and Fridays for dinner.

Darron kept popping and locking his legs, crossing his arms and slapping our shoulders. "How's the Big Apple?" he said. "I love tellin' people you live there."

"It's wonderful," I said, and for a flash I accidently pictured the New York I had in my head before I'd ever been: a cartoon alley cat singing jazz till someone breaks a bottle over its head.

"Well shit, you gotta come to Blue Bear with me tonight!" Darron said.

"Are you still? You can't be," I said.

"Yep, still jivin'." He spun around quick in his black clothes.

"Hey, you cut off your tail!" I said.

He rubbed his neck where it used to hang. "Cause I'm a workin' man now! I went back to college and *all* that. It's why I still live here—I got student loans to pay. Hell, you've been gone forever. I'm the gym teacher at Benson now!" He grabbed a banana from the middle of the table and scarfed it down.

"Wow, somethin' to be proud about," I said. Then I surprised everyone, including myself, by asking a personal question. I said, "Do you have a girlfriend, too?"

Darron and Mother looked at each other, and Darron tossed his banana peel at the sink—it cut the wad of gnats and made them scatter. He said, "Not my kinda thing, if you know what I mean."

Mom stood up quivering her empty plate. She curled a hand back to unhook her blanket from her rump and said, "Are you gonna tell your brother what you meant by that or just leave it as a puzzle?" She checked to see if I would laugh with her but I didn't know what was going on yet, so I couldn't.

Darron said, "Sure! I came out after you left, Bro. I don't know . . . a few years ago? I woulda told you, but you never gave us no address, so." His eyes flicked to our mom.

I said, "You came out to visit me?"

He said, "What? No."

Mom said, "Different kinda comin' out, Junior. He's talkin' closets."

I said, "Oh!" Then I shuddered real hard. I said, "Oh, I thought you said somethin' else."

Darron said, "Nuh-uh. I *wish* I came out to New York, shit! What's that cost though, a million dollars?"

"I don't know, ask Father John. He paid for the tickets when we went out," I said.

Mom set her plate in the sink soundlessly, then sniffed her nose to the side with her arms crossed. "Yep," she said, looking at Darron.

I said, "Well dang, okay. You're talkin' gay."

He said, "Hey, that rhymed." Then he swung his body side-to-side all hard like you're asking a five-year-old what's his favorite color. "Yeah, that's right. Can't do anything about it. *Don't* do anything about it, actually. I just don't have romantic whatcha-macallits." He grimaced. "I just like to dance, don't I."

I huffed a hard chuckle. "Well okay!" I don't mind having close-talk moments, it's just that I don't care about them. I said, "Am I supposed to do anything?" and he laughed, "No, not that I know of."

"He's the way he is," our mother stated, proud to do it so matter-of-fact.

"Ha!" I said.

The three of us looked at each other nodding, then started clearing our throats so we didn't urinate down our legs like satisfied dogs.

"Well sure I'll come to Blue Bear with you tonight. Course," I said.

And then I remembered: CAROL! I'd forgotten about her for a whole twenty minutes! Blue Bear equaled seeing Carol! I suddenly felt my bowels fill with gun powder. I excused myself and went upstairs and my butt shot the toilet.

I went and visited my old room in the attic and took some boxes off my bed. When I pulled down the sheets a spider crawled out and I let him live instead of coming along and claiming the place for myself after all these years. There was a sewing machine on the desk where I used to write and read while drinking Cokes. I used to like it there with just me and my lamp and Cokes and books. Hell—like? It's the only thing I've ever actually enjoyed doing besides haircutting. I even had my own little fridge.

I heard Darron yell, "Hey, Brother John! Check this out!"

I went down to his room, which was exactly the same as it's been his whole life: it smelled like his genital-scented bed, his lava lamp was performing on the dresser, and there were dirty dishes on the wheely TV stand he got for his twelfth birthday. He'd shook so hard with happiness to get that wheely TV stand, he pissed Father John off—Father John kicked it across the room and dented it and Darron later that day was like, "That's okay," and showed how he could put a cluster of Solar System stickers in the dent. He was sitting on his twin bed smiling up at me.

"Look. My new enterprise," he said.

I said, "Where?"

"Under my bed."

I lifted up his new adult-grey bed skirt and pulled out a stuffed potato sack.

"There's a bunch more under there," he said. "Open it up."

I pulled out a rope, a cowboy hat, and a jean jacket from the sack.

"Each one's got a rope and a jacket and a hat," he said. "They're my Imitation Cowboys." He waited with a hanging smile for me to say something. "It's so easy, people buy these up like penny candy! Alls I need to do is go to the Salvation and pick up any old jean jackets and hats! Some rope and a tater sack and you got an Imitation Cowboy!" He put stress on the second part—*Cowboy*. "Tourists love 'em," he said.

"We ain't got tourists comin' through Ten Sleep!" I said.

"We sure as shit do!" Darron said. "I sold ten'a these already and I only been doin' it a week! Thirty bucks a pop! People from Florida?"

I'm still proud of my brother Darron for his Imitation Cowboy enterprise. I patted him on the back, "Looks like you got it all figured out."

He said, "No I don't," and scoffed me off like I'd told him he could fix a rocket.

"Smart move," I said and left his room. Was I whistling? Sure, you can add all that.

I went downstairs to ask Mom where I could find Father John. Though, I've kicked myself ever since because I should've just gone to find Carol and then went for a good night's sleep and woken up in the morning like, Oh, hi Dad, I'm here but I'm leaving. But, stupidity is as stupid does. Or whatever the hell they say for it.

Mom was on the velvet horses couch with a dirty look on her face. She was holding a Romance and I could tell she'd gone up to her vanity and done a shellac on her bangs. She has long brown hair and she'll do a bang and spray it till it's stiff when she nods. Me and Darron always said it looks like a crushed tarantula on her forehead.

I said, "The hell's wrong with you?"

She looked in pain. The horses around her reared their heads to match.

"I'm all bloated now. You made me break my diet."

She started on a coughing fit.

"Where's Father John?" I asked, trying not to sound too interested.

"What's it, five? Down at Willie's then. You gonna pick eem up for me? I can't barely move."

"He still didn't get his license?"

"Hold on," she said, and tipped aside to creak a fart out as if to see if it would sound like, "No," which it did.

I left the house, shocked by the silence of the outdoors.

Going back to Ten Sleep, even in my head, gives me the squirms. Makes me forget about all I've seen since and all I've accomplished. Idiot H.C. standing with his wee-wee in his hand saying, "What's this?" And Father John walks by in dusty boots goin', "It's your vagina, dummy. Is it on its period?"

When I walked into Willie's, it smelled like someone had just bleached the toilet, and *The Cosby Show* was loud on a big TV. Two old vets sat at a square black table with a pitcher of beer on it. Two young men cracked pool in back by the velvet Elvises. My father was alone on a bar stool. He was wearing his tan cowboy hat after all these years: still clean.

I just went up to him and hiked myself up on a stool. He had his head pointing down like a sleeping cow. He had hearing aids.

I watched him in the backbar mirror. A Fun-game somewhere was sounding out a jingle and passing a blue laser over our faces. *Ring-a-ding-ding, it's the year 2000 and look who's back.*

The tender came up and said, "What can I get ya?"

It made my dad turn to look at me. Our eyes still matched, even with all the added age. He looked away for a beat, then looked back at me and his shoulders jumped.

"Didn't recognize you," he said and put out his hand.

"Hello," I said, and I shook it. Then I got giddy about shaking hands, so I squirmed my lips trying not to smile. I smacked myself upside the head with a trout in my mind, the trout growing bigger and bigger after each time till I simply couldn't lift it.

My father said to the tender, "Better make it a Manhattan," and the sudden speech made him hack.

"No, I'll have a whiskey soda," I said.

And after that, I couldn't think of anything else to say, though I technically wasn't thinking. It was like I had my finger in a socket and my brain was stuck on one thought: *you can't think of anything to say.* I felt like that time I went to the store with him on accident when I was twenty-five and I had to think of something to say in line, which I didn't.

"This a visit or are you here to stay?" he said.

"No, just for the night. I got some work to do in the area."

"Kinda work?" he said.

"I was hired to drive a wolf out here? And release him in the wild?"

"A what?"

"A wolf? It's in the lot right now in back'a my truck."

The audience exploded into laughter on *The Cosby Show.*

"It's pacin' in back'a my truck, prolly hungry," I said.

My dad took time between saying things—something men in Wyo do just because they have all day.

I sipped from my cocktail and shivered. I don't like the taste of alcohol.

"You drive it from New York?" he said.

"Yes sir, I did."

He said, "Psh!" and took a big pull on his beer. I looked at the hairs hooking out of his nose pores and felt my own nose to see if I had them—I don't. I squirmed on my stool. I was waiting for questions I knew he'd never ask. I didn't want the scene to end, but I didn't want to sit there like a poop stuck in a rear either.

I drawled a long, "Weeeell. I need to get this wolf back to the house and catch a rest. We leave first thing in the morning."

"Time *is* it?" he said.

I read the Budweiser clock in front of us. "A quarter till."

He picked his bottle up an inch and smacked it back down on the counter. "I asked for the *time,* not a goddamn math problem."

I got up from the stool and tossed a twenty down, the wind from the motion making the straw pop out of my full whiskey soda, which the scene could've done without.

"I'm not ready to go yet, thanks for askin'," my father said.

"I'll be in the lot."

The sun was doing its set. Crickets did a Welcome Back chant, taunting me. I shoed at the gravel and looked through the bullet holes at the wolf. He was curled up sleeping, or meditating?—I wouldn't know. Father John came out holding my whiskey soda. He had a chain connecting his wallet to his belt and it swung lower than his knees. Long enough to give a pickpocket time to go "Woo hoo!" before an old man topples over five feet back and drags on the end of his prize. Anything to make someone feel dumber than they already are. Father John limped on his age-rotted legs, and I counted a limp for each of the eight years he'd abandoned me.

"The hell you lookin' at?" he said, still across the lot, but it sounded like he said it right in my ear.

He didn't compliment me on my truck, he just got in. I drove us home with the windows down and it smelled like the refinery. I was used to the passenger's seat being empty and now my father was in it. He looked around to judge the town while he rode, burping and cracking his teeth on ice, rattling the plastic cup. We didn't say anything until I parked in front of the house.

I said, "You wanna see the wolf?"

"There ain't really a wolf back there."

I climbed my fatass into the back and unstopped the peephole. I opened the food bag and funneled some pellets in. My dad came back to see. He wheezed his face up to the hole and looked in for a while before his eye adjusted.

"Christ!"

I tried a long yawn.

"What're you gonna do with it?" he said with breath so sour the wolf coughed.

"Release it," I said.

"*Release it?!* You're dumber than a box of rocks if you think that's the thing to do."

"I've been hired to take *care* of this wolf. I've been given exact instructions off a *note.*"

"Lemme outta here! If you think I'm a toad! Lemme out!" he said, panicking in that old kid's way of his that always made me feel sick and thirsty.

So I let him out, knowing simple-as-that how this whole "parading a wolf in front of my father" thing went.

The father sat down at the kitchen table with the grace of a hog. He picked up his fork and used it to point at The Haircutter and say, "This jack-in-the-box thinks he's gonna let go of a perfectly good piece'a cash like it ain't weird."

The brother turned on the small TV on the counter and *The Cosby Show* was ending. He changed it to the news.

The father said, "Even though the first thing I saw in that wolf was dollar signs. And same's with that truck."

The mother said, "Father John knows. Trust eem."

The Haircutter closed his eyes and took his scissor to a head of hair in his mind. He felt a rush and rode it. His mother and father and brother flicked their eyes from the TV to him, from the TV to him. The sun came in through the window above the sink and set while they were eating, making long shadows draw out from the salt and pepper shakers and from their moving hands, making the room warm-colored to go with the smell of country pot pies. The mother ate with one arm hugging herself around the middle, and the other arm—white with black hairs—coming out of her shoulder blanket to fork around. The Haircutter noticed she had peanut butter on her cheek from the earlier sandwiches. The father ate with his hearing aid ringing and one wrist resting on the table edge far out from his body. He'd laid his toothpick next to his plate in order to eat.

The news reporter on TV said, "A new study on theory shows evidence of *opinions?* We'll explain after this." The father pointed at her and said, "Now how come she's so homely lookin'?" The mother laughed and it sounded like a turkey gobbling. She put a cube of grey turkey into her mouth, her teeth like grey lace once strung up white but forgotten about, as people forget about what a special occasion it was to be born and go on to never brush their fuckin' teeth.

She cleared her throat and said, "How's the meal, boys?"

"It'll make a turd," is what the father said.

The mother ticked her tongue and smiled.

It was always all about Father John.

The brother brought his plate up to his face and licked it clean. Someone silently farted in order to have something be under the table besides no family dog.

The Haircutter stood, saying, "I've got some paperwork to do out in the truck."

I'd been sitting for an hour or so doing who wrote autobiographies in the '50s, when Darron knocked on the window.

"Can I see the wolf?" he said, and I said, "You bet," and showed him the peephole.

He looked in and said, "Whoa, hi, buddy! See you can tell right away that's a wild animal." He saw *Wolf Fancy* next to him. "Aw cool—*Wolf Fancy*," he pronounced the name and fanned the pages, sticking his face near. "It almost even smells like a wolf."

I said, "Well there you're smelling the wolf, not the damned mag." I said, "Psh!" like our father.

"What a cool animal," he said as he crawled back to the front seat.

He said, "Hey bro, I know you did what you had to do with Jenny."

I flinched. I said, "Ach." I said, "That was damn stupid and you know it." Then I said, "WHOA! Did you see that?! I think that was a turkey buzzard with a cat in its mouth!" pointing to a fake spot in the sky.

Darron craned his neck for a while trying to see, and when it went calm again he said, "We made a grave for her out back. You should check it out."

I went through the bushes on the side of the house instead of cutting through; I didn't want the whole house knowing, Oh, he's going to see the grave. The backyard had an unused shed and a three-wall fence of ivy. I looked around for a grave till I was like,

"*This?*" It was a pathetic little cross made out of two pieces of fire kindler.

When I was in my late twenties, my father traded a chainsaw for a buzz-haired mutt dog named Jenny. When my father was with Jenny, it was like we had a grandchild in the family. It was his precious "Lady Jenny." When he held her, all your attention went to the smile lines shooting out from his eyes. Every single time he came home, he had a McDonald's cheeseburger for Jenny and never one for us. When he sat on the couch and Jenny sat up on the back of it, his hair would lift to point at her—his love was electric. When I was thirty, when I was in love with Carol, I would talk to her about Lit, as I've said. And so there came a day when I asked her to come to my house to see my collection of books. She came. She rang *my* bell. No one was home but me and her. I was horny and excited. I said, "Come on in!" and went straight to the kitchen and opened the fridge to get Cokes. I heard Jenny's nails on the floor and a single bark.

Then I closed the fridge door and saw Jenny's jaw clamped on Carol's leg.

If only the little fridge in my room had been stocked with Cokes that day.

Carol's screams were like death-metal music supporting the horror. I kicked Jenny hard and she yelped but snapped forward to bite that leg again. I kicked her again but she was prepped for it—her jaw held fast. Blood was filling her mouth and spilling out the gaps in her teeth. And there was a knife on the table right next to my hand. Like, "Yoo-hoo!" I stabbed Jenny twice in the potbelly.

She immediately bent up to lick the wounds, but then went all erect like she'd suddenly been stretched taut by invisible hands—her eyes were terrified.

I looked up and Carol was gone. Spots of blood pitter-pattered out the open door. I got the portable phone in my hand and Jenny jerked with her tongue popped out.

The dog was dying on the plastic floral floor.

I called information and asked for a vet's number. The nails from one of her paws dinged on the metal table leg as if to keep my attention. Her hyperventilation blew blood bubbles out of the knife slits in her potbelly—they rose in the air and drifted away or popped.

I yelled, "Stop it Jenny!"

And in a while more, she stopped.

Father John came home and the scream that he made was the most horrifying sound I've ever heard in my life, and I've woken up to the sound of a mouse writhing on a sticky trap under my bed till it ripped its stomach and its guts slipped out. Father John got down and gave her CPR (as his last kiss from Lady Jenny). He looked at me with blood around his mouth like Ronald McDonald—"The fuck'd you do?!"

The Fair Fare seats looked like someone had doused them in acid. Dirty yellow foam showed through. My sneakers stuck to the floor mat.

Darron was telling a boring story, at which he was an Olympian. "Cotton, I think. But wait—he went to Toledo, he might've said—I *think* he said his nephew lives there—oh wait, *Tampa*? Hold on, I'll look on my globe later."

Here was the same scene that had played out every night before I left Ten Sleep for good: Mom was driving me and Darron to the Blue Bear and I was sweating over seeing Carol. I was so nervous my teeth started chattering. I had on a plain white

T-shirt that I'd picked up on the road. Cause Carol once said, "Guys look great in plain white T-shirts."

We pulled up in front of the massive oak doors, "Bye Mom!" like two children. A neon sign hung over the top: Blue Bear Saloon. I saw Darron in that blue light again. This time with a heap of potato sacks on his back. I hate how the poor kids say "Santy Clause" like me and Darron did.

It smelled the same: sawdust and cigarettes. Twinkle lights dangled and a moon-shaped dance floor took up half the room. Darron clasped his hands behind his back and did a footstep down the length of it, a couple whoops coming out from waitresses like, "Darron's here!" I looked for Carol. I weaved through the big black tables and got to the bar and sat down.

"Coke please," I said to a young, blond bartender.

When she gave it to me, I said, "Hey, is Carol workin' tonight?"

She looked at the other end of the bar and lightning struck when she called, "Carol!"

From the back it could've been Carol on a big weight gain. But when she spun around I saw a druggie old lady like from out of a mug shot. Her jugs swung back and forth for a sec from having spun around. Her eyes pointed in whichever direction they damn well pleased. She grunted, "What?" with spaces in her teeth.

"No! Carol Mary Mathers! Carol Mathers! She's young!"

"Oh that's the only Carol that works here," the tender said.

"Are you sure?"

"This place is like Cheers bar, everyone knows everyone," she said.

My heart decomposed. I looked at her again in case she'd been ravaged by time. I shouted, "You're not Carol Mathers are you?"

"Huh-uh!" the woman grunted. "Carol Couch. Who's askin'."

I sucked down my entire Coke through the straw and pushed it away from me. I heard Carol Couch go, "Psh. I don't know what that guy thinks he wants!" She said to her friend, "I don't know—there's a guy down there bein' an asshole."

Carol.

I heard the buttery countryman on the sound system spread "I'm gonna love you forever" all over the room. I went to the table where Darron had laid out his Imitation Cowboys. I sat down and burped out loud as a *fuck you* to the situation.

Darron was wearing black pants, black shoes, a black long-sleeved half turtleneck tucked in, and a black belt. Same outfit he's always worn. I ordered another Coke from a waitress who passed by. Why not? I had a show right there.

He was finishing up a dance with one of the waitresses. You could tell they'd done that dance a million times, but she still had on a proud, quiet smile, with her big butt swollen inside of her light denim jeans, her cowboy boots scurrying, and her big hair getting in Darron's face sometimes when they switched directions. When the song finished, he kissed her hand and she walked off the dance floor holding her lips in her mouth.

A faster-paced song came on and Darron's sweaty hair flopped and followed his jerky movements—till three ugly girls went and had their pictures taken with him. I heard them yell, "What's your name?" and he winked a stupid amount of times saying, "Think *Bewitched.*" And they were like, "*What?*" After they sat down, Darron did a succession of kicks for them. He'd pump himself up with his tongue stuck out on his cheek and then run for a jump-kick in front of their table. They took pictures, the flash going off when his leg was midair and his hair was swooping to meet his tucked head. Patrons watched with their cigarettes up near their raised brows—"Are y'all catchin' what them girls are doin' to Darron?"

I was finishing my second Coke when he came over, panting, to ask why I wasn't dancing. The way he said it, "Wanna dance, brotha?" while moving his hips, made me ache for him. Like, *That's my brother and he's not a bad guy.* The song changed and he clapped and threw his arms up, flung his head around and yelled along to the lyrics, "Freedom like a BLACK HOLE!" He sprang off like a cat, ran toward the table of girls, and just when it looked like he'd hit the wooden fence surrounding the dance floor, he did an air kick, throwing his head forward to touch his knee—their camera flashed just in time. The girls screamed and bent over to laugh; one girl fell out of her chair and you could see her underpannies. Some patrons hooted, some stubbed out their cigs like they were going to take a stand, but then only hopped in their chairs clucking like chickens till they let out their smiles and relaxed, lighting up again, loving the show, because they know that it might be the only thing that'll *happen* tonight.

I went to the foyer and used the pay phone to call my mother. She was like, "Already?"

I said, "I'm tired. It's been a long day."

I hung up and stood there listening to the wind whistle through the leaks in the door. I'll admit, I nearly cried thinking about Carol. The cling she had on my heart was maddening. I was completely in love with her. And was she married? Did she still live in Ten Sleep? Was she still *alive?* I didn't know.

In all the years I'd lived in New York I just never got around to dating. If I was feeling sexed, I'd jack one to the thoughts from when I used to jack one when I was in love with Carol. Carol Mary Mathers! I had to find her! And just then, I saw a broken chord hanging from the pay phone and I shouted, "PHONEBOOK!"

I tore back inside and hurried to the bar and asked the tender girl, "You got a phonebook, please?"

She shook her head and said, "Got stole."

I asked every waitress if they knew Carol and I got *no*'s all around. I went to Darron and he was handing out Imitation Cowboys to the drunk girls. They immediately put on the hats and went on the dance floor to rope each other. Darron licked his fingers as he counted their cash, germs building up on his tongue. A poopy-smelling lady poked him and said, "How much? It's my grandson's birthdee next Wendsdee."

I said, "Darron, you remember a girl named Carol who worked here?"

He said, "Is that that lifeguard girl from the pool? She dudn't work here, I can sense athletes usually. Wait—how would *you* know her? Oh, her name's Carrie. Who's Carol? Oh, is that that one girl! Hell yeah, I remember her—what ever happened to her?"

I floated away on a wave of rage.

When my mom pulled up there was a drunk in the van with her. We drove to the emergency room cause he had tickled someone in the bathroom and had gotten smacked so hard he cut his head on the paper towel dispenser.

"Why'd you tickle eem?" Patty asked.

"Cause he was bein' a cunt!" Earl said.

"Do you know Carol Mathers? Either of you?" I said.

They both said, "Who?" and Mom said, comfortably, "You coulda brought a rag, Earl. You're gettin' blood on my new seat cover."

"That's what it's plastic for!" he grouched.

Mom chuckled, "You wanna get tickled too? Cause I will!"

Ten o'clock on a two-lane highway. Cars flashed past with the cast of a bobcat bolting because he knows the Wyos think his beauty looks best stuffed and posed in a pouncing position. The wake of the passing bobcat cars vibrated the phrase *Carol Mary Mathers.*

After the emergency room, Mom said, "So you seen him dance? That entertain ya?"

"I had a fine time watching him," I said.

"So you're still talkin' like that, huh?" She had her hands on the tan shag steering wheel and she was straining up to look in the rearview.

"Talkin' like what?"

"I don't know. Like a fancy pants," she said.

"I don't talk like—"

And she suddenly did a U-turn.

I fell against the door and said, "Whoa! What in the dang hell!"

"It's a good time to get the van warshed. Everyone's out drinkin'."

And then I saw, above a row of oak trees, the yellow-suited cowboy laughing, spinning away now to show the rest of the town. Mom smirked proud and turned into Brother and Son's Carwash.

I used to run the register, and once I ran the buttons for a month, and once they had me on dry duty for about a year. They let me read while I worked, and I had my own shelf in the fridge in the break room, so I liked that job very much.

We pulled up and waited in line. I was like, "Ha! Alright."

A maroon sedan was in front of us and it had little kids slapping the windows screaming about how fun it was to be in a carwash. When the soap valves squirted, the kids screamed and pointed, smiling so hard they gagged. When my mother and I took their spot, we too tried pointing appreciatively at those squiggle squirts, but it felt like we were trying to be hippy-dippy, so we kept quiet until the light dinged green. We advanced into the dark where barrel-sized brushes came down to buff—it made the van rock, and out of the corner of my eye I saw my mom jiggling like jello, so I pretended to look out my window. Then the rinse jets came on and I said, "Is there a phonebook back at home?" My mom said, "Well yeah, but I don't know how current it is." The stomach ladies winked, whispering, *Carol!* I would get home and start calling every Mathers there was.

The light dinged *Done!* and we drove through long black flaps that parted lazily off the face of the van like we were a Goth whose mom was introducing us to someone. Someone sauntered out of a door by my side of the van with a rag. Dry Duty. She came around front so we could see her. "Would you like a dry-down?" said Carol.

It was *Carol.*

I went, "Whoa!"

I rolled my window down and stuck my head out, "Carol!"

Mist dazzled in the lot lights and made rainbows on the concrete, oiled ground.

She said, "Who's that?" and when I got out of the van and "jogged" to her she screamed, "John!"

She hugged me and we held it.

Carol's blond head seeped a dolly smell up to me until she took it away.

"You work here?"

My mom turned the van until the headlights shone on us. She rolled her window down, "Who's that?"

"Carol Mary Mathers!" I yelled, belligerently. "I was just lookin' for you over at Blue Bear and here you are!"

"Oh, Blue Bear!" Carol said.

"There's Shane!" I said.

I saw Shane, one of the sons from Brother and Son's, hanging air freshener trees on the wall inside the shop.

"I'm gonna stay here and talk to Shane and Carol, k?" I yelled to my mom.

Carol wore coveralls and her hair was in a braid with baby hairs for the wind.

We walked down the cement hall that led past the old break room I loved. Carol was ahead of me, her figure hidden beneath the coveralls.

She spun around and grabbed my wrist, "I'm sorry I ran off that day. I've felt bad about it since."

I hoped she wasn't thinking about how fat my wrist felt in her little hand.

"It's okay!" I said.

"Right away I just thought *Emergency Room*. You know? So I just ran to my car and you didn't come and I was all bleedin' and stuff so's I just took off. And then my *mom* was all up in my face takin' care of me so I didn't call you till a ways after when your dad said you moved to New *York,* so I've *got* to hear about *that* because I *love* New York even if I've never been."

I said, "How's your leg?"

"Oh!" She pulled up a pant of the coverall to show two puffy scars looking like pink caterpillars stuck on her leg. She shrugged, "It's fine."

"Your leg dudn't deserve that," I said.

"Who cares!" she said.

I sensed her wanting to give me a hug, but she kept on walking like *who cares.* She never asked about how Jenny had responded to getting stabbed.

We entered the store part of the carwash. It had the same sag ceiling with the same bugs dying in clumps in the sizzling light fixtures. Shane looked at me with a stack of pine trees in his hand.

I said, "Shane, nice to see you. How's your dad, huh?"

"Uh, he's good," Shane said with acne so hard it looked like he was rotting.

"Tell him sorry for leavin' without notice. I got abducted pretty much," I said.

"What, like aliens?" Shane said.

"By my own father actually, but one time his face turned green, so hell. Maybe."

"Whoa," Shane said, interested.

I ate a candy-caramel and leaned on the counter while Carol spun on a stool behind it asking me about New York and flicking her eyes around my face.

"I actually came out here to release a wolf," I said.

"Now that's gonna need an explanation."

I spread my arms wider on the counter and drawled, "It's an underground favor for a rich acquaintance."

"Dang!"

I heard my subconscious say, "That posture ain't right," so I clapped above my head and relaxed into a different fake pose where the candy-caramel was sticking out of my cheek like a tumor. I said, "But I wanna know what *you've* been up to, Girly."

"Aww, I went to, Oh! I student-taught for a year, then I got my own class, and I quit after the first year. I didn't know I hate kids! Honestly that's the worst job anyone could ever have, a teacher. Then, shit. Tendin' bar cause'a student loans. Then I went to nursin' school for a little bit and had to quit cause I can't do blood. Then, shit, more tendin'—the whole time actually. Then I started workin' here pretty much like two years ago now? And it's good cause I pick my own hours, so that's cool. I work all the time—I'm serious. Cause I live with my mom and everyone at the bars are in *college,* so hell, why not. Hey, I'm writin' a novel like you said I should!"

Her top teeth were long and they slanted invitingly into her mouth. When she smiled it showed her pink gums above them. Her cheeks bunched up ruby. Rabbit-like.

"I'm off now, actually," she said. "Do you want a ride home or wherever you was goin'?"

"Well hell yeah!" I said. "Then we could keep talkin'."

"Yeah," she said, grooving like a ferret. And when you're in the middle of scenes like that, you're like: I'm *alive.*

We drove down the same road that my mother and I had just taken. I was breathing Carol's special car air. I watched her pay attention to the road, pressing her turn signal to sound out its prissy ticks. She had peach fuzz covering her entire face and it sparkled in the passing streetlights. Her eyes flicked over at me.

"I was always wondering what happened to you," she said.

I swelled up lusty, "I couldn't wait to see you. I thought about you all these eight years."

"No you didn't!" she flirted. "You live in New York."

"I *did.* You're Carol Mary Mathers. I ain't never talked to someone so much as I talked to you. And you're the only *girl* where I ever thought, *Now here's a girl . . .*"

She smiled hard, showing me the new wrinkles she'd gotten.

"It's why I came out to find you. And now I'm sittin' here thinkin', there's Carol, pretty as hell, just more wrinkles," I said.

"Hey!" She slapped my arm.

"It's like an old queen but better."

"Hey I could be mad at you for that!" she twitted.

I chuckled hard.

"I bet I look so old, you're right. Eight years? Yeah I was twenty-two! Oh god, I must look like a hag," Carol said.

"You look damn fine to me, Girly."

She slapped my arm again, "Shut up," which made me laugh.

We came to a red light and stopped.

She sighed, jiggling the gearstick, smiling.

I said, "So you got a boyfriend I'm assuming?"

I kept breathing slowly, and I regret, loudly.

"No," she said.

The light bled onto her face heart-red.

"Haha, why?" she said.

I said, "Cause that's the right answer."

I picked her hand up off the gearstick and kissed it.

Her smile faded and her eyes went wide. She wrapped a single hair around her tongue and strangled it.

"That looks like a sausage," I said.

She spat the hair out.

We leaned in and met lips.

And before they knew it, H.C. and Carol were parked in a slot at a Taco Bell restaurant and she was climbing over her seat to sit next to him. Two kids making mouth love. Two adults with hearts beating wildly being honest about the way they felt.

Sweat spurted from my pores; my legs went numb. My pants set up tent for the night. My seat disappeared from under me and I hovered in a void where the portal to everything was in Carol's little mouth. My lips were trembling so hard I had to stop kissing to bite them still. I held her face and it felt covered in hot velvet.

She pulled away, "Wait, stop! I got lopsided titties, before you see! One's for an A cup and one's a B."

I felt them to see.

I was feeling more than I'd ever felt before in my life.

The cars on the road said, "Yes. YES. yes. YeSSS."

We took a break, our tongues hanging limp from our mouths, absolutely abused. I told her about the wolf job.

"I wanna come release it too!" she said, yanking my chest hairs.

"Okay! Are you an early riser?"

"No, but whatever you want! I'll wake up right now if you want it!"

I said, "Well, let's mosey then. It's midnight. I say we leave around five."

She whimpered, "But what happens *after* five? I gotta say goodbye once we drop the wolf?"

I reached down my jeans to squeeze my boner and said, "Well I thought either I'm staying in Ten Sleep or you're comin' back with me is how it's gonna work, Girly."

She screamed. That animal scream for her rabbit-like features—like a bunny getting slaughtered is what I would come to think of it as.

"I COULD COME WITH YOU?!" she said.

"Well hell yeah! I got a big truck and a big apartment all ready for you." I was quick to say, "Well, I don't know about *all ready*. I bet the apartment could use a major clean, but . . ."

Then she was like a bunny that got injected with a test medicine. Flapping her body around, making scary noises.

She dropped me off at home and said, "Is that your flippin' truck?!"

I said, "There's a wolf in back."

"Fuck!" She gripped the steering wheel and looked at me with stars in her irises. "I always knew I'd catch my big break! I've just always wanted to get *out* there! I ain't got *nothin'* here holdin' me down!"

After I kissed Carol goodnight, I floated inside. I went straight to get my dick out and came in one stroke.

I laid with my eyes pinned open in my childhood bed. A bomb of vitality had exploded in me. I fell asleep with my hands placed beat-heavy over my new heart.

When the alarm clock rang it went, "Girlfriend! You have a girl-friend now!" Yow! I showered and it was over before I realized I was showering.

I went downstairs and my mom was in the kitchen wearing a pink bathrobe. We watched the coffee maker with our arms crossed. It was dark out. A cold wind sucked the curtains against the window screens, then billowed them halfway across the room like they were spirits trying to tap our shoulders.

I said, "Well," and turned for a hug.

She said, "Gol dang it, so that's it huh?"

"It unfortunately is. I didn't take Monday off, so."

"What're you doin' for work," she said more than asked.

I told her, "I work in a law office."

"Well that sounds major," she said sincerely.

I saw the old familiar sight of Father John's stocking feet bobbing in the doorway to the den—he was kicked back in his La-Z-Boy.

The coffee maker made its last hiss and Mom poured me a thermos. "This is my good thermos. But I want you to take it."

I said, "No Ma, I couldn't do that."

She smoothed her robe and said, "Well, you missed all those Christmases anyways, so."

I went upstairs and tapped on Darron's door.

I opened it and said, "Bro, I'm leavin'."

He sat up in bed wearing an undertank, "What?! What the?"

I went and stood above him and he smelled like an infected dick that had dropped off a body.

"I seriously have work that I have to get back for," I said.

He stood up out of bed and hugged me, saying, "Well try to come back again soon, for hell's sake." And when he pulled away from me he was crying.

I said, "Geez, Darron. Don't cry."

"Aw, shut the hell up!"

He flopped back into bed and pulled the covers up to his red, glistening eyes. I stood at the door slowly closing it, seeing his eyes just watching. I mouthed, "Bye," and he brought out his frowning, quivering lips to say, "Bye, Brother John."

I went back downstairs and stood in the lamplight by Father John's La-Z-Boy. He looked up over his glasses, over the paper, and waited for me to say something. I acted out of breath and said, "Hittin' the road." He folded the paper and stood up, grunting minimally. My mom handed me a rip of paper, saying, "Write your address down so's we can send letters." I was proud to write New York City, New York in front of my father but I didn't look to see if he was seeing. I wished I had a hat to put on to signal my departure in a mature way.

Instead I just held out my hand, scared as hell that Father John would laugh at it, but he shook it and said, "Still could sell that wolf. I got a guy in Rainer who might be interested."

"I can't. I can't," I said, "Good idea, though."

I hugged my mother and she walked with me to the door pulling tight on her shoulder blanket (which was over her pink robe) saying, "Alrighty, watch the road then. There's wrecks a lot on I-80. Evidently. Come back soon if you can, it'd be nice to have you for longer. Alright, Junior. This is too bad you're leavin' so soon."

I cut across the dew-wet grass. Disbanded birdsong. I pulled on the cold moist handle of the door to my truck and hoisted my fatass in. I put Mom's good thermos in the space between me and where Carol would sit. I went in back and unstopped the peephole and funneled a last meal in to the wolf. I said, "Today's the day, by the way. You're about to get along little doggy." I couldn't see his body, but his eyes gleamed and his claws ticked over to get the grub. I rolled the top of the food bag closed and, for the first time, saw a picture of a Cocker Spaniel on it. I sat there about ready to cry, hearing the wolf crunch on Cocker Spaniel's pellets, until I heard Mom open the screen door. She came out to wave again. I crawled in front and looked up at Darron's window and saw his curtain peeled in one corner. I waved. I started up the truck with its big-dick sound. My wilted mother stood in the yard as I drove away, her shawl fringes blowing in the wind. My father, I guess, had gone back to the paper.

I pulled up in front of Carol's address and she was yawning at the curb with suitcases and her mom.

"We just seen a raccoon," Carol said when I got out of the truck.

"Hi, I'm John Reilly Junior," I said, and Carol's mom Trish had a hairstyle so high and blond you could see right through it, so if you squinted it looked like she didn't have any hair whatsoever. She was crying so hard she couldn't say one intelligible thing. She gave me the limpest hug in the world and tried to communicate how low-strength she was out of rapture that I was giving her daughter a big break. Carol looked asleep. I didn't try to kiss her—I just moved her stuff to the back bench of the truck.

"I know it!" Carol said when she hugged her mom goodbye.

Trish broke through the blubber to bellow a crackling, ominous-sounding, "I love you two!" as we pulled away.

Carol made a nest on her side of the bench with pillows and afghans and slept as I drove toward the Bighorn Mountains. The wolf truck headlights casted orange as road-life darted out of their way. I quietly opened the thermos and got some coffee down my neck. I looked over at the blanket bundle next to me and thought, well this ain't bad. I don't mind having to get used to this.

When we reached Casey Canyon, the sun had risen palely all around us. When I cracked my window, mountain air tingled on my nose hairs. Carol stirred and I looked and said, "You all right there, gorgeous?"

She came out from the blankets and pushed her hair off her face. "My ears are poppin'."

She looked around at where we were. We rode like that for a while, me thinking, *Okay, that's fine, we'll take it slow.*

"I can't believe it but I'm tryin'," I heard. "Do I smell coffee?"

I said, "Yeah!" and handed her the thermos.

After she drank, I said, "You wanna see the wolf?"

She smiled. Finally.

She said, "Do you wanna see the wolf, he says."

"Climb in back and unstop that peephole."

Carol climbed in back and looked in.

"Eew! What's all them piles?"

"His poop!" I said.

She plugged the hole right back up again.

"Did you see its eyes flash?" I said.

"No."

"You coulda waited till you seen its eyes flash!"

"I'll take your word for it," she said.

And as she was climbing back to her seat, she kissed me on my cheek. Euphoria sang a high note down to my pelvis and rang my dick like a bell. *Yes!*, I said to myself.

Once the sun was bright as sin, it hailed for about three minutes. Carol squealed and clapped, and the wolf more than likely lifted his head, thinking, "Now what the hell's this?"

"There's a rainbow!" I said.

"Where!" Carol said and got her camera out of her soft white purse.

You know.

We were a few miles into the Bighorns when the woods felt thick enough for wolves. I pulled off down a side road that barely fit the semi. Trees ten times taller than the truck parted to let us through. I stopped and killed the engine.

I said, "Alright, Carol. This looks good. Now do me a favor and when I say go you press that yellow button right there with the back door symbol on it."

I crawled in back hoping Carol wouldn't notice how hard it was for me to climb back there. I unstopped the peephole.

The wolf paced in the rods of sunlight striping through the bullet holes.

"Okay, go," I said.

The back door slid up with a rolling sound. A line of light moved across the wolf quarters, revealing shit piles and clumps of hair and Cocker Spaniel food pellets scattered everywhere.

The wolf went very slowly to stand at the edge of the haul.

Carol tapped my shoulder and said, "Take a pitcher!"

I took her camera and put it up to the hole. In the pic, his spiky silver body is facing deep green trees, greyish-blue pine fronds, brown flaky trunks. There's a puff of breath coming off his profile.

His unhinged nostrils worked the air. His coat rose and flattened. A sluice of cold wind came through the peephole and I could smell the wolf in it—a separate smell from the pine and the piss and shit.

He was statue-still.

"Go on!" I said, and he looked back at me. He saw a long-lashed girly eye watching him through his food hole. I saw a current of tension run through his body and he leapt out of the truck, his hind legs in a comical diving posture. I felt for a moment that I'd just lost something. Then I caught a glimpse of him running away. Running!

"Woooohoo!" I went. "Yeah!"

Carol crawled in back and put her hands on my face and said, "Aw, did you cry?" and she kissed me. "It's so handsome you had a big job like this!" she said and kissed me again, which started the hardest makeout session I'd ever been a part of. We "made love" amongst her suitcases and perfume smell. She was humping me all curvy-like as the birds outside twiddled in branches crisp. Her skin had goose bumps from my cracked window. Her nipples responded accordingly. And her face became drawn down and sleepy-seeming as it ascended the stairs of pleasure that lead to her orgasm.

The law office I worked at in New York made me see a psychiatrist as protocol. After concluding that I seek my father's approval, he rated me "immature on matters of sex" and it always bothered me. But there in that truck having sex with Carol, I saw how sex is about as immature as it gets, so that lock-eyed psychiatrist's comment didn't make sense. I could go wave my dick in his face saying, "Someone humped this and she was all sleepy-looking like someone falling asleep trying to watch a movie past her bedtime," and *that* wouldn't be more immature than sex.

But I'm not saying I didn't like it. I loved seeing Carol like that. I thought, *You can do this anytime you want and I'll be here to let you.* I thought, *Now if this ain't me being a man, then I don't know what is,* and then I orgasmed, which pretty much scared the hell out of me it felt so good. I yelled, "DANG GIRLYYYYY!"

("Is he losing his virginity in this scene?") No, it was my second time, but thanks for asking. While the yellow-suited cowboy mockingly spins. And while Carol and I had no idea that in four hundred sex sessions later the very woods around us would ruin our lives forever, making it so we'd never have normal sex again. You'll see what I mean, and thanks for being confused.

CHAPTER THREE

TWO FLOWERS BLOOMING IN EACH OTHER'S FACES

They drew a straight line through Nebraska and curled through the Iowan bluffs. Morning sun silhouetted trees and telephone wires. Sunsets made backroads golden. The Haircutter drove the truck between the guidelines while his fat heart fainted repeatedly within him.

Carol: rabbit-like. Long front teeth that slope into her mouth. Solid legs that hyperextend—pop backwards at the knee. She's short and blond. Her brown eyes seem pinched toward (as if attracted to) a pearl that rests or rolls on her protruding sternum. I'd say, "You're so beautiful," and she'd say, "Not really, but I know what you mean." She laughs at the slightest invitation, in giggles that thump like a rabbit's foot. She coughs up her heart and it sits cross-legged on her lips for a chat. She's chipper and prim. So rabbit-like, you nearly expect a butterfly to land on her nose. When she opens her legs, you nearly expect a butterfly to be burped from her pussy. Butterflies nearly equal pussies anyway.

We cut through heat haze in our empty truck, smiling. "Man I can't believe my luck," I'd say and say. Talk about a joy ride. Carol shouted to me over radio songs with her feet stuck out the high window. Her legs coming out of her cutoff shorts were as hyperextended as my thoughts. I thought about haircutting and how I'd no doubt have to tell her everything. I wondered what sorts of horrors I'd left lying around my apartment. Deflated socks here and there? An unflushed toilet? Pages of bad writing? All my tables! I thought, Will Carol still love me when she sees I need to use Gold Bond? *Does* she love me? I thought, What *is* love? I even asked myself what is *what?* What *is?* And all that kinky stuff from an astrology textbook you'd find in an antiques store.

Cattle dotted hills the color of their grassy shit patties. I'd smooth my hair in Men's Room mirrors, I'd suck in my stomach and huff it loose again. Every time I'd eat from her bag of road snacks I'd sneak a look at my teeth in the rearview after. I had no idea how close to or how far away from being kiss-worthy I was. Had I known that she'd one day be *begging* me to fiddle her diddle in the back of a cab, demanding that I look in her eyes while doing it so she could "come for my pretty lashes" I would have been much more relaxed.

The first time we checked into a motel and laid in that bed together I realized why life is worth living. When a pink little lady runs her dangling cartilage-hard nipples through your chest hair while you pet her rump, while she squeals, finding the pleasure hilarious, while she drips wetness onto your prick, beckoning it, you are touching heaven.

During sex, she flipped and wiggled like a hooked fish. I'm sure I just panted with a startled look on my face wondering, "Is this how?" After sex, her china hand rested on my chest and she told me about the outer space adventure novel she was working on. Her legs wrapped around mine and her feet wrapped too and she was all, "Oozy is a Rootaloid and Romo is a Magazoid and they have a baby named Woomalee Amatrist." The motel room started dripping a faucet like, "Are y'all done yet?" We went out to the parking lot to cool our sweat. Chiggers bit our bare legs. Semis honked night farts on the interstate. Moths ticked against the lot light overhead and Carol tapped a cigarette. I kept putting my fingers up to smell them when she wasn't looking. I thought,

Wow, "making love" is right. I thought, *Dang Girly.* I thought, *Talk about Cupid.* And all that crap.

In those motel mornings, we'd watch a news program on TV while the sun puked its deal out on the world. I'd open the curtain of the large lot window and truckers and families would pass by and look in at us for a flash just to see. Good, I thought. Get some reality mixed into this sick story of a guy who ate his boss's face off. Carol sat with little pink socks on, eating vending machine doughnuts with crust in her eyes. She always had a certain seriousness for the first hour of the morning, like she'd been with her dead grandma in her dreams and needed to respect that for a while. I'd gather our things and take them out to the truck, which would be attic-hot and smelling like wolf pee. Back in the room, I'd open the map on a bedspread and chew a toothpick waiting for Carol. She'd finally come out of the bathroom steam smiling and smelling like she'd scrubbed with flowers, brushing knots out of her wet hair, which looked like sheering sheep. She'd dress in her cutoff shorts, a spaghetti tank, and the little black high heels with the pointy toe triangles. She'd top it all off with a cig.

Yes, Carol smoked. It disturbed me, until I was like, "Whoa, you smoke?" and she looked at my fat belly and said, "We all got vices." Talk about putting your foot in your mouth, along with too much food.

Carol and The Haircutter drove the billboarded interstate smile-bent for New York City. They passed ads for cosmetic surgery, for theme parks, for McDonald's, etcetera. They used the ads to find lodging at night when H.C. could barely see and when Carol's valentine radiance was wearing. In the mornings they'd hippity-hop to the wolf-stained truck, recharged and in charge of the sets of charms they'd show like flashcards throughout the new day. They stopped at gas stations for road snacks and Carol let The Haircutter pay. They ate at a diner and The Haircutter, for the first time, felt the royal flush of pride. People saw: her, him, touching, smiling. Bills came and The Haircutter unflinchingly paid. Carol saw a sign on the road in Iowa that said Premise Picked Cherries!; they drove thirty-five miles off-course to a farm where they bought a ten-dollar bag from a genderless blob who had its short-haired head through a hole in a floral bed sheet and who sat in a chair they couldn't see. Carol asked if it could snap their pic while they were tasting cherries, but it grunted about how since it rained last night "my chair's stuck in the mud." H.C. and Carol helped it out of its chair, then loosened its chair from the mud. As it snapped their pic, it said, "Wish I could use y'all every day instead of knockin' my chair off with a porch post."

It was about getting food down our necks and about stopping at rest stops. She trickled pee from her little vagina like simply squeezing a lemon, while I sat down on darkness and unfolded a stained hole to plop steaming piles out like some sort of monster's function in a demented dream. And it was about talking as much as we could to teach each other about who we were and what we liked. Carol had a deep indent between her nose and lips and showed me in a diner how she could hold a cigarette there as a trick. I showed her my trick of being able to make it look like there's a little bird perched on my finger and I'm petting it. I smelled that my breath smelt like a sponge, so I laughed with my mouth closed, which felt like I was trying to look like a wise-ol' Santy Clause. Carol tickled my birdy under its chin, saying, "Can I be your Mommy?" Then the bill came and the waitress said, "Y'all two love birds have a nice day," and I pretty much hit Carol in the face with a sponge—I was drunk with open-mouthed laughter like, "Carol did you *hear* that?!"

She called Brother and Son's from a pay phone and lit the cigarette. I came out of the john and saw her across the restaurant, short and blond. I watched her grimace as she told about not being able to come to work anymore. I watched her stub her cig out in a single woman's ashtray and thank her. Then when we were leaving, I held the door for an old man who was entering with his family and he shouted, "Was it good?" I stated, "Best french toast I ever had in my life." And later, Carol was all, "You were so nice to that old man!" It was about charming each other like that.

Two kids on the road is what it looked like. Singing along to songs, eating sunflower seeds, "My lips are numb from the salt, let's try kissing!" But what it felt like was Fat. I felt fat and uncomfortable not being able to fart when I had to, not being able to burp rough when I needed to, and every time we came to a door and I held it open for Carol why'd I feel so stupid? I wasn't used to it all yet. Girls had always been something I snarled at, not something I was allowed to touch and to take pleasure from. She kept coming over to my side of the bench to cuddle up to my gassy, mewing gut, and I'd think, *How the hell's that something you want to do, Girly?* She'd take my hand off the steering wheel and put it up the leg of her shorts. And I'd just kind of sniffle and clear my throat thinking, *Please don't make me fail again!* I didn't know how to pussy-play back then, so I'd just spread the petals, part the sea, and wiggle my fingers in there, but she liked it anyway. She thought it was funny.

Even though I felt uncomfortable, I like those memories very much. She'd need to do a standing hug every time we stopped the truck for whatever reason. Get a little hug session in where I'd stand there confused and laughing. Then she'd need a picture of herself in front of whatever dumb thing—a bronze eagle at some rest stop—and she'd want the pic to be of her pretending to kiss it. Later, when we got the film back, all the pictures of her were just of her head and the sky because I kept smiling when I'd see her pose and my cheek moved the camera up. "Don't quit your day job," she said when she saw them. In all the pics of us where she'd held the camera out in front of our faces it looked like she was at Walt Disney World having her pic with that Hunchback of Notre Dame.

I sensed that I would get used to it, though, and that's what kept me faithful and excited. I knew that I would find comfort sooner or later. Same as I had come to find comfort in New York. You're the same person no matter what the scenery is, and the scenery is the same scenery no matter what person's in it. So as long as you're slept and fed, stuff's gonna do what stuff's gonna do. I treated us the same way. As long as I took care of my prize Carol, stuff was gonna do what stuff was gonna do. I just did my best, is what I'm saying. I let myself feel uncomfortable, and I let myself feel comfortable when that happened too. At a motel one night, I was petting her head and I was like, "Man, I love you." She flailed in the bedskins going, "No! Shh! Not yet! I wanna wait till you rilly fill it!" I was like, Okay whatever, Girly.

When she saw the New York skyline she squealed. It was raining. It was night. The streets were slick and shining different colors. ("It's *just* like the movies!") She cracked her window and held a cig out the crack and sat up straight to drag from it. She pumped her legs and looked around, releasing smoke through her smile *and* nostrils which was the ugliest she got. We had hip pain and rocks of road snacks in our stomachs. Our buttholes lisped the names of all the processed chemicals. I drove to the area where I'd found the truck; I pulled into a spot and unloaded Carol's things. I left the keys under the floor mat as instructed. Then, hunched in the rain, I patted the side of the truck and said a little goodbye, and I flinched when Carol saw. Then I was like, She'll think you have a sensitive side, so I kept going, and she was all, "You got a sensitive side, huh?" There's the word "man" in "manipulation," but there's the word "man" in "woman" too, so I wouldn't go trusting formulas like those. We took a cab to my apartment with my last few bucks.

What should I tell you about what followed my sudden abandonment in Times Square in '93? That I serendipitously found a poetry club after walking for two hours and that I met a lady there who listened to my story? That she got me a job working at the shop part of the club because I could name all the English poets and what they wrote and when they wrote it? That I overheard a customer who was serendipitously looking for someone to rent her freshly-dead old aunt's apartment?

The niece had inherited the apartment and wanted to rent it out for cash. Eight years I lived there on 37th and 6th and I never saw that girl again; I just paid the bills that were sent. It was an old warehouse building, so the elevators were oversized, the ceilings high as trees, the common hallways dark and labyrinthine. The apartment had two big rooms—one, the main room with a three-step elevated kitchen in the corner; the other, the bedroom. They were separated by an optional wooden door that could be pulled out of a slit-hole in the wall. That was my hairboard.

The kitchen was on a triangular dark wooden platform in the corner, raised to the height of three old wooden stairs. This was the apartment's charming feature. It's where I wrote under the ceiling-high window on a swivel chair pulled up to my writing table. By the light of the city I tried to write something good, and I never did. Behind my back then was the fridge, sink, and stove in a strip. Above the sink was the old aunt's portrait. The apartment came with some of her stuff, which I was glad for because I've never been one to have stuff, but I've always appreciated stuff's "homey" feel. When I washed my hands at the kitchen sink, I faced Old Auntie. Her white hair was butt-parted and tied back like Virginia Woolf, which I'd found to be so fitting for the writing room that I'd snapped when I first realized it, and shouted "Yes!" believing it was a sign I would write something good. I mostly just wrote lists of writers and what they wrote and when they wrote it to see if I could remember, and I always did.

The rest of this main room had windows that filled the wall facing 6th Avenue. I taped sheets up to cover them because it was too bright otherwise. No one wants to have to squint in their own main room. And I didn't want insomniacs across the street standing at their windows unfocusing their eyes on my hairboard either.

I think I had around fifteen tables and they filled that main room. If you saw, you'd think I was some sort of table freak. ("Oh there goes that table freak guy.") I got into buying tables because I wanted the perfect one to write at. When I'd stepped into the apartment for the first time, I saw that perfect writing spot under the kitchen window so I went straight to Macy's to shop for a writing table. I bought one there and didn't write anything good at it, and a few days later I saw a table in a restaurant that was more Lit-like so I paid a thousand dollars for it on the spot— almost half my Brother and Son's savings. Once I got it home, though, I found that I couldn't write as much as I wanted to. So the next day I bought a table from a catalog with the credit card I'd received. It went on like that. I bought tables at flea markets, I bought tables out of restaurants, I bought tables from people selling stuff off tables on the street, I bought tables at furniture stores. I tried every kind. All I spent my money on was food and tables. Little did I know, all I needed in order to write well was to have something to write about instead of just lists. Either way, I had an apartment full of tables.

My bedroom was called The Chambers even though I was the only one who knew. The Chambers had a double window next to the bed that I shaded with a red sheet, which later provided me and Carol with a place to make love where it felt like we were doing it inside of a heart. My bed was Old Auntie's wooden sleigh bed with the curl parts sawed off. The bark was sharp and you had to watch out not to touch it, but better that than trying to get a girl with a sleigh bed.

The floor was a shiny black plastic that had been in place since the 1940s. It came up in places as little bubbles that crackled when you tapped on them. The fireplace hearth was marble—fit for a panther to lie by—and had gold pokers and a grate that watched you like a monster with an underbite. I had my outfits in the closet, and your basic hygiene products on the bathroom sink. I had papers and Old Auntie's record player with a simple selection of recs. I had my scissor, which I'd bought at a barbershop straight out of the barber's hands. There was Old Auntie's leather couch in a corner by the fireplace, and a telephone stand in the foyer probably with Old Auntie's earwax still in the hearing holes on the phone. There were cars honking ten flights down, and old-timey music coming from the apartment above where the singer sounded like he had a dinner roll stuck in his mouth and didn't care.

That's the sound that Carol and I could faintly hear as we carried her crap down the hall to my door. Then the old sound of my keys turning the lock, "Ah, home sweet home."

The apartment was hot and fuzzy. I took her in by the shoulders and guided her around, "This is the main room. This is the kitchen. These are the tables. This is The Chambers—" She shrieked when she saw the sawed sleigh bed with its stained sheets. She stepped into the bathroom and opened the medicine cabinet, which I hadn't done since moving in. She saw cobwebs and a dead spider and Old Auntie's denture glue in there; I was so embarrassed. She lifted the red sheet that covered the bedroom window, breaking cobwebs that connected it to the glass. Outside, the wind growled like territorial cats. She went to wash her hands in the kitchen and snarled at Old Auntie's portrait. "I bet her ghost's in the wall spyin' through them eyes." Carol made me take down all the bedsheet curtains in the main room and she opened a window and whipped her hair in the wind, "It needs to keep us on our toes!" She wiped down the leather couch I had never sat on, then made it so the tables fanned out from it on both sides. It made you be able to walk freely around the room and stop to sit on the couch if you wanted to.

All this she did while I, casual as a con man, taped up the slit-hole where my hairboard was kept.

"Whatcha doin'?" she said.

"Oh this hole gets mold comin' through here that's bad for the lungs, so it needs to stay taped shut. I took it off before I left town cause I knew we were gonna get a heat wave. You know—tape meltin' to the wood here? Not good."

Because I liked her and wanted to keep her.

I said, "Hey them sheets on the bed are just stained, they ain't dirty."

I looked at her and she wasn't even listening—she was choosing a rec to play, "Ooh fun! Records!"

I kept on with my task, covering my secret with Old Auntie's duct tape, her dead cat's hair and piss-box gravel still stuck in the ridges on the side of the roll.

We cleaned the apartment like it had never been cleaned before. I sanded down the sleigh bed. We even thought to scrape gum off the undersides of the tables that had it. We bought food, flowers, firewood, and wine. ("Ooh *wine!*" she'd said.) Carol found the stand of Old Auntie's that I'm pretty sure was used to hang an IV bag from, and she wheeled it up to the bed and hung a fern plant from it. The tentacles wept halfway to the floor.

"What was once used for death is now a breathing organism," Carol said and I was like *man* it's nice to have a woman's touch. But she came to use that plant as her bedside ashtray. She'd stub out in it, and it'd swing and smoke like that thing for Catholics.

I had to go to work. I had worked at the poetry shop for a short time, then the law office for six years. I sat alone on a swivel stool in the empty basement of a thick building in Midtown and had tubes pointing at me in a 360. My job was to remove a canister from a tube when it lit up to redirect it to another tube and press a button for it to get sucked up into the body of the corporation where someone received it in their office. Spinning circles and counter-circles, using my hairy arms to do an ape's task, in the darkness of that workspace I'd think: *This isn't real! That situation with Carol up there! My life has a second heartbeat in it now!* I still had to go shit all the time—that love sickness thing. I kept telling myself, "You *do not* have to poop again, you *just* pooped." But al*ass*, there I was running with my pants half-down to and from the private john I had, yelling at those blinking tubes, "I'm comin'!" I'd shit with the door open, looking across the empty dungeon at my tube circle, grunting, "Just a sec . . . !" The john had a pink shag seat cover that matched the reason for having to shit—*Love,* and even matched the types of shits they were—*girly.* Because there wasn't much left to shit out after a while—it even made a sound like a girl going, "*Blech.*" But I'd laugh at the sound thinking, *Carol!*, as if she's teasing me, trying to make me laugh. I even pretended it was her who'd picked out that pink shag seat cover in an alternate life where she's the janitor. Seeing it alone when I wasn't on it—in its own shaggy foo-foo world—I fell in love with it like family, understanding fully what it's like to have a baby girl.

On Saturdays, we'd drink a bunch of coffee and do music on the record player. I signed up to have Old Auntie's telephone turned on so Carol could call her mom to shout, "I can't barely hear! We got jazz on full blast!" She'd cozy up on the couch to write more for her space adventure novel. She'd ask questions like, "Does *Woomalee Amatrist* sound too pretentious for a title or does it sound creative?" or "I'm gonna make three themes in this and not just one. Is that my call?" She'd sometimes try to write a poem to share at the open mic night we went to on Sundays. She had this whole list of city things she wanted to do—she got ideas from a magazine called *Now York.* ("Where's my *Now York?*")

That first time she decidedly said, "We're *going* to a poetry club and I'm *wearing* all black—don't judge me!" I saw her profile lined red by the light of that embarrassing stage, and she was so impressed, so humbled, that it made me squirm and feel home-sick. It was like, Hey, Carol what about us! She never did get up to share a poem. (I said, "Aren't you gonna do one?" and she tossed a hand, "Oh noooo. I didn't realize the caliber.") After the first time we went, I caught her reading *Woomalee Amatrist* when we got home. When I walked in the room, she shoved the man-uscript under her pillow and slept on it until she thought I was asleep. Then I heard her carefully slip it out like the tooth fairy and very slowly put it under the bed. She was beyond impressed by those open mic nights. We went back and went back. She asked people, "Hey, do you know what time this starts?" knowing perfectly well what time it started. Sparking conversation became her thing. Walking toward the subway afterward, she'd lift up off the ground, choking on her squeals, and I'd have to hold her down huffing like an alcoholic overaged balloon salesman. "You can't know what you're missing till you know what it is!" she'd say. "John, those are my people! Let's go to Xavier's reading on Wednesday! I think he was the best, but I liked that Asian girl too!"

Carol carried a watermelon home from the store, saying "DANG this is fun!" when H.C. pinched her rump. Carol made potato salad, saying, "I carried a watermelon," in all different ways. She said her period looked like a hatchet wound, and laid a whole day shivering in bed while I slipped chocolate bars under the door, proud to be so mature. We were freshly arrived in New York and our new relationship was in fragrant bloom. We weren't used to each other yet, so when I did a spittle piece that landed on Carol's plate, she ignored it and only blinked, keeping eye contact. We were courteous and complimentary. We'd make love and say, This is like nothing else, This is like our bodies were meant for each other, We're like puzzle pieces, and This is like fate.

We boarded a subway train and sat down smiling, holding hands. The conductor said, "Next stop West Fourth Street, transfers to the A, B, C, D, F, and M trains, stand clear of the closing doors," and while he said that speech, I looked at Carol and mouthed along with his words, not missing a beat.

"Nuh-uh!" she said, shocked and laughing.

"I just saw your hangy-ball," I pointed into her mouth.

"Eww," she said. "My uvula? I don't like that mine's pointy."

We rode on, and at West Fourth street we transferred to the F train. And while waiting on the platform I swelled with love for her. In the storm of our approaching train I said I love you to the back of her head. I said it again, and she turned around like, "What?" and I said, "I got somethin' in my eye." We boarded and sat across from a bum who smelled like hamster bedding and who was humming in a voice so high I thought he was a woman until Carol got done looking in my eye.

New York: the hustle and bustle, the bags of trash, the fast-moving loud-talking people mixed with cloudy-eyed people at the ends of their lives walking like prunes holding groceries. The shaken world spilled on the color grey—the people that landed and built their buildings and peddled their wares while eating their flavors of stinking foods fuck in foreign tongues right next to each other, separated by a wall a granny could punch through. New York: the little Italian part hugging the Chinese part, the suited Jewish men with their curlicues bouncing. Skyscrapers rise dick-like, like dicks covered in jewels showing off. Tourists shoot up the centers to stand in the heads to take pics of other jewely-dicks whistling, "What a man-made marvel." A hippie lady sits on the spit-strewn sidewalk coloring in the word *abusive* on a sign: *Left Abusive Man.* Sally forth, pigeons flapping out of your way. Pass a musical genius on the corner playing violin like it's the tool used to call heaven and God is on the line. Unsupervised school kids kick his coin cup and run away screaming, holding pizza. Young men drink from full-sized containers of juice. People look up, and people who pass them look up to see what they're looking at; people take pictures, and people who pass them say *I've taken that exact same picture before.* Trash bags blow through the streets and say *Thank You* on them. Lightning branches above buildings in which politicians conduct the world, perhaps even the lightning. Nannies push babies like swaddled bundles of hundred-dollar bills. Tomato, tomahto, tornado—call it what you were raised calling it, but here it's all the same. Every last one of us looks at the same numbers when we look at a clock, the numbers are just in different fonts trying to make our worlds *seem* unique. How many people in New York are seeing it for the first time? How many people have lived in New York their whole lives and can't afford vacation? How many people are just letting their dog stop to sniff another? One owner smiles down at them, the other owner stands quarter-grinning, looking around.

How many times did Carol and I meet after work on a certain street when I got to watch her walk towards me from half-a-block away—saw her blushing and looking down at her functioning legs, looking up at me, then down, then around semi-seriously, then down at her legs again, holding her lips in her mouth till she arrived at me squealing? You walk in the Fashion District arm-in-arm with your fresh new Love and when she sees a man selling belts she tugs at yours saying, "You wear your belt kinda high, don't you?" And that's the day you realize you've been wearing your belt mid-waist. In the mirror at home you move it down to the smell of the flowers you can't stop buying. They quiver, "Voila!" Every table has a vase of them in a certain stage of rot—New York: you and your girlfriend like to spend. Check the bank account and see that it's so low a goldfish couldn't even swim in it. You peek in the purse of your Love while she's showering and see two twenties and a bank card and you wonder when she'll start paying for things. And then slowly, slowly, the two of you get to the place where you start talking about things like that, though you never actually did talk about *that*—it comes at the same time you spit on accident at dinner when you're talking and she points to where it lands and laughs. Comes at the same time she says, "Yes, fuck it!" when you're "makin' L." Comes at the same time she automatically grabs the cart at the grocery store because she knows pushing one makes you feel absurd. New York: you're laying in bed with your Love and a cockroach drops from the ceiling onto your chest. Hind legs like a frog and a loud crunch when you kill it. And later, when you say, "I'll make a fire, it's cold in here," and Carol says, "It's cloudy with a chance of cockroaches," you think: *Impossible! She can't be so perfect and so funny and so happy to be with me!* You were right: impossible.

We couldn't walk an avenue without stopping to kiss. Two flowers blooming in each other's faces—one with a longer stem. I used to cut hair from couples who did that.

—

She liked to wear baby-pink lipstick. She wore that when I watched her lips say, "I heard you in the subway. I love you too."

I rolled my eyes, "Better call the press."

I love you. Three threaded words that turn you neither more woman nor more man. They're veritable spurts of semen—drops of concentrated relief, release. That's it. While Carol says it when she shows the $100 piece of sushi between her legs. While I say it when I see a singlet of her golden hair slip like a tip to the furniture, or when I see a singlet hanging from my beard and leave it there. "Aw, I love you!" Three threaded words that mean, "Thank you so much for letting me touch you whenever I want and for not thinking I'm gross even though I'm a shriveled piece of snail meat without no shell!"

Carol Mary Mathers never eats the last bite of her banana because it "has that piece of poop in it."

She said I was manly, I wasn't fat. I had never thought of that.

One morning she was sitting at the kitchen table while I was doing up some eggs and she opened a book to a random page and read it to me. She paused at paragraph breaks to sip from her coffee, and the snap that came from swallowing then parting her lips to speak—I was soothed and coddled and my eyes drooped and I fell in love with her on another level: as a boy does with his mother.

She quit smoking for me. Instead of smoking, she'd close her eyes and meditate on the burn of one, and if I spoke she'd say, "Shh! I'm having a cigarette."

I'd run to the work phone on blink breaks to call her:

"I miss you! It's only two o'clock!"

"I miss you too! I never wanna let these butterflies go!"

Sick stuff like that—all that Love crap that makes you say to the camera as you're hailing a cab, "Save your breath, I've seen a movie before."

Here's what you do to keep a good girl like that: support your bunny rabbit and take her to see poetry. Watch people on stage with pimples and beer-breath roll their eyes in self-disgust when they flub. Watch them unconsciously tap their foot to the off-beat of their words, watch their stance be like a cricket that got stepped on but survived. Watch Carol quietly say, "It's okay!" wincing with prayer-hands covering her eyes. She cares. When musicians are on the street begging, she gets as close to them as she can. She crosses her arms and pops her legs backwards and nods. She turns to me at clap breaks saying, "This is my kind of town, man. My kind of town," when normally she never says "man."

One day, when I got to work, I was waiting for the elevator to take me down to the basement and my boss made an appearance. He'd gone grey since the last time I'd seen him.

Says, "Mr. Reilly, I've got to let you go."

I say, "Who's going to do my job?"

He says, "Robotic arms."

I say, "But it's been six years, and I'm good at this job."

And he says, as he's putting an envelope into my human hand, "Well it's the year 2000 now, and we've got computers for most about everything."

And just like that, I was fired because of some robotic arms.

I went straight to the bank and faced the screen. Two hundred dollars. I went to the teller and deposited my check saying, "Can you put *double* that amount in?" She cackled back with her hairstyle like a nest of snakes on her head, "Honey if I could do that I'd be rich myself!"

I walked home with $1,873.16 to my name. Then when I got home I had to write a check out to the poet girl because it was the first of October the next day. I was like, "Onnnnnne thousaaaaand siiiix huuuuundreeeed annnnnd zerooo over one hundreeed," with my fat hand and my favorite pen. So there. All that to say that I had $273.16 when Carol and I were at our happiest.

I had to go out looking for work, but everything reminded me of Carol and of sex. Reading a book on the subway train—the way the parted pages bobbed with the bumps in the track—of course I thought of Carol bouncing on top of me! Her voice sounding babyish and in pain before her horror-movie orgasms. Her saying, "I think my sexual peak's now instead of thirty-six, I'm serious!" I would smile at my book and sort of coo, then I'd realize I was doing it, so I'd look around to deal with who saw. ("This book's hilarious!" showing them the cover.)

"I didn't do anything all day except wait for you!" she'd say when I got home.

I'd lick the tears of ecstasy off her face and call it "Mamma cat."

"I'm glad you stayed inside all day," I'd say, petting her greasy hair. "This way no one can steal you away."

We took a bath and plucked the spider webs that connected the tub to the wall like harp strings, and Carol got out to pee, and then sat on the pot staring at me for so long she peed again. A cockroach walked across the ceiling while hissing like Cupid was covertly checking on us while whistling.

"Boyfriend and girlfriend" became my favorite thing.

Then one day I was walking down the street after dropping off a failed job application—it was on 47th between 5th and 6th—and I was smiling at a thought of Carol, and I stopped dead in my tracks. I realized then and there that I was *actually* in love with her. I realized that I hadn't been before. Not at the motel, not even in the subway when I'd said it the second time. But *now* I was in love with her. And then I realized—really *realized*—that all this Love stuff was happening to *me*. *To me.* It was in *my* life; it was *me*. I was lucky. I was new.

And what did my mind go to?

To that duct-taped slit-hole in my apartment. Like tape over her eyes. She hadn't yet seen me.

I went home and got her off the couch and led her by the hands to the middle of the room.

She said, "You're ice cold, but you're sweating! You're shakin' like a leaf!"

I said, "Now listen here I'm gonna tell you somethin' I shoulda told you long ago, Girly. WHOA here we go—"

If you're ever wondering about why someone does something, and you're thinking, "Why would that person *do* that?" and you're judging the act on a scale of what's *normal* and what's *not normal,* stop right there and put your ruler away and get that pencil out from behind your ear. People do what they do for *reasons.* And more often than not, the reason is none of your business and it's not even something you'd understand. It's not your job to point out "flaws" in people. Like when there's an apple in the grocery store with someone's fingernail print stamped into it, you don't take the apple to the manager and chuck it at his jaw, you just choose another apple or get that one and cut the fingernail part out. Or hell, if you're a sicko, you eat the fingernail part along with whatever was under the person's fingernail.

"Carol," I said, "I'm gonna tell you somethin' about myself that you might think's shocking."

She said, "What?"

"It was a sort of therapy I did."

"Therapy?! You ain't a psycho right?"

"No, not therapy like that." I grimaced. "Sit down."

She put her butt on a table meant for lawns.

I said, "It was when me and Father John were on the bus out here."

"*What?*" she said.

"He was sleepin' in front of me one night. And I was lookin' at the back of his head through the gap between the seat and the window, you know. I was just like *hating* his head. Because you know what he said to me at that McDonald's stop? He was like, 'I want you outta me and your mom's hair.' So when he said that, right away I pictured myself walkin' on his scalp through his hair like it's some woods I'm lost in? Like with—I saw I had a piece of broken toothpick for a walkin' stick?"

"Okay?" Carol said.

"It doesn't matter, but I was sittin' there lookin' at his hair and he was asleep, so—" I stopped to chuckle, trying things, "—I took out my Swiss army knife and cut off a piece of his hair."

"Ha! Good!" she said, clapping.

"It made me feel kinda good though, in a funny way. Like orgasms, but not that weird." I farted fast, "No, not that weird at all, hell Carol. The point is, the next time I had the opportunity, I cut off a piece of someone else's hair." I tried shrugging.

"Who was it?" she said.

"Well, it goes on and on though."

She blinked and put a hand up to her pearl.

"I did it a lot," I said. "Hell, like every day I'd say."

"No, you didn't!" she said.

"Yeah, I did."

A sickening pause; a sickened look on her face.

Yes, to complete the weirdery I said this to myself often, sometimes aloud: "I'm The Haircutter, and I like it!" I cut hair with the confidence of a serial killer. It was my thing. It didn't make me proud, but it didn't make me ashamed either. It didn't make me masturbate, it just made me do it again. Locks frayed off with the sound of my father's gasp if he'd witnessed the scene.

There came a rush. Built up like fat and equaled a habit. Like saying I'm The Haircutter and I like it. Pull me up a chair and I'll take my scissor out of my back pocket in order to sit down. Put me in a movie theater and I'll snip from the head in front of me. Put me on the subway during sardine hour and I'll snip from the hair trusting me. Put me in a bar and I'll snip from your hairstyle, then order a Coke while inserting the lock into that miniature pocket jeans have. Put me on a toilet and I'll connect those freckles on my thighs with my fingernail to see a red vacuum cleaner outline for a second. See? It's nonsense, so who cares.

Except Carol.

"To strangers?"

"Yeah," I said. "And I can't say why. I just didn't have anything else to do or somethin'. It started bein' a habit. But I'm done with it now that I have you!"

"You cut off their hair?!" she said.

"No! Just a lock!"

"What do you mean? How'd you cut off their hair? Didn't they fill it?"

"No they didn't feel it. I never got caught. I just got good at it. You'd be so surprised how many times someone's hair is right in front of you just trusting you not to cut it, Carol."

"But it takes rill guts to do something like that, John! *Weird* guts," she said.

This pained me. I went to her and gathered her hands in mine and told her, "I know Carol, and I really hope it's somethin' you can accept about me. And it's over with too, it's totally done and over with, so what's the big deal? It was just somethin' that made me feel somethin' when I didn't have anything else in my life that made me feel. You know what I mean, *feel?* Like how I feel lovin' you." And at that cheesy admission, I felt so unlike myself

I released her hands and paced with my brows furrowed, grinding my teeth.

"You're lyin'," she said.

"Why would I lie?" I said.

"Cause you're a good guy!" she said.

"Well, maybe I'm not if I cut all that hair."

"But normal people don't do things like that!" she said.

"Unless they don't have nothin' else to do?" I tried.

"No! They go out with friends, they have hobbies!"

"That *was* my hobby! I even call myself The Haircutter, or H.C. for short! *Everyone* calls me H.C.! My name feels like it *is* The Haircutter. Carol, I had this whole life here without you and I'm just fillin' you in on it is all."

Then I thought, *No! I won't have this!* I got angry and said, "No! Now this here's dumb is what! I don't have weird guts, I just had a weird thing for a while." I picked up my keys and tossed them onto another table. She lowered her chin and writhed a bit, finding it sexy that my voice was raised.

"Okay! It's okay with me. It's fine," she said.

I panted; she bit her lip and her legs twitched open an inch.

"Well, look first. Before you say that," I said.

I went to the slit-hole and peeled off all the tape.

I said, shrugging, "God, I don't know why the hell I didn't tell you this when I was taping this hole up. I was all focused on the mold."

I balled the tape up and tossed it at the kitchen. I cleared my throat and slid out the door. That old feel of sliding it out again.

Carol gasped.

There it was: 3,017 locks of hair in every color taped to that old piece of wood, dated and noted, looking like the coat of a wild animal if you squint. The coat of the beast that is New York.

She put her hand over her mouth. It made me wince and look away. I was frozen inside, waiting. I tried to look at myself judgmentally to see if I thought I was weird, but it all felt normal to me—that's my hairboard, so what? Except it's pretty.

Carol tapped her toe triangles over to stand before it.

"This is my hairboard," I said, and faster than you can say Creepy she yanked me to the bedroom. And that's the first time we really "fucked."

So came the day when The Haircutter thought to stop in to Biggest Browse Bookstore to show Carol off as the product of the wolf job. They found the artistic boy Finn running a register.

"Why didn't you check in after completing the job?" Finn said.

The Haircutter said, "Was there something wrong with my mission?"

"I don't know. I just have your payment. I almost spent it."

"Payment?"

"Yeah I've had to carry your cash around waiting for you to come in. I was broke last week, you're lucky I didn't spend it."

Finn opened a drawer and handed The Haircutter two thousand dollars. The Haircutter went, "Yee haw!" on accident, then stuffed it in his pocket, stuttering and looking around. "I thought the per diem was my payment," he said.

"I don't know. But hey, come to an opening Mr. Christmas is having at his gallery tonight. Come by, you have to. It's the Thank You Gallery on 20th and 10th."

"Oh yeah?" The Haircutter said, "Well hell, I'll bring Carol. Here, this is my girlfriend Carol."

Carol said, "How do you do," and her heart fluttered beneath her protruding sternum—it was the first friend H.C. had introduced her to. And the last he ever would, because it was his only one.

Snow fell fast as rain the night we went to the Thank You Gallery. A crackling fire licked its shadows up the walls of Old Auntie's apartment. The windows were tall and sweating; the city outside was covered in crystalline. Carol made mulled wine to fragrance the evening with cinnamon and the snagging smell of alcohol. Lace at the hem of her dress dusted the 1940s floor as she padded around on black-bottomed bare feet, getting ready for the opening. She squatted with a compact to use the fire as a light on her lips; she applied lipstick. I sat before a table of roses in a chair that had curling, metal legs and a split, yellow seat. Her spine was to me. She saw me watching her in the compact—she jerked it away so I couldn't see, then she slowly glided it back and we held eyes seriously. Her hair was in one solid curl, matching the rose petals befallen before me. She stood up slowly, clashing with the flow of snow. I dug my fingernails into the table. She turned around to me blushing to show.

The chests of two "young people" pumped the air, tenderizing it.

A *Love Songs* record wobbled beside her, gleaming, matching her lips.

She looked like a protagonist.

I said, "You're the cat's pajamas," being careful to pronounce pajamas pa*jaw*mas as aristocrats do, and realizing with a fading smile that I don't in fact actually know what an aristocrat *is*.

Stuff like that. She wore a long blue dress, her black high heels, and for warmth her fur hunting coat. I wore the suit that I'd been wearing daily for job interviews. It smelled in the pits, but what're you gonna do.

The snow melted when it touched the ground, but blew straight into us before it did. Clouds of steam came out of grates in the street like ghosts of past-century bushes. Carol's high heels kept pace, tick-tocking the concrete. We had to stop in a deli to ask for a napkin so she could blow her runny bunny nose. Her makeup job looked nullified in the lime-green light. I loved her though, and she loved me. We hopped over puddles of slush, conquering them. A man shouted over the rumble of traffic and through the gusting white, "Do you mind if I tell you about the word of The Lord Jesus Christ?"

I said, "Look, we're here!" and pointed across the street.

The Thank You Gallery was a square white room with *Thank You* gilded a thousand times on the window. It was packed with people inside. Carol and I shook off our coats, shouting over the din. The floor had a layer of grey slush that people extinguished their cigarettes in. A smiling girl offered us free glasses of champagne. A man wearing horse blinders turned to his friend and hit him in the head with them, "Ooh sorry! You just became a fashion victim." His friend said, "That's okay. This is amazing. It's lovely, really. People are very gently on drugs."

The whole thing was strange to Carol and me—a square room stuffed with smokers and free champagne. What for? What's "an opening" mean? I thought, *Well, I guess it means opening up and socializing. Okay.*

I looked at Carol and she was brushing off her dress, drinking fast sips of her champagne. It was a tougher crowd than the one at the poetry houses. Where those people would suck pens and hunch and cross their legs doubley where you do the foot too, these people would glance at you with a look that could cut your next birthday cake.

I took Carol's arm and led her to a couple who were linked together by a chain that was hooked to a nose piercing on her and an ear piercing on him.

"Hi, I'm H.C. and this is my girlfriend, Carol."

I took a mouthful of champagne, then I saw something that made me spit it out so hard it dissipated completely and got nothing wet.

The girl on the chain shrieked and tugged her boyfriend away.

Carol and I stood before a pair of human lips sticking out of a hole in the wall.

Real lips.

"Oh my god, John! Weird! Is that rill?"

"There's another!"

Each of the three walls of the room had some holes with lips sticking out of them.

"Excuse me," someone said. It was a man who wanted to view the lips in front of us.

He stepped up to them and kissed them. A little peck.

"What's he doing?" Carol said.

We looked around—there was someone else kissing. A completely normal lady was on a stepping stool kissing one of the lip sets too. Someone took her picture.

"John! What *is* this?"

"It's the damned weirdest thing I've ever seen in my life, that's what."

"It's thrilling!" she said, like it was urgent to say so. Like she was saying, I'm gonna puke, gimme that trashcan!

It's thrilling!

The crowd parted to show a man in a blue suit kissing a hole in the wall while caressing it as if combing the fronds of a weeping willow. A bald man stood beside him howling, loving the love scene. He was in a checkered suit that was red and green, so right away I thought: *Christmas.*

I approached him with a finger pointed at him.

"I drove the wolf," I said.

"You're my wolf man!" he said, laughing eight feet taller than me.

I felt a surprise sting of jealousy upon realizing that the wolf was as much *his* as it was mine, if not more.

"Leslie Christmas," he said, shaking my hand and spitting in my eye. He had piles of spittle in the corners of his little mouth like piles of silver bullets.

"I'm H.C. and this is my girlfriend Carol."

"Hi!" Mr. Christmas said and kissed her hand.

Christmas had turtle's lips and his head looked enormous because it was hairless and his face seemed to take up only a very small area of the head. He looked like an ultrasound. But tall— *very* tall, and very thin. And when he laughed, which he did a lot, his eyes starred and his top lip gathered even pointier and flipped up a bit.

"What do you think of the piece? Isn't it a gas? She's one of my favorite artists. Blaise DonRobison. She's over there."

"What? It's an art piece?" I said.

He burst out laughing. "Yes! An interactive installation. The kissers will be here every day. Hi, how are ya?" he said to someone else.

I said, "What?"

"Yeah," Carol said with her jaw dropped, smiling, "How's that art?"

Christmas popped a laugh, "I like you two!"

Once more—his face was placed discretely on a small area of skin that protected his king-sized brain. It made me stand there thinking about how brains are stored inside of faces—or behind faces? Or simply how faces are placed on the skin that protects brains. And, as if this weren't odd enough, these "faces" act like labels on boxes with ever-changing contents—as minds change their contents, facial expressions label the change—see what I mean? The brain is Sad; the brain is Horny. And, because women love ultrasounds, Christmas was a womanizer and all that. The man is A Baby; the brain Likey. Most everyone's brains held charm for him—their labels clearly indicated such. He's the kind of man who stands on the edges of skyscrapers to get high.

"You are inside of the Thank You Gallery, *my* gallery, an *art gallery* and the artist is Blaise Don*Robison* and this is her *art* piece." He stopped to laugh sincerely and hike his pant legs up by the pockets. "It's a comment on the ambiguities of sexual pleasure in the year 2000."

I said, "Huh?" snarling.

Carol said, "I'm not accustomed to art ideas or ads or whatever, but any dummy knows art is sold in museums, so what's an interactive installation then? And what's an art gallery?"

"It's all the same! Art *is* art. This *is* a museum!"

"I thought it was an art gallery," I said.

"Yeah!" Carol shouted, pointing at me.

Mr. Christmas pushed us out of the way and ferociously kissed a set of lips, having to bend his legs to their height. Then he sucked away from them and looked at us half cross-eyed as if the scene was supposed to make us understand.

"It's art because the artist says so," he said quietly. "You can read about it on the sheet, it's around here somewhere. The idea inspired the artist enough to see it to fruition. She's letting us inside her mind. Hi, how are you," he said to a man in a wheelchair who had his wrists floating up around his head like gnats on a peach.

"Your hairboard is art," Carol said.

Carol had a black eye booger in the corner of her left eye and H.C. permeated body odor at a radius of five people and had one of his pant legs caught in the heel of one of his shoes when their lives changed forever.

Carol said, "I've been tellin' him, Mr. Christmas. He's got this giant board of *hair locks.*" Her fingers oogled the words like she was talking endangered crystals.

"Carol!"

"I've been tellin' him he should do somethin' with it," she poked Mr. Christmas to keep his attention. "It's a big huge sliding door at our apartment and he's got all these locks of hair that he cut off people on the street taped on it."

Mr. Christmas looked me up and down. His face labeled that his brain/box contained interest. "Is that right?" he said.

I set my champagne glass on a table and a dwarf took it and put it in a bin.

I said, "Carol, can I talk to you?"

"No, tell him John! How many hair locks you got, like, what's it, three thousand?"

"Is this true?" Mr. Christmas said, "May I see it?"

I stood huffing and said, "Are you serious?"

Mr. Christmas grabbed our shoulders, "Have a smooch and let's go."

"Now? Tonight?" I said.

"Do you really have this hairboard?" he was like.

And I was like, "Well yeah, I do."

"Then let me call my driver," he was like.

Impossible? I tell you, it happened just like that.

We were at my apartment in fewer than ten minutes from when Carol told him about the hairboard. I slid it out while we were still panting from the walk down the hall.

Carol said, "See?" and he told her, "Shh!" which made her choke on her gaping smile and go wait up the stairs in the kitchen, watching from there, wringing a dishrag.

He absorbed a big long look, then started pacing before it, scratching his shave. He stopped to mouth along to some of the notes—*Female, 12th and 2nd Ave, April 7th, 1994, 3:19 p.m.*— and then zipped his head forward and kept pacing before it. He finally spun around on his toes to say, "You did this. Over the course of eight years?"

I said, "Ach," and continued stripping shreds of bark off logs by the fireplace. My fingertips were nearly bleeding.

Carol said, "You makin' a fire?"

I thought fast, "No, just doin' up some kindler."

She said, "I never seen you do that."

I grouched, "It's cause I had a bunch made already!"

Mr. Christmas looked at the hairboard and went "Uuuuuuh!" like a man dying a death that he doesn't want to. I stripped the logs even faster, harder, watching him out of the corners of my eyes. It was silent, but for the sound of his shoes crackling on the black floor, but for the sound of me laboring over the wood.

"Why do you have so many tables?" he finally said.

"I was just trying to find the perfect one."

He nodded and walked penis-first toward me, "Let's have a seat at one."

I chose the table with the freshest vase of flowers on it.

Mr. Christmas said, "Why did you do this?"

"Ach," I waved him off.

"There's no need to be shy."

When he said "shy" a piece of his spit landed on my bottom lip. I swiped it off, disgusted with him. I said, "I didn't mean to hurt anyone." I said, "I just did it once, and then after a few times I realized I was a specialist at it, so. I always wanted to be a specialist at something, so that pretty much sold me on it." I got out a toothpick from my breast pocket and scraped my ear canal. "And plus, you know—watch the collection grow just like hair? Them locks look pretty don't they? And I don't even *do* pretty, but hell."

"Mr. H.C., I'd like to represent you," he said.

"What's that mean?" I said.

"I'd like to have you as one of my artists. I'd like to sell your hairboard."

"Sell my hairboard! What? I'm not an artist." You know.

He narrowed his eyes at me, then he burst out laughing and they flew apart. "Yes! Yes you are!"

My legs shrunk inside my pants and the hairs on my face stood out like spikes on a blowfish.

That night I lay in bed with Carol and she fiddled with my dead balloon penis and told me everything was going to be the way she'd always wanted. I had said yes to him. He said he would have an opening for the board just like the one for Blaise DonRobison. He said we'd have to prepare statements about why the board was important, and we'd have to find things to say that it's like or that it's a "comment on." He said that someone would buy the board and put it in their home as a piece of art. He said that after it was sold, I could come to him with another piece of art and he would try to sell it too, because it'd be part of my body of work as an artist. He said all that I had to do was admit that I'm an artist because people would be interviewing me and expecting me to care about art and my projects after. And I just sat there like a bird who flew into a window. I was like, "Okay." And I became an artist. After he left I looked sideways at the table where we'd sat and saw five droplets of spit that had been shot from his mouth during our conversation—sitting there like diamonds.

Two days after Christmas's visit to see my hairboard, Carol and I were coming home from a walk when the doorman, Doorman Diego, handed me an envelope.

"Zees was lef for you, Mr. H.C."

It said *Mr. H.C.* on the front and it was the first time I'd ever received a personal letter in New York.

"What's this?" I said.

Inside was a plain white card with gold lettering:

Mr. Christmas requests your presence at a cocktail
hour
at his home on Tuesday.
Four o'clock, Old Station West, Portsmouth.
Ask for Charlie Quick.

"Where's Old Station West, Portsmouth?" I said.

"Well, getcher phonebook out and look!" Carol said, squeezing my arm. "A *cocktail hour?*" she said, "Exciting!"

An elderly neighbor lady passed us snarling, clutching her pocketbook tight and telling her dog not to sniff us, "Don't, Kevin!"

Portsmouth was a forty-five–minute train ride out of the city. We swayed past blinding fields of snow, horses steaming under blankets, townfolk waiting like figurines on slippery station platforms. The sun set winter-early and made me a golden Carol. She kept putting her toe triangle up to flute my cobra.

"Stop, or it's gonna strike, Girly."

Carol had dyed her blue dress black and had unstitched the lace duster to use as a bow around her head. Her hair was in a shellacked braid and she wore her single white sternum pearl necklace, as she always did. I wore my regular clothes—one of my collared shirts and my jean jacket.

We took a taxi through Portsmouth to Old Station West and were shocked to see that it was an old train station made into a museum. We were like, "Is this right?" We entered and asked the ticket taker for Charlie Quick, and the lady picked up a phone and said stuff quietly. Her chin connected to her neck and made her tongue pop out and her eyes bulge like she was choking on her own face.

She hung up and said, "Okay."

We stepped into the main area like, "Okay." It was long and narrow with a high round ceiling. An empty train station. There were glass cases on both sides of the hall with artifacts and papers in them. Laughter echoed eerily—a little girl was skipping circles around her grandpa who was spinning a bookrack and who probably had Werther's in his pockets. And they were probably all ghosts, along with the lady who died by choking on her own face. There was a staircase that curled a grand wooden banister down into darkness. We heard clicks on the floor and looked and saw a man coming. He reached out to shake my hand when he was still a good fifty feet away, making him look either professional or ridiculous—I wouldn't know which.

"Mr. H.C.," he said, "It's a pleasure. I'm Charlie Quick." He was a plain blond Englishman in a plain blue suit. "And you must be Carol."

We clicked down the staircase and the downstairs floor was identical to the upstairs floor but without the round ceiling. We walked a long hall, Charlie Quick's hands in the pockets of his soft suit pants, Carol's high heels keeping pace, and The Haircutter trying not to wheeze. We turned right and started another small hall—it had the same glass cases on one side and a picture of a deconstructed black-and-white train on the other, and at the end of this hall was a dead end with some chairs and a couch and a statue of a conductor waving. This end, however, was anything but dead. Charlie Quick glanced back at us once with a smile as we came closer and closer to the couch and chairs. When we reached them, we were not gestured to sit down—rather, Charlie Quick walked behind the couch, stepped over a *lamp cord,* and stood in the four feet of space behind the couch and the wall, looking down at a miniature wooden door.

"What the?" I said.

Carol threw her arms up delighted and said, "I'm just gonna wait and see!"

"It's a unique home. Mr. Christmas owns this museum."

We stood in our tall bodies looking down at the little door. It was shaped like a mouse hole, it went up to our thighs, and had an engraving of a Christmas tree on it. Charlie Quick pulled up his pant legs and squatted to turn the little brass knob. It opened out towards us as thick as a vault and an unseen bell jangled roughly.

Inside was a straight, blue velvet tunnel with a pearl of white light at the end. I'm saying there was a royal blue velvet mouse hole tunnel behind that miniature door behind that couch in the basement of that train station museum. And you bet we were told to get down on our hands and knees and crawl into it. But before we did, I thought of my Carol and said, "Now wait a minute here, what's this all about?" but then from the pearl of white light came a camera flash, "Is that my wolf man?! Welcome to my home, Mr. H.C.!"

I went first and then Carol. Halfway down, she sneezed and Charlie Quick said, "Bless you," and I realized he could see her butt wrapped tight and wiggling in her dress so I looked back at him with bared teeth, but he was just kneeling at the door with a pleasant expression on, making sure we got through all right. I thought, *Okay, relax and just see.* Another camera flash— Christmas was taking our picture. "Don't let him see down your cleavage!" I said to Carol, ticked off. At the end of the tunnel was another door and Christmas was there squatting.

"You came! You actually came!" he said.

The ceiling touched my hair. Mr. Christmas had to walk with his head bent in his own home. Home? It was a small room lit by a Christmas tree and a murky aquarium that hummed like a background tenor for a Christmas song. There were white cats everywhere—walking around or sleeping on the furniture. There was a low blue velvet couch, there was a low glass table that you

could see the black carpet through. Across from the couch there
was a kitchen that made you let out a sigh of relief because it
looked like a regular apartment kitchen from New York City—a
strip of stove, fridge, and sink with the normal light that a kitchen
has, though it was sickly dim.

Mr. Christmas opened the door to his bedroom for a second,
saying, "The bedroom," and we saw a black room with a black
bed with white cats walking over it. Sleeping on it. And when
Carol later used the bathroom, accessed by the bedroom, she said
there were two cats shitting in the litter box at the same time,
growling at her while she peed. The place was a real dump, a real
eccentric's lair—even had a computer on the floor with graphs on
the screen. I sneezed and heard it slap the glass table. Carol said,
"Lookit!—the aquatic fish match the ornaments on the tree!" and
when Christmas and I looked, she wiped my snot up off the table
and petted it onto a cat's back.

We were given goblets of wine. We were told to sit on the
couch, which was so sunken in our knees went up to our chins. Mr.
Christmas sat in a puffy TV chair and screamed, "WATCH!"—
we jolted and wine splashed out of our goblets. He demonstrated
how his chair electronically reclined. A buzz harmonized with the
fish tank as he reclined all the way straight, holding his goblet
aloft, then slowly came back up to sit. And of course as soon as he
was upright he burst out laughing.

Christmas will burst out laughing at something or other in his
head and he'll howl and grip whatever's handy. He bursted out
laughing and slouched down in his chair laughing so hard he had
to chew the armrest. (Once, months later during one of his laughs
in a steak restaurant, he picked up a knife and stabbed it into the
wallpaper and it stayed there bobbing, then fell and knocked over

his glass of wine which Charlie Quick *sucked up* off the edge of the table so it wouldn't get on Christmas's suit.)

"Wait—you live here?" I said.

"I live in many places," he said.

I was like, "Okay."

A cat jumped up on my lap and meowed, wondering, "Can I be petted?" I saw my snot on its back—what a coincidence that it was the same cat. I stood up to make it drop off and it clung for a sec looking up at me; then it dropped off and I sat back down, grunting louder than I would've liked, but that couch was low. I looked at Christmas and he was blowing on a cat that was perched next to his chair on a side table. His top lip flipped up ridiculously as he blew on the squinting cat so hard its fur parted down to the skin. He turned to look at us and seemed slightly drunk from the exertion.

He said, "Oh, you have to see my scales if you come here, that's the rule. I do these voice lessons." He did a lung-clearing cough and swallowed the produce. "Scales in G-alternate-minor," he announced and a passing cat meowed like, "Oh, goody, I love this song!" Christmas clashed with his fish tank doing singing scales like a nervous person telling a stranger about their morning poop because the stranger is an artist and the person can't even so much as sing. I was sitting there like, "*Huh?*" Carol clapped dramatically when he was done.

"You should perform out!" she said.

He buzzed his chair back to recline, sipping his wine from there as a game to see if it wouldn't spill on his face.

"Are you married? Cause I bet girls go crazy for that!" Carol said.

"I'm not married. Having one body is burden enough," he said.

I said, "Huh?"

"I detest having a body," he said. "Isn't it a pest? I have to distract myself from it."

"What do you got all these cats for then if you don't like pests? I don't care for animals, but I like meat," Carol said. "Get in my stomach," she said to a passing cat.

Christmas asked about my hairboard.

"Are you ready to sell that door?"

I had thought about it. I'd thought: if I sell that board, you can't argue it'd be a manly move. Especially since I like the board so much. It'd be a sacrifice for my girl. I'd have this great girl, I'd have money, and I'd have a "job." It made sense.

"I'm ready when you are."

"Good!" he said.

And it was hot in the lair, and I don't like wine, so I said, "How long is this cocktail hour?"

Christmas laughed like a female seal barking in the background of Carol saying, "Jonathan Reilly Junior that is the rudest thing I ever heard you say! I'm sorry, Mr. Christmas, or Leslie? What should we call you, X-mas?" And he just laughed at her, not deigning to answer a question that his Charlie Quick should've taken care of.

He did a speech about my hairboard then. His purpled lips sampled the words soundlessly before he spoke them. He sat up straight: "If someone feels compelled to create something, then the something created is art. Because, where did that compulsion come from? The only explanation is that it came from art itself. Art is everywhere. Babies are art, or at least the ones that weren't accidents. Your hair thing, yes. People want to look at it! Because they're compelled to! Compulsion is born of art, as art is born of compulsion. My apartment here is a work of art; I felt compelled to create it." A cat jumped up on his lap and he swatted it off, disgusted. "Synonyms for compulsion: Obligation. Urge. Obsession. *Need.*" When he said "need" he pointed at me.

"See now that's interesting," Carol said. "You're opening me and John's eyes up. He told you we're from Wyoming? See, cause most stuff just takes longer to get over there."

Christmas was fingering his goblet rim, smiling at me.

"Oh, tell me," he said, "what does Mr. H.C. stand for?"

"It's not Mr. H.C., it's just plain H.C. Actually, I'm The Haircutter, but most people ask me what that means, so I go by H.C."

"THE *HAIRCUTTER?!*" he screamed, his cats hissing and running to hide.

He got down and chewed the carpet.

CHAPTER FOUR

THE DICK OF FATE

We left Christmas's museum with bellies gurgling the dregs of mostly peed-out wine. We ate Tic Tacs and yawned all the way home. Even Carol was tired of it.

The next day I was knotting my tie when Carol said from the bed, "What are you doing? You found a job! You're an artist, remember?" She undressed me piece by piece like a little ceremony and we smoothed our goose bumps by getting back under the covers and rubbing up against each other. "I love your chest hair!" she screamed.

In order for Christmas to sell my hairboard I had to dust it off. I made a fire and Carol made a Jell-O mold. I blew on the board a few times, then Carol walked the length of it with her hands behind her back like Christmas. She popped her legs backwards for balance before she straightened a lock—her floor-length dress looked weird in the back accordingly.

"Aren't you sad to see this thing go?" she said.

"I don't really *do* sad."

I guess if I had my way I'd keep my hairboard where it was and I'd go on Monday to get my old job back. I liked the peace I had in Wyoming when I just did my carwash job and went to see my crush and no one bothered me. A "leave me alone" kind of thing. I wanted what I've always wanted: nothing. And Carol. I wanted Carol and nothing else. But it was a Christmas who stole the Grinch situation.

—

Christmas sent Charlie Quick and some "art handlers" to get my hairboard. They put plastic over it and unscrewed it from its track. Charlie Quick lifted his sunglasses up to show how elitist his eyes were when he said, "Mr. Christmas would like you to come to the gallery now to sign papers." Carol waved goodbye to me and the hairboard with a silk hanky.

The Thank You Gallery looked completely different in the light of day. Only "the kissers" were still there. Their lips were through their holes, their whack-job minds and bodies were on the other side of the walls waiting. Charlie Quick motioned for one of the handler men to kiss a set, and I watched the man slowly understand what it meant and by the time I left, he was down to an undertank and had a radio out and an arm up on the wall, and the back of his head squirmed and I heard sucking at musical pauses.

Mr. Christmas was on the phone, but he motioned for me to come into his little office.

I stuffed my fatass into an artsy chair and watched him cover his phone in spit. Everything he said sounded like an airplane door ripping off at forty thousand feet. The words seemed like they'd stick to a fridge. He spoke from a glitch in time and space. When the person on the other line had a turn, Christmas lightly whistled with his brows in tide with what he heard.

He said, "Caboose!" and hung up the phone and clapped and said, "Artist's Statement." He poked his tongue out to wet a finger and opened a drawer to peel out a piece of paper. He handed me a pen and sat on his desk with his fingers on his temple veins.

"Why," he said. "We're going to need to know why you cut all that hair, *why* you then cataloged them on the hairboard, *why* you got pleasure from seeing them up there. We're going to need to know *what*. *What* does cutting hair do for you, do for the victim. How. *How* does it relate to life and how does it communicate with society as a *whole*."

I don't remember a lot of what we wrote, but it was in a writing style totally unlike mine and had comparisons to humanity that I completely disagreed with.

I said, "There's only one reason why I did it. It was the only thing that made me feel."

He wet his eyes in appreciation. He said, "Good. You can tell them that, but tell them this too," tapping the paper.

He took my picture to have in the corner of the Artist's Statement, which would be printed and handed out at the opening. Later, when I saw the pic, I saw I looked like my thighs were glued together and my whole body was completely held up by my feet pointing out like I think I'm a ballet dancer. My palms were pointing backwards and my eyes were like, "What are you looking at?" And next to my pic was a close-up of the hairlock from *Male, F-train, March 12, 1998, 12:45 a.m.*

I got another one of those white cards from Charlie Quick:

> You and a guest are cordially invited
> to the Thank You Gallery's unveiling of
> The Haircutter's *The Hairboard*.

Carol made herself an arty purse to carry for the night—a jack-o-lantern. She slapped its guts onto a long wooden table with a smile on her face. She unstitched the lace duster from her dress and used half of it as the purse handle. The other half she sewed to the neckline of her dress, and her little cleavage heaved against it when she breathed, making the lace turn up and down. I had my suit washed with the last of our wolf job money.

The room was packed with the same sort of people and the same slush floor all over again. Everyone clapped when we walked in. Carol said, "It sounds like rain!" I took her silk hanky from her pumpkin and used it to sop up my sweat. Someone said, "Don't be nervous, brother! You're awesome!" Carol's baby hairs looked drawn on her face—that was her only jewelry besides her sternum pearl. She held a hand over her womb and waved with the other. The jack-o-lantern swung, watching the scene. I fed the hanky back in through one of his eyes and my fat hand burst through it.

"Sorry, Carol!"

"Shut up! Smile, dang it! Everyone's watchin'!"

I smiled, my nostrils flaring as hard as I could make them flare.

The room was a bouquet of glasses clinking, of the sexes laughing, of the muddled melody of a song beating, of the cutting perfumes on all the ladies. I started shaking hands, having no idea how long I'd be at it. "NICE PIECE!" "I LOVE THE PIECE!" Their words beat toddler-hard on my eardrums. A flashbulb went off in the direction of "the piece"—it was somehow mounted on a wall. It matched the fur coats socially dancing crisscross through the room. I went to stand before it. There were spotlights shining on it. Someone stepped up next to me and I automatically held out my hand—he shook it without having to look down to find it. He had two rows of dictionary-definition teeth and a cigarette pinched between them. He talked and smiled without having to take the cig out of his mouth or squint, "Nice piece. I'm with Christmas too."

I said, "Oh! You're an artist too?"

He said, "I just had a show here three months ago. The one with the wolf? You didn't see it?"

He wore shiny black shoes with matching hair; he wore a soft red sweater fit for a wolf. His shave was blinding. And his eyes were two spheres halved by lids. The lids looked like dick skin, but purple. His irises hung half moons to do the law's minimum.

He said, "I'm Scott Harp, you didn't see my wolf piece?"

I said, "No. Sounds like cruelty to animals," and went straight to the john.

There was a line to use it so I got on the end and was standing there for a beat before someone at the front said, "Cut the line! Please, by all means!" and the special treatment started.

There was a scented candle on the sink. I stood in the mirror. Saw fat, clear-headed H.C. got scared by a wolf man and ran to hide with a scented candle. I saw that I was bothered by this man—*why?* Call it *ego* or call it *lego*—they both can build a house (in which a nighty dress hangs on an Arctic Tundra Grey who pads around on hind legs salivating). I slapped my cheek and saw it ripple. I decided I needed that hairboard to be sold at a price so high opera singers would fall flat trying to reach it.

I left the bathroom and started ferociously shaking hands with whoever I saw, confusing some people, delighting others. I went up to Christmas and slapped his back and yelled, "Come on! Take our picture! Over here, over here!" Christmas hooted hard and I smiled "proudly," feeling the foreign pull on my face, wondering *Is this how?* I even forgot about Carol. *Forgot about Carol.* At one point I turned around and saw her jut out her hand at a passing girl and state, "Hi. I'm Carol." The girl laid her hand in Carol's as if giving her a dead rat, then changed her mind and took it back ("Actually, that's my dead rat—I just had its nails polished.").

The camera flashes popped. People pointed saying, "That's the guy!" or "Hi, Haircutter!" Women held their hearts with hands jeweling brightly. Charlie Quick came and said something in Christmas's ear, something that made Christmas burst out laughing, which made a passing woman flinch so hard her wine slipped out of her glass. People were already asking to buy my next piece.

"It was one of them whirlwind-type dills," I heard Carol say and say.

Carol and The Haircutter talked to the press and to potential buyers and to anyone else who approached them with their hand out like a bayonet. *The Hairboard* sat quietly exposed on the wall, absorbing smoke. The next day, it was on the cover of the paper under the heading: *CUT IT OUT! New York artist cuts hair of 3,017 oblivious pedestrians!*

That night in bed, I saw flashbulbs in the center of Carol's *O* mouth and flashbulbs flashing at flashbulbs when I came into her. My hairboard sold for $XXX,XXX.XX—to the elderly couple covered in so many jewels they couldn't even lift their arms to shake my hand. Carol jumped screaming around the apartment while I dug a hole in my mind and filled it with $XXX,XXX.XX and tried to get it to make me feel. I even sat down on a table and said to myself, "Be happy about it like people do." I've just never been one for money, or for numbers for that matter. I never even knew my own phone number since I always had to look it up, so I never had to memorize it.

Christmas "sent a car" to take us to a celebratory dinner. It was in a restaurant covered in splattered paint—walls, tables, and chairs. Candles dripped their honeyed glow on the clapping hands of supporters as we entered. We walked a long table saying, "Hi, how are ya, okay that's nice there, alright thanks so much, well isn't that something I wasn't even an artist just one month ago." I spotted the wolf man Scott Harp, and I puffed my chest out. Christmas pointed at me and Carol and rang a gold bell with a bow on it. Charlie Quick appeared and stood on a chair to hold a mistletoe over us. "Kiss!" they shouted. I flicked my tongue at Carol like a snake and she flicked too. Everyone laughed. Carol laughed so hard, her head fell back and I licked the length of her accordionic neck. I looked at Scott Harp—he was clapping, liking our act. I lifted a leg and farted hard. Carol said, "Let's sit down! I need a drink after all this!"

We ate like a king and a queen. We didn't even know what we were eating. All's I know is it tasted good, while Carol sat next to me, saying, "John, all these people are here cause'a you. I can't wait to make L next. You look so handsome sittin' up like that in your suit. You're makin' my pussy twitch." She masturbated me with her words. While down the table Scott Harp used a pocket knife to clean paint out from under his fingernails. He then produced an *orange* and used the same knife to peel it with. The citrus spurts intersected the chit-chat sung like bird warbles from the Adam's appley necks of the most perfumed and jeweled up ladies I'd ever so closely seen. More dinners and more events followed. A train of decadency crossed our lives and we hopped on.

Fame. Fame in New York. Fat vibrating to the beat of the song. You see women so tall and so beautiful it makes you believe in extraterrestrials. Restaurant owners whisper with voices as hot as hell, "She'll go home with you for free. She's Brazilian. Really fun. No? How about some more bread?" He shouts, "Carol, you are stunning tonight!" while your ear drips his breath off in droplets that could no doubt poison children.

Carol and The Haircutter fought like black-and-white camera crews were hidden in potted plants around the city. It was "glam" to fight. Carol's curls bouncing in slow-mo when she slaps me. Mascara smeared cinematically when we arrive at a party— Carol sometimes spending it on the host's bed. Women went to the bedroom to "see if Carol's okay" and they all hung out in there. "Someone go get a bottle of champagne. Someone get Carol chocolates." Carol complained about how The Haircutter loves her the way she is and always goes with the flow like a girl. "Carol, you use a handkerchief?" And she'd say, "It's my hanky. I wave to John with it when he leaves. I always keep it between my breasts." And an ugly-faced lady sips her champagne thinking, "*What* breasts?" I can't remember a single reason why Carol and I fought, but I remember teardrops caught in her curls, and me going, "Hey cool, look at how your tears are just sitting on your hair," and she was like, "Pretty, they're like pearls!"

We panthered around the city in a shiny black car, bottles of champagne foaming. We went to openings, to restaurants, to lounges, to parties, and to events. Carol poked me constantly to whisper, "Manners." I'd "snap" at anyone who came to our table. ("What, you like the hairboard? Good. That's fine. Thanks. No, I'm quite happy with Mr. Christmas, thanks. No I don't have any inspirations, no. Alright, see this here's a *steak* and alls I'm trying to do is get it down my *neck,* so if you'll have some manners and scram the hell outta here . . .") Carol cried in bathrooms, tipping towel-givers all her cash, telling them her crow caw story about the big mean man she's stuck with cause he fucks her just so.

Then show us at home! With each hump, Carol says, "I'm gonna cry, I'm gonna cry, I'm gonna cry!" And with her orgasm comes a blubber of tears, "I'm livin' in a dream! I love you!" I roll over to get her hanky from the nightstand and see a cockroach on the floor—it had been watching us the whole time. I know if I get out of bed to kill it, it'll run out of the room. So let it watch.

The island couldn't contain the breadth of our love—it made tea of the rivers and all the birds drank it, getting fucked up. It could "only be so." (You know.) It was impossible that, if even for a moment so slight it could masturbate on the tip of a candlewick, our love wasn't the most important thing going on in the world.

I bought a pole and a paintbrush and taped the paintbrush to the end of the pole and wrote with pink paint *I LOVE YOU CAROL* on the brick building ten feet across from our bedroom window. With her hair resting on one shoulder in a solid curl and with the snow polka-dotting between the message and the window, Carol said, "Take a pitcher of me in front of it." She stroked her curl like it was a mink stole and smiled with her eyes closed for the pic. A bird flew into the window, absolutely wasted.

Carol's mouth around my rod—like a fish on a hook.

Carol's boobies bouncing so hard they're blurry—ha ha, you're hilarious, keep going. The Haircutter needs a relief to the weight and almost melancholic state of being so in love. And from feeling such suffocating contentment. If I passed a mirror I'd stop to see what expressions Carol might like. You know how it goes. A long and lasting pull on the prettiest cello string. We slept with smiles on our faces. Ring in the new year with a bell on a cat for all we cared. We were busy tossing spaghetti at the wall—if it stuck, she'd go, "Supper's ready!" Then we'd "fuck" and it'd go cold. Stuff like that—that like stuff. Every act was mirrored as: Everything! Everything! Everything!

One day Christmas called me into the gallery and had me spend an hour in a closet painting. He had little canvases and he said, "Whatever you do, don't try to make a scene. Don't paint a mountain and a tree or whatever. And no house. Just pick a color and paint a shape on the canvas." He held my fat hand and showed me how we could lay down a stripe of green and then put a blob of yellow near it and call it done.

I said, "Really?"

He was like, "Yeah, that's fine. We just need these to go with the body of work. A few Haircutter paintings."

He left me alone for an hour and when he came back I had twenty-five paintings filled with who wrote novels in first-person present tense and when they wrote them. He grabbed the yellow blob painting and burst his head through it, well pleased.

Once they were dry, he called me back into the gallery and told me to bring Carol. ("She's your gimmick.") We stood beside a woman who smelled clean and who furrowed her brows at my paintings, which Christmas had hung on a wall. She splayed red fingernails on her throat and dangled a hand of them over a hipbone. How powdered was her hairy skin, how insectile were her lashes. How puckered were her lips—enough to resemble a butthole. Carol was narcotized. She complimented the woman on her colorless clothes. "I like your plain tan skirt," she said slowly, sincerely admiring it.

"I have to catch a plane," the woman said *(in an accent)*. And with the sky star-spangled above the Thank You Gallery as if Charlie Quick had washed it for her visit, she told Christmas, "He's absolutely fabulous."

"Haircutter paintings!" everyone said, or whispered if we were around. Carol wore glittery green all the way up to her brows. She styled and sewed her lace duster dress in all different ways. She smiled with her shoulders raised when she finished a conversation, and uncoiled like a snake when starting one. She *listened* while slithering between the words that she heard with her eyes slitted. She allowed people to talk to her for minutes upon minutes straight and she'd say, "Interesting! Huh, isn't that interesting? Now THAT'S interesting," nodding her head so hard her hairstyle slumped. She'd roll her compliments in sugar before serving them. ("See, and I don't mean this just cause I'm *sayin'* it, but I *love* that.") A napkin doodle would get a standing ovation from Carol. "YOU ARE . . . the real thing." She made people blush so hard their faces caught fire. She liked the whole thing. Appreciating. Liking the laughter, participating, saying, "Sure!" when someone offered more champagne. She got out a little notebook when she met someone to record their first and last names. And H.C.? I wanted to start all conversations with: "You've got the wrong guy." If someone asked about art, I'd tell them about Old Auntie's portrait above my sink or I'd just list colors I like, and say, "Is that what you mean?" I was a coin someone had tossed into a fountain after kissing it with their uppermost wish. Underwater, unmagical, and idiot-still. But they didn't care. If a dog laid a purple crap and you asked him how it happened, you wouldn't think the crap was any less purple if he couldn't answer you, right? Still—at lounges I'd eat the provided snacks and chew to the beat of songs like, Will this do? I'd drop my jeans and wiggle my butt as my signature dance move. You know. Going through a beaded curtain and not knowing if you should hold them spread for the next person. Stuff that makes you go, Hey this ain't me so I don't know. And in your head a blimp as fat as you goes by with a banner: *They Can't Polish No Turd.* I finally had Christmas give me a sheet with the answers to the questions on it. When reporters called, I just read from the sheet while Carol sat on a table smiling like that dog probably looked when he was laying the purple crap, or else for sure how he looked when he turned around and saw it was purple.

They loved and loved while becoming more and more famous. The paintings sold and sold. Christmas dove and dove from a high board into a room full of gold coins. Collectors heard and heard The Haircutter's name. Articles were written and written about him. *I Got My Hair Cut By The Haircutter and Now I Have PTSD: How Far is Too Far to Go in the Name of Art? By Jamie Talentless Civilian.*

My paintings sold and sold. Then they resold and resold, making my worth increase. Carol and I spent the money on dinners and "drinks on us" moments where the bill was more than we made in a week at the carwash. We bought so much food at the grocery store we had to have it delivered. We ate and ate, getting fatter and fatter.

I said, "Don't you wanna buy a new dress?"

And Carol panicked, "You don't like my dress?!"

I told her the truth, "That's the sexiest damned dress I ever seen. And I love how you change up what you do with that lace duster thing. It's creative and fun."

She thought I'd chosen the right words—she came and kissed me, "I love your suit and jean jacket, too. Let's always just wear the same stuff."

As for our apartment—same thing. We just weren't ones for shopping. We didn't feel right being in stores and picking out stuff. Carol bought a red silk robe the one and only time we went shopping, and it hung like a bloody loogie in our empty closet for months till she wore it. So our apartment remained the same, while our bodies bulged against our same old clothes as if to hug them.

Carol and The Haircutter were everyone's favorite. Carol and The Haircutter were the model of love. People drew their cartoons. Carol started smoking to "handle the pressure," and soon, her cartoon always had her with a cig. Soon, when we'd pose for pics she'd say, "Don't crush my cigarette, Puss."

"You got a whole pack!"

"Doesn't mean I want 'em all crushed."

We'd look around—*where were we?* Somewhere between an invitation and a car ride home. Somewhere between Wyo and Mars. Somewhere between a marble floor and a cat—it peed on a supermodel's fur coat and arched across the room, its own fur grazing the ceiling. It hit a politician in the head and made his security guard shriek, "*What the FUCK?!*" It slinked away with its mouth oddly open and someone snapped its pic.

"Let's just stay for one more drink" became the thing.

"Let's go F in the john so we can stay" became a tactic.

So we'd F in the john and then I'd go find a couch to sit on while Carol walked the room doing our socializing. I sat below one of my own paintings once and didn't know it. Someone was like, "Can I snap a pic?" Till I figured it out and said, "Oh. Fine." Popped a fart out to put some color in the face, to fluff the couch, to assure the photographer wouldn't sit to chat after his camera flashed. He sat right down in the fart.

He said, "I'm Keith. I was named after a belt buckle in the hospital gift shop."

A passerby said, "Oh, cool! That's so white trash!"

Keith said, "Excuse me? Thanks a lot? Don't you think it's inappropriate to apply that term to a complete stranger?"

"*I think* it doesn't matter," the passerby challenged back.

They sworded with limp penises trying to get them into boners so someone could win. The Haircutter chuckled, making Keith lightly bounce. A cheeseball arched cat-like across the room and a man caught it in his mouth like a politician's head. First thing he did was turn to see if The Haircutter saw, and said, "Score."

One day, I got another white card from Charlie Quick:

Please come to the gallery to speak to Mr. Christmas.

I said to Doorman Diego, "They're telling me to go to the gallery again."

He nodded and pressed some buttons on his controller.

"Famous," he said, pointing at me.

I laughed, "Haha!"

I went to the Thank You Gallery and found Christmas standing before a painting. The painting was: *The End?*

He was wearing his red-and-green plaid suit. When he saw me come in, he said, "This is stupid, get rid of it," and Charlie Quick appeared to take the painting out of sight.

"What are you doing next?" Christmas said, and a piece of spit landed on the back of my hand like it was tapping it to ask a question.

I said, "Uuuuuh?"

"The next piece in your body of work. What's next, what have you thought of?"

I said, "What?"

He howled and went to a wall and slid halfway down it to speak to me in an invisible chair. "It's easy, Haircutter. Your excuse for the hairboard was that cutting hair was the only thing that made you *feel.*" He grunted from the strain of holding his pose. "Perfect," he said. His face got redder and redder and his long thin thighs began to quiver, then he shot up bouncing and said, "Your next project will be what makes you feel *now.* You say you aren't cutting hair anymore because of your new girlfriend, is that right? Because you don't *need* to cut anymore. Well, *why.* What has replaced your *feeling.*" His veiny hands shot up to rub his veiny brain, while his cufflinks flashed in the polluted sunset coming from the Hudson River down the block. "And I don't want you to go to *museums,* okay, I want this to be as virginal as you are. I want you to tell me, to *show* me, what it is *now* that makes you most feel. I want you to decide on a way to present that, and I want it *presented,* and I want to *sell* it, and I want you to create *another* piece after that. This is what I'm doing with you.

Let's play. I know how to play, do you? You create the oeuvre of The Haircutter and I'm going to sell it for you."

I said, "Huh. Well I don't know what the hell else is making me feel except Carol."

Laughter and a snap that told me to follow his dress shoes peeling beneath his swagger.

We went into his office and he made us both espressos (to make me crap when I fart). He took his espresso back like a shot and rolled his enormous head around on his neck, making him almost fall backwards since most of his head is on the back side of his neck. I flinched and reached out to catch it, but he was suddenly putting chapstick on his turtle's lips and rubbing them together. He said, "If it's Carol, then what is it *about* her that makes you feel?"

I said, "Oh hell, *what?* See I just don't speak that language is what."

His eyes puckered into stars and he laughed. "Well what would *you* do for another art piece? What do you like to do most with your time?"

I said, "Oh hell, just hang with Carol. She's the one who does the datebook, so. I can have her bring it in if you let me use the phone."

He squirmed and spoke then in a voice I'd never heard him use: it was a normal person speaking honestly, politely. His ego hung in the air around us, flapping its wings, letting Christmas be frank[incense].

"Confidence . . . equals . . . pretend you're from the future," he said.

I put a hand to my chin and nodded, pretending I was understanding. This perked him up again, and put him back in his standard deportment, which was the kind you felt compelled to toss a cane to.

I said, "What's the deal here? So what makes me feel's the question? Coming into Carol, pretty much. She's on birth control, so."

His barking laughter. "Do me a sex project!"

I said, "Huh?"

He screamed, "Go home! Go home and think about it!"

Sex. A disgusting ritual. There were two times—two?—where I folded up over myself like a snake shedding skin and like a skinned penis I throbbed in the color pink with my eyes drooped and I was like *I get it, I get it.* Maybe that was the time or two that we touched "making love." Otherwise, it was all just fucking, with Carol's round rabbit eyes darting. Using our piss and poop holes to get to the Human Nature button inside of us, to press press press it, losing our ages and identities. "Fucking." You're rubbing up against a tree trunk while onlookers at the zoo go, "Eew!" Your eyes droop and then you "come" and then your red penis retracts back into your fur as you walk your cage with your butt still faintly humping like the bumblebee that flew over to sniff your semen puddle. It should be embarrassing, but it's celebrated instead. *I fucked today!* like that sticker for voters. Whistlers in the morning office say someone had a good night last night. People are weird. Neverthefuck, we fucked nonstop.

She'd throw herself on me like she was the sea and I was a sea rock to be engulfed, massaged, and dripped on. We got more and more vocal during sex—we explained it, poked at it, told it to roll over so we could tickle its belly; we affectionately stroked it while we ate.

You think I'm kidding about that? Later we'd whisper: Man we were horny, huh? Haha yeah weird, I ate my whole plate. Haha yeah I sall that. I almost stabbed the back of my throat with my fork when you did your comin' thrust. Oh no!, I'm glad you didn't.

We were on the same page of the same sick book. Titled *Sex by Fuck*. I'd fuck her with my deflated socks on. My thing was more in a boner than not. Was it sore? Felt about ready to fall off. There's a mental aspect that controls you when you're in a groove like that, just like shooting heroin into the same over-used volcano on your arm, I'd imagine. My penis is seven inches when erect, it's 5.75" in circumference, and it's unclipped.

Waiting for her to orgasm was like waiting for a stampede of mixed animals to come charging through the room. I sometimes winced watching it come around the bend. She'd flail her arms, screaming, with her mechanical pumping rump keeping her attached to me by the dick. Afterwards, she'd slide her legs off the bed and her body would follow like water. She'd go "tinkle" and come back to stand on the rug saying, "That was goooood," pushing baby hairs off her face with her clity hanging from her flaps like an exasperated tongue.

And so, we began forming our sex sessions into a presentable format for Christmas. I went out and bought a bunch of petri dishes to ejaculate into so we could make a big artful heart made out of petri dishes with sex essence in them. Carol, smiling widely, would hold a dish up to my thing and get it to come in there. Or we'd be doing it at the stove, say, while she was cooking, and I'd open a cupboard like I'm looking for spice, but I'd pull out a petri dish and I'd pull out of Carol and try to get the dish to catch my come. It was disgusting, but so is coming into petri dishes in the name of Art. As a counting system, we unwrapped a condom every time we had sex and tied it to a condom chain for Christmas to hang up banner-like at the opening.

Carol, loving the entire thing more than a person would ever think, wore the condom banner as a scarf/necklace jig that she would have just *loved* to wear outside of the house, but we had to be clandestine so no one would copy. I recorded our heart rates with watches that we'd put on before we'd start and I logged them later and did charts of comparison using a ruler, glitter, and glue (Carol's idea). During her orgasms, I'd photograph her with her black camera, which we kept by the bed. I think we had around seventy orgasm pics of Carol, sometimes looking in the lens, which looks more like she's about to puke then it looks like she's in the middle of an org. One day Carol was writing and I came up and braided her hair (best I could) and I was like, "About what?" and she told me she's doing a sort of "wife-of-the-artist biography." She said that while I'm working on *The Sex Project,* she'd be journaling about it.

I told her, "Let's put it in the project then!"

And she was like, "Exactly!"

Later in bed I was like, *wife?* It made me smirk so hard I rolled over and asked to make L.

I recorded our moaning with a tape recorder when we were at the height of our moaning and I was careful to press Stop before any orgasms so that the tape was entirely of moaning from all different sessions. To pair with the tape we purchased a video camera and had Charlie Quick film us having sex outdoors with a blanket over us. It was a scratchy black blanket of Old Auntie's that probably had her dead skin cells shaking from it when we humped. We sprinkled her cells all over town. We'd stop on whatever corner and say, "This'll do," and Carol would spit on her hand and get herself open, and Charlie Quick would toss the blanket over us and cross the street to get a good shot of our black mass amongst the pedestrians. I'd hump away, the both of us laughing like donkeys. Till we'd start liking it and we'd get all serious and moany. I told Charlie Quick to film the part of us running away too. Carol shouting, "Go, go, go!" with her hair flying back and with one of her titties hanging out of her shirt. Once, we did it on the subway right at the foot of people's feet. Bing, bang, boom. Carol put on a show for them with her *Oohs* climbing a scale of pleasure. The final high note she sang graduated mega-cum-loud from our Insanitute. It all sounds crazy, but when you put us next to a pic of a leper beggar pulling himself down the subway car by the arms with his lower body draped over a skateboard, it's pennies. I called the project, blandly, *The Sex Project*. And Christmas later changed it to *Private Particulars.*

One stormy Sunday, when we were getting ready for a sex session, I watched Carol put on her heart rate watch. She was standing by the window in flashes of lightning at 4:00 p.m. I came up behind her and touched her forearm—she froze. I slowly slipped the watch off her wrist and it dropped to the floor. I slowly turned her around and saw her eyes and mouth be like, "What's he about to show me that's new?" We passionately kissed, the thunder clapping. I didn't come into a petri dish, we didn't snap her orgasm pic. We laid in bed smiling after. I shouted, "*Man*, I love you!" over the rain. "No, *I* do!" she said. We both knew then that it was time for *The Sex Project* to come.

(If only I had known the horror in store for me. I would've skipped all this "art project" bullshit.)

We put everything in a cardboard box meant for office files and brought it in to the gallery. When we walked in the door,

Christmas said, "Shh!" and proceeded to search for a cricket stuck in the room. Carol unpacked the petri dishes, arranging them in the shape of a heart (which Christmas later showed us how to "mount" so it could be hung on a wall). I saw the cricket hop past Christmas's office so I shouted, "By your office!" Christmas hopped across the room with one pointy dress shoe up and ready—he killed the cricket, then swiped his fingers through the juice and laughed with spirals in his eyes. In France, a pretty teacher wrote *cliché* on the blackboard.

He walked toward us then, smooth as water, until he realized what we'd brought in. His hands shot up to his brain and he yelled, "Quick!" Charlie Quick appeared with a magnifying glass. Christmas looked through the stack of Carol's orgasm pics, he saw our petri heart, he saw the crafty heart rate chart, he read Carol's biography which was only two-and-a-half pages long and ended mid-sentence mid-word on the word "artistic."

. . . *brushing his teeth more often, I've been having harder orgasms. Maybe if I had known that banging was so artis*

I had Charlie Quick hold one end of the condom banner and walked across the room holding the other end for Christmas to see. He clapped for fifteen minutes. Till Carol said, "Wait, not yet!" Charlie Quick wheeled out a TV and I put in the black blanket porn. Carol pressed play on our moaning tape at the same time that I pressed play. Christmas held his brain and paced with his legs bent, "Yes."

"Yes," he said.

I already had my arms crossed, but I spread my stance wider.

Before we emerged from our black car the night of the opening, Carol said, "Speak quotably." She'd tied her lace duster around her neck like a leash for me to hold during pics.

When we walked in it sounded like a sudden downpour. ("PSH!!!!!") They clapped curls out of the smoky air, slapping their palms together so hard it jiggled their faces, making some women's clip-on earrings drop off. Flashbulbs popped and popped. I held Carol's lace duster leash and walked her around the square room. People tossed words at us like confetti. I was like, "Okay, thanks." Carol was like, "Thanks-uhhhh!!! Thanks so muuuuch-uuuuh!" Our video was projected on the wall where *The Hairboard* had hung, and speakers framed it projecting our moaning tape. Carol's orgasms framed the room in frames. The condom banner hung wall-to-wall. Old Auntie's black blanket was pinned up bat-like having no choice in the matter. There were several glass cases for the memoir and the heart rate chart. On the third wall hung our petri heart. People were looking at me every time I looked around for the catering boys who had little hot dogs. The oldest man I've ever seen put a lit cigar in my mouth and I spat it out shocked. He said, "Cripes!" and his grandson came to say, "I'm sorry, I thought you'd like that!" A lady with a shaved head wanted our autographs on the old Artist's Statement from *The Hairboard* opening, and then a lineup grew where people wanted us to sign this opening's invitation and the Artist's Statement that Christmas and Carol had drawn up. Blah, blah, blah. In Ten Sleep, my father sucked jelly off the sleeve of his flannel shirt, saying, "This place is a fuckin' pigsty, Patty." Patty Reilly in her purple sweatsuit brushed her hair and it made a crackling sound in electric harmony with the velvet horses couch she sat on. Darron spun circles at the saloon, and the yellow-suited cowboy spun in the fresh, cold, Wyo air. On 37th and 6th Avenue in Manhattan, my papers went crisp in the same fresh cold coming through the rattling window frame above my writing table. On 20th and 10th, I ate a hot dog and watched myself

have sex on a subway train under a blanket. Everyone around me laughed so heartily at the passengers' reactions, they bent in half and tangled their legs to clutch their champagne in. Ting, ting, ting—they asked for a kiss by tapping their pussy little glasses. Carol came to flick tongues. Someone put a garland around our heads. Everyone sighed collectively, flashbulbs going off. Carol and I spread apart and strained against the garland until it burst undone, petals spraying.

After the opening, Christmas threw a party at the top of a building on Broadway Street. I had never seen the building before. Everything with him was like it was made specially for a scene in a movie and, come morning, would disappear. Carol and I saw out over the sparkling New York skyline holding the familiar weight of champagne glasses in the hands we gutted deer with as children.

"We're standin' on top'a this town," Carol said.

A boa constrictor slithered by with a video camera on its "back."

"You're happy then?" I said.

She said, "I'm only just gettin' started. Your bow's my life's work."

She'd pronounced *bow* like in a doggie's *bow-wow*.

"My *bow?*" I said.

"Your body of work."

"*Your* body's a work of art," I said, and she kissed me, "Thank you!"

Carol then played Twister, genital crabs jumping sprightly from player to player, crawling up their legs and finding they've already been in those pubes before.

Scott Harp approached me with his tie slung over his shoulder saying, "Carol is amazing."

I said, "I ain't blind! I'm the one who went to Wyo and caught her!"

That wolf was *my* wolf and then there was some black-haired man with eyelids like dick skin saying it was *his* wolf. Or some shit like that. Whatever it was, I hated him.

"Nice piece," he said. "I love that Carol's so dedicated."

"I know it!" I grouched, and walked away to go stand by a butch lesbian who'd just entered the party on a pogo stick.

"I get around town like this," she said and twitched her head so hard, her hair cleared off her freckled forehead. "Are you the guy whose show it was?" she asked casually in a low, out-of-breath voice as she collapsed her pogo stick and put it in a special carrying case.

"You're my favorite person I've met in a long time. I knew it right away," I said, and she yanked her face in toward her neck, confused.

Just then, a human-sized hamster ball rolled into the room. People had to jump out of the way. Inside was a little *elf*, with unwrapped candy bars clacking around to make like turds. People screamed, and he rolled around until people started cheering. "That's Siedle!" I heard. "That's Siedle the elf. He's rad!" I heard. "He's a good listener!" I heard.

Later, the elf walked the party biting butts and assisting anyone who wanted to try being a hamster. Women in sequined gowns toppled around in the scratched plastic globe, then busted their lips or laughed so hard they pissed. One lady rolled it Olympically around the room in high heels with a burst of orange hair, a gold dress, pink makeup on. Photographers jumped out in front

of her to shoot this flash of fashion and they jumped away before she rolled over them. I was happy to see them grunting hard when they landed trying to hold their cameras aloft.

"Siedle!" Carol said, "The Haircutter wants his pic with you!"

I had always thought that elves were like unicorns and asteroids and didn't exist, so I had Carol use up her whole roll of film on us.

"Excuse me sir, let me please get another pic with you," I'd say and I'd catch him again, feeling dumb like he's better than me. "Thank you," I'd say to him, letting him go.

His little high voice was like, "You're welcome!"

I wanted him to take off his curly shoes so I could see if his feet were curly too, but I somehow couldn't just say it and ask. My champagne quivered in a bloodless fist—Siedle's curly shoes passed me again and again—I was thinking: *Now! . . . Go! Ask when he passes by! . . . Go!* All I would've had to do was politely point and say, "Hey are your feet *actually* curly?" But I never did. Later in bed Carol said of course his feet aren't curly, "Don't let anyone find out you're a bigot please." I never saw that pogo stick woman again, though every time I saw a construction worker on a jackhammer I thought of her.

Private Particulars sold for $XXX,XXX.XX to a German collector named Hanz Polke, who has the type of breath that spreads out like a fart and who's bald, but for a little tuft of hair on top like something to hang him by. The sales number went into the *New York Times,* along with a picture of The Haircutter and Carol beside an orgasm pic. People outside the lines of the art scene got all colored: "Did you get a load of those artist freaks?" "Who, The

Haircutter? I just invited them to the gala." "Shirley Steinfarb! You take too much Xanax and you damn well know it." And things started changing.

There's The Haircutter lying fat-stuffed on a table. There's New York swishing cars through the cold mouth of Sixth Avenue. It's nighttime in April. There's one lamp on in the room. Carol clacks her high heels over to her purse to get a gold lighter and a cig. The room air presses very very gently on her cheek telling her before she flicks the lighter which way she'll turn her face for the flame. She inhales, bats her lashes, rattles her thin gold watch higher up on her wrist.

The Haircutter says, "You're so perdy we should take you to be put in a museum."

She says, "I can't believe how fat I am," each word chewing on smoke.

Carol crosses the room again, her breath smelling like pubic slop, and cig, and lipstick, and her new perfume called *Bad Influence*. She kisses her John goodbye, "Ciao, Puss." When the front door slams, Puss's stomach rattles. A spider sinks from the ceiling to tick on its string beside John Reilly's long-lashed girly eyes—he's no longer a free man.

Ten floors down, Doorman Diego says, "Bye, Miss Carol."

"Bye, Love."

Her black high "hills" tick-tock on city grit, her rump responds accordingly. She hails a cab by whistling like she's seen done in movies. She looks out the window while she rides, snapping pics with her little black camera. The destination is a rotting brick building that houses million-dollar works of art. *Like a clam and a pearl*, Carol thinks as she leaves a blond hair and a light fart in the taxi. Pigeons part just for her—she smiles like an actress. Friends of all shapes and sizes greet her fawningly when she enters the party. Is there jazz playing? Or is it all about laughter and lighters flicking? Does one even notice jazz when in each partygoer there's a chorus of words to memorize, of gestures to pretend you were the first to do? Uptown, the spider watches The Haircutter do a set of push-up reps for the first time ever. H.C. feels proud about it for two weeks after, telling Doorman Diego, "I'm actually working out now? It's been good," nodding, twitching a breast like he's seen done in movies.

With the showers of spring, I started accepting it. Carol and I liked different things. I liked that my writing papers shriveled in the mist coming through the window in front of my desk; I liked that when it rained, the smell got puffed up by the heat—if I were a lady I'd get out some test tubes and beakers to try to make a candle out of it; I liked to write in peace; I liked that I could walk around the house and see Carol's things because it reminded me that she lived here and would be home soon; I liked cracking a can of Coke—I liked the cold feel of it in my hand; I liked sitting as long as I wanted to on the john, or "The Namesake" as I called it once to make Carol laugh. One afternoon I'd been sitting at my desk doing who wrote novels in 1979 in Asia when I thought, "It's been a while since I've seen Carol." I got up and hiked my belt up around my stomach and descended the three kitchen steps and went to The Chambers to see if Carol was in the bathroom—she was usually in there "getting ready" if she was home. I found her curling her hair, topless. Her puffy pink nipples matched her lips. And when she sprayed each curl with hairspray she scrunched her face up in protection and all her wrinkles flashed, and I thought I'll love her with no lesser power once those wrinkles are stamped permanent. I thought, *Get old, get fat, I'm here to love you anyway.* She winked at me in the mirror and said, "Stargazin'?" I did a grin all sincere, "Sure as hell am." Carol Haircutter: two hands dangling off the mechanics of two wrists. She clears her throat more often now. Looks like she's on a postcard from Paris. But scratch her chin and rodeo dirt will smell up off the paper.

"You look damn perdy like that," I said.

"My period's about to burst outta me any second."

I walked away to go do Asia in '80.

The rain started coming down in sheets.

Carol called, "It's clappin' hard out there, huh? My poor hair. Maybe I'll have people over *here* tonight?"

A month later, every table was covered in bottles, clothes, trash, paintings people left, balloon animals, our wilted roses, half-eaten steaks with ashtrays dumped on them, panties everywhere—some with used maxi pads in them. Lines of "coke" laid on my precious tables—one line laid on a negative pregnancy stick. There were drum snares coming from an unseen radio, there was a small fire in a bucket with a diary in it. There was a snot rocket that looked like a Hershey Kiss—the lining of a nostril with a snot tail for the little tag sat lonesome on an empty table, and someone had written near it: "The Sneeze", there was a goldfish, there was a ten-foot pole for someone to not touch someone else with.

I'd wake up to the sound of a fly stuck in the main room, until I'd adjust and realize it was someone talking. Damp heat came up off piles of people as though they were fresh piles of dog shit. I'd make my breakfast, and when I farted they'd crawl across the floor with beakers and tests tubes trying to make a candle out of it. Carol sauntered out in her red silk robe saying, "Morning, X

X," getting everyone's first and last names right. She'd spend the day eating with them, clipping toenails with them, braiding their armpit hairs, while I picked up around the house with a garbage bag, thinking *Charlie Quick should be doing this.* One day, a lady in a corner with a pigeon on a leash stood up and left, and I saw that her nest had been made of *Woomalee Amatrist.*

"Hey Carol, check this."

I gathered the 92 pages. They were stained and crumpled with boot prints and pigeon shit.

Carol and them were meditating. "We're as light as a feather, as stiff as a board," she said with her back to me.

Slump-shouldered H.C. shuffled son-like into his bedroom holding Carol's manuscript.

I put it in order and read it on the pot. I thought, *How'd we get into this mess?* I was The Haircutter and I liked it. Carol Mary Mathers was a sci-fi writer. Now it's Carol with a ribboning cig, charming parties of people into hypnosis with the unintentional elegance of someone who's driving and charming at the same time. Now it's H.C. writing in his closet with a candle and a sack dinner. ("Don't no one go in the closet—my man's workin'!") The yellow-suited cowboy tauntingly spins. I set *Woomalee* on the floor and dropped my pants and sat back down. While down the block, a journalist sat lamp-lit and alcoholic, hunched like a semicolon over a typewriter writing about the new art world star: some fatty weirdo who, in each splatter of paint, shows artistic umph and poignant understanding. While said fatty weirdo shat a hard fart into his toilet saying, "Splatter *that.*"

One normal night, when too many people started taking my pic in my own home, I took my cue and went to the fridge and got my sack dinner, then I gathered up some writing supplies, and went to The Chambers. And when I opened my closet door Hanz Polke was in there masturbating. I put a sign on the front door after that: *Please everyone come over less often. I don't like it. Signed, The Haircutter.* The sign seemed to work, because one night I noticed no one was home. I looked around and noticed a TV under a table. I turned it on and sat down. While Carol walked the light-throbbing, lettuce-wilting streets of New York, I watched a blond lady show me her part and go, "I'm embarrassed about my thinning hair!" I laughed so hard I threw a nearby pizza at the screen.

It took me a while to notice that there had been something under the pizza. When I stood up to get a Coke from the fridge, there was an envelope of photos on the floor labeled "John and Siedle."

"Who's Siedle?" I said, as I opened the envelope and my scalp shrank in horror. They were pics of me holding an *elf* and it had the face of a sixty-year-old health nut who rapes people. It was from a land far far away, and I was *holding it,* vulnerable and happy. *What had I become?* My belly button felt like someone was sticking their finger in it. My arm hairs rose. I threw the stack of pics out the window. I vowed to stick to humans and animals from then on; I'd have interest in nothing in between, not even robots, no matter how essential they became. I went to The Chambers and into my sock drawer where I kept the envelopes of photos labeled "Sex Pro Doubles."

What sex? It had always been *her* obsession more than mine, but now when I entered Carol she felt like a colt scrambling up and standing for the first time. It often hurt her so bad we had to stop. While the dick of fate carried on: it fucked and fucked us. When she came home, I showed her the old orgasm doubles from the sex project and said, "Whoa, your face looks perdy like this!" She ran away crying.

Summer. Sun shining on the brick wall message: *I love you Carol.* Heat muffled the car sounds, and bird chirps came through lettuce crisply. All we had left were mornings in bed. I would lay listening to the drain drip in the bathroom while she slept hard. I'd watch her neck tick, sometimes in beat with the drips. I'd lift her hair, like lifting cooked pasta, and look through its glittering strands to focus on the brick wall message out the window—*I love you Carol.* Then I'd refocus on the strands—back and forth, sometimes in beat with the drips begging brass instruments to release it into proper song. That's all we had left in the way of what's intimate. Even still—I felt attached to her by a stalk, and I'm not talking a dick. She was an extension of me, and I of her. Even still—I started cutting her hair and storing the locks in my sock drawer. It gave me merely a pre-cum's worth of the old rush: everything wasn't *enough.* I remembered a time when I didn't *do* sad. I wanted to jump off a sea cliff now. Die by a hard slap from Mother Nature. See The Haircutter's lifeless body bobbing and coldly decomposing like his heart.

One day, she burst through the front door screaming, "Oh my God, Scott is doing the coolest art project ever!!!"

I bellowed in my underwear and nineteen-day beard, "HOW DARE YOU USE ONLY HIS FIRST NAME!"

Her face blew off its skull and she darted to The Chambers. I worked my way up off the pile of clothes I lounged on when I watched TV. She was shivering like a bunny under the bedskins.

I tip-toed in like a fairy's godmother and caressed her curls saying, "There there!" in a high voice. She bought it. She was like, "Without you snappin' off my head, can I just tell you somethin' I wanna share since I think it's cool and poetic?" Her puffy child's face with its matching voice was poetry enough. I thought, *Hell, what's wrong with me?* I thought, *Here's this little Girly I love trying to tell me her interest.* I sat and listened to her talk about Harp's new project. My face fought so hard not to snarl it had to snarl just for the fight. I gripped the mattress and watched her hairbrush the whole time—it was sitting on her dresser like a rat spine.

Scott Harp did a press release announcing his new art project, which he was calling a "heartache hunger strike" entitled: *Flee, Thee.* For thirty artistic days he would be locked in a glass box inside the Thank You Gallery, nakedly exposed to the public for all to see his probably-large penis and his starvation. After the thirty days, Christmas would smash the box with a mallet. Harp would be allowed a stack of crackers and a glass of orange juice once a day so he wouldn't die. There would be a discrete toilet in the corner, and a glass chair center-front that he'd sit on, staring into the depths of heartache abyss. He said in a statement: *I have been experiencing a heartache so keenly felt as to render me depressed for the last five months. The purpose of my project is to purge my body and mind of said heartache by meditating on it being a dependence-based egoic attachment that needn't be fed.* He would go into the box in two days.

I immediately went to shave.

Here's Carol and me out that night with all the yappers and swooners and perfumers, all of them saying, "Eat up, Scotty! Try this!" I walked straight up to Harp and grabbed the nearest piece of food and stuffed it in his mouth while he was in the middle of saying hi to me.

Everyone erupted, "Oh my god, The Haircutter's here!"

Carol said, "Scott, we should sit with you!"

I roared, squeezing Carol's ass hard, "Why are you being nice to him?"

"Because he's my friend! These are my friends!"

The wolf man punctuated her statement with a gluey wink. I chucked a bread roll across the room and it landed in a bread basket while two people were kissing; they parted heads and the man picked up the roll and buttered it. Harp lifted his wine glass and wept on his cheesy reason for going "in the box," while The Haircutter got up and laid on the dinner table, face-down on top of everyone's plates of food. Stuff burned me lightly here and there on parts of my body while I heard Carol plead, "John, stop, please." A couple people clapped, but not many. When I stood up, some mashed potatoes fell off my chest and I saw Harp just ignore it—he lifted his glass for Cheers. I spent the rest of the night mumbling who wrote what and when they wrote it, and two people followed me around, scissor-stepping with their ear as close to my mouth as they could get it—a man in a top hat, a woman with curly hair that looked wet but when it brushed my hand I felt it was dry and rock-solid.

When we got home, I showered, and when I came out Carol was "asleep" even though I could see smoke rising off a stubbed cig in her fern. I got in bed and saw if she would say something but she never did. I turned around so my back faced her, and the bedsprings responded accordingly. A siren wailed and turned the walls red. Carol's stomach growled. I turned around and whispered, "Are you hungry?" She didn't respond. I heard her pillow when she blinked. I turned back around and settled in. The bedsprings responded accordingly.

CHAPTER FIVE

HUSH,
HOWLER—
HUNT

Harp had been in the box some twenty days and didn't seem to have a bigger penis than me, and Carol said she was so disgusted by the idea of his starving body that she couldn't go to see, and she'd been staying home with me a few nights a week, so I had been in a much better mood—I'd even given that TV to Doorman Diego.

I was in the kitchen one afternoon doing up some eggs, when Carol came out of The Chambers wearing a green complexion mask, clapping.

She said, "John, I just got the best idea!"

I said, "Look at you! What is it?"

"It's a complexion mask," she said, and I said, "No, what's the *idea?*"

As we laughed she (suspiciously?) took a single teacup from the dry dishes pile and put its sole entity away, then stopped dishes to twist my arm hairs saying, "I got an idea for your next art project."

I said, "Hell, I forgot about all that."

She said, "I think you should go out to Wyo like you did with that wolf, but *you* should be the wolf."

Right away I said, "I don't like that at all! That's someone else's art project I'd be usin'."

"Scott's?" she said.

"Excuse me if you don't mind me asking you to not use his first name basis?" I said, flipping an egg and not breaking the yolk. I flicked my eyes halfway to Carol to see if she saw—she did.

"Scott *Harp,* sorry," she said.

I poked the yolk with my spatula to show how I won't abide by hearing about him. "It's bad enough I was *used* to dump off *his* art piece like I'm some kinda *garbage man*."

"But you loved doin' the wolf job," she said.

"Ach. I don't wanna hear about Scott Harp."

She started twisting my arm hairs harder, "Well, think about it. You could *make* somethin' outta that experience. You could *use him back* like he used *you*. Plus—show it's more *your* wolf than *his*?"

And that's when she got me.

I turned around and said, "Huh."

She said, "Yeah!"

The eggs chatted in the pan about how they thought we were onto something.

I said, "So what, so I'll just drive out there like the wolf? Like someone will basically do the wolf job all over again, but I'll be the wolf?"

"Yes!" she said.

"HE should drive me!" I said.

"Harp? Oh he'd never do that," she said.

"YOU should drive me!" I said.

"Well that ain't fun for me, Puss."

I said, "Hell, we should BOTH be in it! We'll both be wolves!"

"I don't wanna be a wolf!"

"I got it!" I picked her up and sat her on my writing table. "We get driven out to Wyo by Charlie Quick, and we act JUST like wolves, alright? No talkin'! And he sets us loose in the wild and we have to live like wolves to see what that wolf went through!"

"Why do *I* have to go along? It ain't like you drove *two* wolves," Carol said, waving a giant red flag I was blind to.

"Cause I don't give a bum's hoot about art and you know it," I said. "Come on, we can be love wolves and nuzzle a bunch."

"You gotta do a new project! We need money!" she said.

"So help me get it, Feminist!"

She walked away, taking her pussy with her.

That is how it came to be that Carol, freshly showered and with her face puffed up from crying, told me an hour later that we'd ride out there like love wolves, communicating only with our hearts—*no talkin'!*—and we'd get dropped off in the woods at separate places far apart, and that the art would be: we'd have to find each other using only our hearts. "No cheatin'! No callin' out! However long it takes!"

We went to Biggest Browse to purchase wilderness survival books. We looked for Finn and found him shelving on the basement level. As we approached him, his face took on the expression of a lottery winner who's in shock about winning.

"*H.C.?!*"

He barely shelved the book that was flapping in his trembling hands. "Oh my god!" He stepped forward on sickly-thin corduroy legs and kissed Carol's cheeks, breathing heavily, "You're so beautiful!"

I said, "We're looking for—"

And he interrupted, "You two, fuck! I gotta say you guys are inspiring! I'm totally changed! Like SO inspired! H.C.!" He grabbed the sides of his reddening face, "That whole time you were coming in here I had no idea you were an artist! I *really* respect how you could just do that and not have to talk about it and not show your stuff off like most artists. God, and your WORK, man, the PIECES!"

I automatically put out my hand, and he shook it, looking down at it. When I yanked it back, he fell against a shelf and a book popped out and landed cover-up at our feet—*Seven Steps toward a Healthier Mane on Your Horse.* Carol picked it up, "Ooh! John we should get horses when we get back!"

Finn said, "Where are you going?"

I said, "Well that's what we need your help with. It's for the next art piece."

"Oh my god!" Finn squeaked.

"We're gonna get Charlie Quick to drive us out to Wyoming same route as the wolf job, and then me and Carol are gonna do a hunt for each other in the woods without shouting out using only our hearts. So we're gonna need literature on how to camp and do your basic survival skills."

Finn bit his too-thin lower lip, pressing his teeth into a chin pimple. He brought his hands up to obstruct his blushing face and clapped them. I looked at Carol and she was beaming, giggling.

I said, "Now snap out of it. That's enough there. Take us to the section."

Finn took one step, saying, "Right this way," and his foot didn't work—he collapsed right there in the aisle. His boss passed by with a clipboard, then reappeared walking backwards with his glasses on the tip of his nose, "*Finn?*" he said.

Carol picked up Finn's head and his eyes were rolled back to the whites. He looked like a dead baby bird on a sidewalk.

We studied in The Chambers, slapping at mosquitoes, saying, "We'd better get used to them!" The city blew hot breath in through the window screens. Carol sat on a toss pillow on the floor in front of the fan reading about plants—her own plant a vagina, wet and living, too. I didn't read hard on my survival book because I knew that as soon as I got dropped off I'd call

Darron. My plan was, I'd spend three or four days in a motel and then I'd have Darron take me back out to the woods again and drop me off closer to Carol. As long as she didn't know that I'd cheated, it was fine.

Carol said, "Let's have flare guns."

Carol said, "Let's have real guns too."

I said, "We can just go with the *flare*."

We'd shoot a flare gun off when we found each other and Darron would be waiting with a camera to snap a pic of the sky (we'd alert him using a cell that Charlie Quick would deliver). The presentation—the proof that we had done the hunt honestly—would be that we'd just *say* we'd done it, and that would be artistic too because the audience would have to *trust* we'd done it. So it was a project on both love and trust, with a minor in acting like wolves, and a major in hunting. It was a new way of hunting that no one had thought of before. We'd have Charlie Quick do a photojournalism through the peephole when he dropped us off. We'd sleep in tents that we'd hitch alone, we'd use camping stoves to boil creek water for rice, and we'd "use our hearts" to find each other. We decided to name the piece *Hush, Howler—Hunt* even though I felt dumb when we told people. ("It's hush comma howler and then dash hunt.") The more people we told about the new project, the more Carol got haughty about it. People said, "I can't believe you're going to do that!" They said, "Aren't you scared?" And she'd say, "That's what bear mace and pony tills are for!" They'd tick their tongues and shake their heads, "You are so supportive." Then she'd seriously say, "I'm lookin' forward to the Zen." She always said that when she told people. ("I'm lookin' forward to the Zen.") I had to admit—I was looking forward to the "Zen" too. Peace and quiet like when I'd come home from Brother and Son's and I'd sit at my desk and the only sound was my slurping pop or turning the page of a book while Jenny barked at the living room window.

I just remembered that I killed Jenny.

We went to Kmart and bought two pup tents for $16.99 a piece (they were on clearance). We bought long backpacks and all the stuff to stuff them with that the survival book said. I chose a brown backpack and Carol chose red, so if anyone saw us in the woods they'd know we like poops and bloody tampons.

"Nobody's gonna think that," Carol said at the checkout, annoyed with me. My hands hung at my sides, their palms facing the person behind us in line. I yawned and Carol saw my gold fillings—I could've known that's all she saw in me.

The day we went to the Thank You Gallery to tell Christmas, I was pleased to see that Carol didn't even glance at Harp in his glass box. I hadn't seen him since the opening (at the start of which he disrobed dramatically and took a seat on his glass chair and leaked tears out, etc., while onlookers said, "What are we doing after this?" or "Don't you think it's more chic if I just have *one* glass of champagne tonight?") He looked completely different. He looked like when Darron used to play with dead squirrels till Father John would make him bury them, and when we were bored we'd go dig them up. He looked like one of those squirrels if we'd thought to shave it and prop it up.

Christmas emerged from his office clapping.

"I heard, I heard," he said. "Everyone's talking about it. So when do you leave? Do you want Quick to drive you?"

Charlie Quick was in a corner picking up dog poop with a plastic kid's shovel. He froze when he heard his name. I saw his face turn red to match the shovel.

"Eew," Carol said.

"Someone's dog shit in here," Christmas said. Then he went, "Speaking of which!" He tiptoed over to a chute on Harp's glass box and opened it and looked in. He grimaced and slowly closed it. He snapped at Charlie Quick, "Empty that fucking thing. It's distracting the artist. Deal with that dog's shit later."

Did I wonder about Christmas and Charlie Quick? About their relationship? I and everyone else in New York did, the difference is I didn't care. From what I had gathered, they lived together in a penthouse on the Upper West Side. They slept in separate bedrooms, but Charlie Quick got into bed with Christmas and his cats if he felt like working from home with trays of brats and kraut. They met in Dusseldorf in 1984 as two young mustard lovers who saw the spark of loneliness in each other, and soon discovered that they were both orphaned only children of only children. They took care of each other when sick from then on out, yadda ya. The Thank You Gallery was Charlie Quick's but he didn't have the bells to run it, so his oil-money friend Christmas bought it up and started his circus. Christmas was a celibate for no particular reason, and Charlie Quick fancied no-nonsense American black women, so the penthouse dinner table often had his female guest—perhaps the three of them were laughing at whatever-the-hoot and cheersing, eating goose necks, drinking Riesling from crystal goblets. But what did they *want* from this art stuff? They were like purebred bloodhounds playing Sniff The Cat's Butt; I always thought, "Go do something *else!*" But as Christmas once said in an interview, "There isn't a reason for anything, Jesus Christ. Can we stop this insanity yet? How could there be a *reason* for anything? What does that even mean? Every day is simply Christmas. And everything is a present. Haven't you noticed?"

We followed Christmas into his little office. He has a butt the size of a little boy's. Carol sat down in one of his little arty chairs for his butt and she cleared her throat and sat up straighter. She'd never gotten used to Christmas. Her smile had a melted quality around him. She thought he was the coolest person in the art world because he never went to parties that weren't his own. He didn't even smoke. She once called him a mirage on the plane of artistic existence, and when I asked her what the hell that was supposed to mean, she said, "I don't know, it's what some artist said about him," and I upturned a table and kicked one of the legs off to show how I won't abide by anyone calling Christmas a mirage on the plane of artistic existence, even though I didn't care, or didn't know what that saying meant. (I was so confused back then.)

Christmas got out a spray bottle and sprayed his face and head until he was a glistening penis, then he got out a towel with a Santy on it and wiped himself down. "Disgusting," he said. "There's a week left on this thing," gesturing toward Harp's box.

"Disgusting," I said, and spat on the floor.

Christmas looked at it and burst out laughing.

We'd leave the next day at six in the morning—Quick would pick us up in the wolf job truck. I looked at Christmas and Carol as they were going over a papered detail that I wasn't interested in, and I thought, *Huh.* I thought, *Will you look at that.* I thought, *A year ago, the only people I knew were Doorman Diego and that dead baby bird on the floor of the bookstore. Now I have a Christmas Carol.*

Carol said, "Sign here," and I signed a document. Christmas got out his pearl-handled pistol and shot the doc on his dotted line. Carol and I just put our pointers in our ears and didn't say anything about it, because it was the third or fourth time we'd seen him do that and we were comfortable now like, That's Christmas and his office floor of bullet holes that women's high heels get stuck in. I felt a wash of satisfaction in the wake of the gunshot, like the final rinse in a carwash. I felt so good that, on the way out the door, I let me and Carol stop in front of Harp since I knew she liked art and since I'd heard someone at the opening describe how Harp "looks into the eyes of the viewer and then into their soul, and then into the infinity that their soul came from, and then he rides the wave of infinity *with you.* And then he drools, and if you look closely at the pinhead of the drool, it has the universe in it." Sure enough, I saw a puddle of drool between his feet with some galaxy in it. Sure enough, I saw his eyes scramble up off the floor and snake up Carol's body. When they landed on her face, she inhaled so hard her protruding sternum creaked. I covered her face from him and punched her sternum in.

"Let's go!" I roared.

The crack of dawn. Sun reaching into the main room to illuminate tables. To flick shadows off our silhouettes as we moved around the apartment. For breakfast I did up everything we had left in the fridge. One last savory meal. Charlie Quick would be feeding us granola through the peephole. Doorman Diego rang up when Quick was downstairs—it was a hard, loud buzz—like a bee farting hard until it pops. Carol and I looked at each other.

"Here we go."

"Here we do."

"I love you. Last chance to say it," I said.

"Same here, let's go, he prolly doesn't got parkin'."

Down we went in the elevator with our backpacks and nothing else. I felt stupid, so I put my backpack on one shoulder like a junior higher. I didn't want to go on this art project, but the fact that Carol would be next to me for the drive there and back was a big bone I looked forward to enjoying.

We stepped out of the elevator, "Goodbye, Doorman Diego."

"Where are you going?" he asked.

"Hunting."

"God bless!" he called.

We stepped out onto the sidewalk—an early summer morning. Quick flicked his cigarette into the street and helped us load the haul—our sleeping bags spread out nicely, our backpacks in a corner. I handed him a letter and a map for Darron, Carol's little black camera, a black cell phone, and a note detailing the details for him. Carol and I climbed into the haul and looked at each other. We put our fingers to our lips as Quick shut us in, my finger like lifting the Empire State Building to my lips, Carol's finger like pressing a polished, scented twig to her lips to pose with. Charlie Quick started up the truck and it lurched forward—we braced ourselves. Carol squealed to show how *this will be fun, actually!*

Dear Charlie Quick,

Drive the speed limit and all that. There is a bag of granola that you should've purchased that's up there with you in the cab. Remove the stopper on the peephole and funnel granola in to us until we whimper like wolves which means for you to stop pouring. Feed us six times a day. We have urination contraptions with which to urinate (mine is a dick of course; Carol's is a special contraption for women), but when we need to lay craps we'll knock three times and you should glide the truck to the nearest rest stop or gas station. Keep all music off—we don't want to be tempted to hum along. Anything that wolves don't do is what you should support. Do not stop very often to sleep. It will be very uncomfortable for us to sleep on the hard floor of the haul, so we want to get out to Wyo as soon as possible, but don't fall asleep at the wheel and crash either, as cops would arrest us.

When we get to Carol's drop spot (DIRECTIONS AND MAP UNDERNEATH THIS PAPER) you'll unstop the peephole and photograph us using the little black camera I handed you. Do more and more shots where we do different poses, until I whine like a wolf, which means stop. Then Carol will get out and you'll close the haul door electronically. Drive to my drop spot then and, same routine, with the photographs and on and on. THEN, go into town at Ten Sleep and go to 6183 LARDY STREET between 4:00 p.m. and 7:00 p.m. to deliver the cell phone to Darron Reilly, my little brother. Also, give him the letter that's in the pile here in an envelope labeled "Darron." If my mother answers the door, tell her: "I'm trading this cell with Darron for some Imitation Cowboys and I wrote him a Thank You. Please see that he gets these," then leave. Then you have completed your mission, and you may return to New York at whatever pace you please, though something tells me you'll choose "quick." Carol and I will take the bus back once we've completed *Hush, Howler—Hunt.*

Signed,

The Haircutter

Sunlight shot through the bullet holes around us.

"It's like we're in Outer Space!" Carol said.

"Just call me Woomalee Amatrist!" I said, and she said, "Hey I thought we weren't talkin'!" We went all silent, then snickered hard at the Amatrist joke.

There we were—going back to Ten Sleep on the same road we rode in on, in the same truck, but now in the back where the wolf and his piss and shit rode.

Art!

I swung my tongue like a wolf and Carol licked her hand some. We smiled like, See—we're doing it, and we're not gonna be embarrassed. We got on our knees to look through the bullet holes. Cars coasted next to us unaware of the truck's inner life. I waited until there was no one next to us, and I stood up and lined my pisshole up to a bullet hole and peed. I farted on accident and turned around and Carol was there getting the contraption that she'd purchased tucked good between her legs. She lined it up to a hole. The pee ran down the wall for both of us, and that's the second to the last time we peed that way. I wrote a note and rolled it scroll-like to send through the peephole next time Charlie Quick fed us. It said: *Glide to a gas station or a rest stop when we knock three times FOR PEEING TOO.*

We'd pop out the haul like two quick fish poops and float away toward the johns. We'd collapse onto pots that collected our collapsed internal debris. We'd jog back to the haul howling, as if to feed the truck's ass two wolves.

It was about picking at stuff (your shoes, the splotches of paint on the floor, your scalp zits, your thoughts). Carol often watched her thoughts on a screen in front of her like a movie. She reacted and blushed. She had muted conversations—her lips lightly moved. I got her attention once and made a gesture like *what are you smiling about?* She flinched hard. Then she scooched over to kiss and make L. It felt like the "old days." I went, "Whoa Girly," all soft on accident. We rocked that truck. Afterwards, Carol had a cig out one of the bullet holes. She put her lips over a hole to exhale. I thought, *We've got a smoking wolf here, folks.* We were getting way too much granola in, what with it being six times a day, so I had a corner pile of granola that I laid munching on popcorn-style with my head propped up on an elbow. I thought, *We've got a lounging hamster here, folks.* We were careful to remember to howl now and then—Carol lightly shaking her hair back, clearing her throat, doing a howl. H.C. howling through a mouthful of granola. A couple of artists getting some howls in. (And shit like that.)

We rode lying down, snuggling. Carol's limbs wrapped around my fat body. She was a net and I was a beached whale someone was hauling.

As we got closer and closer to Wyoming, Carol cried more and more. It was alarming, but I didn't hear the alarm going off. It got so bad that every time I looked at her she had tears dripping from her face. "I don't wanna split up!" she'd whisper. She was in real heart pain. She'd scratch at her heart as if to stop it from itching. The skin over her heart looked like one of my paintings where I took some red and made a motion like the brush couldn't stop signing a check (over which I painted *Perry Sufo wrote Serious on a Tuesday in 1991 in present tense*). Carol crawled across the haul floor crying and saying "John" like the word hurt to say.

"We don't have to do this."

She said, "Yes, we do."

Then she shook her hair and howled to show: *Let's get back on track.*

Carol and The Haircutter crossed America with their cheeks vibrating in the steel haul as they held their heads in ways that made the vibrating least unflattering. Charlie Quick in his driver's seat felt a foreign sense of relaxation. He started whistling, but caught himself and bit his hand white. He hadn't grown up with happiness, so he always thought that people thought he was trying to act like Christmas if he showed some. At a sleep stop one night, he was disgusted by the truck rocking like a Hush Little Charlie, so he got out and went to the bar at the edge of the lot they were parked in. Around the top of the bar ran a choo-choo train, and when Quick walked in, the tender lady did a trick where she hollered and it came out sounding like a train. Around the carpeted floor of the bar, mouse droppings five years old mingled with mouse droppings five seconds fresh. Charlie Quick bought a beer and felt patrons look at his blue suit. He shrugged to drape it better. A news anchor on TV said, "The Middle East is falling apart." A patron grunted and Charlie Quick looked at her—she had a fuzzy birthmark around one of her eyes like her name was Spot and the tender let her eat out of the dumpster at night. Quick blushed his English cheeks. He looked at the other patron, who was wearing rose-colored glasses and spitting tobacco juice through a missing tooth to arch toward the TV but land with a rattle in a bucket behind the bar labeled *Dip spit "here" and no where's else!* Charlie Quick's heart palpitated. He was a scared man; that's why he was companions with Christmas. Christmas equaled power, which equaled protection, which equaled companion-ship. The bar he was in? It made him feel unprotected. He couldn't do normal things; he couldn't even finish his beer. He left an enormous tip and left his bar stool spinning. He burst through a swarm of moths. He heard the tender lady make her train sound through the window screens. He ran back to the truck, his suit coat flapping like chicken wings. He settled into the cab and, rock-a-bye Charlie, fell asleep.

And in the haul, Carol came. In orchestral, silent-sex fashion, the orgasm had many layers—it ended with an oboe of all instruments holding out a note softly retarding. The oboe player, Carol saw for a flash second, had a lazy eye, and stood knock-kneed while he piped. She shook the image out of her head and her vagina throbbed herself to sleep—rock-a-bye Carol. The Haircutter handled his shriveling balls and looked at the roof of the haul, which had scratches on it from hauling art, and thought, *This is an art truck and this is my girlfriend, and this is an art project I have to do.* He thought, *Ma-ma!* He thought, *I miss my old life with my Cokes and books and car wash job. But then I'd have to give up Carol.* He thought, *Well then I'd have to kill her.* He smelled the top of her head and said, "I'd rather she be asleep than somewhere awake and without me." Outside of the truck, the Midwest crickets throbbed the word weird weird weird weird weird weird weird weird weird.

ACTION.

Carol and The Haircutter bouncing so hard their bodies come up off the floor. Fat-stuffed H.C.'s not used to feeling weightlessness—he's giggling. Carol lifts her shirt to show how her boobs are responding—blurry. Quick rips up backroads terrain.

H.C. sees through a bullet hole, "This is it!"

Carol cries, "I ain't ready yet!"

The truck halts to a stop, making Carol and H.C. scatter.

The haul door rolls up to the sound of Carol shrieking.

Quick moves about in the cab.

Carol blows her nose on H.C.'s sleeping bag.

A *POP!* as Quick unstops the peephole. A camera lens blinks in its center.

Carol presses The Haircutter's head to her protruding sternum—he finds her pearl and sucks it. She shakes her hair and howls. The electronic turning of the film roll inside the black camera captures the scene.

They can smell the color scale of the trees. From wet to dry. From wild flowers to wild animal feces. They flick their tongues for a kiss. Two snakes—one fat, one thin, one male, one female, both from Wyoming.

H.C. pulls his body walrus-like by the palms to the corner where Carol's backpack is. The camera captures the scene—Carol and The Haircutter, in camping clothes clean, attach her sleeping bag to her pack, thread her arms through the straps. The Haircutter smashes his face into hers. The camera shyly blinks.

Carol says, "I wish I could talk right now!"

H.C. says, "Me too! What would *you* say?"

And with a surprising amount of heft and gathered strength, Carol Mary Mathers leaps from the truck. Two female-sized hiking boots land *HUFF* on the earth. A female spine responds accordingly. A thirty-year-old blond makes a ponytail.

She looks back to see the face of one fat Haircutter and the lens-eye of one drilled peephole, which she—barely detected, but captured on film—winks at.

The truck lurches forward before the haul door is even half-closed.

I let out a roar of misery when we pulled away. Every thought of what we didn't learn about survival was an electric shock. I started clutching my head like I was going crazy in a movie—I was like, Whoa, this is actually pretty serious. I was like, I just left my girl in the woods.

I ferociously ate granola all the way to my drop spot. Some tears piddle-paddled—fine, add all that. I blew my nose in the same place Carol blew hers on my sleeping bag to see if later a flower would grow.

When the truck finally stopped I fell face-first into the granola pile. When I pulled my head out, the haul door was rolled up—hello nightmare.

Pop went the peephole plug above my head. I scurried to my sleeping bag and rolled it up. The camera whirred. I sucked in my stomach so hard it made me cough. I put on my backpack and went to take two handfuls of granola, then I walked on my knees to the end of the haul and worked on sliding out—I scraped my forearms. The camera whirred once more when I was outside. It's an ugly pic—you can only see my head off the end of the haul looking in the lens, thinking, "I'm getting this head photographed so I might as well close its mouth." The haul door closed electronically and the truck pulled away. What had we gotten ourselves into.

The wilderness watched me from the corners of its eyes to show how it's more important than me but wonders why I'm there. Or did it wave with its branches saying, "You're a part of us!" Either way, I put the granola in my mouth, but realized I didn't want it, so I spat it out (like that same hamster). I took off my backpack and got out the cell. What's the use wasting time?

Riiiiiiing, riiiiiiiing—you know.

"Hello?"

"John Junior here."

"This is Charlie Quick."

I was like, "Oh!"

And told him nevermind and waited forty-five minutes.

Riiiiiiiiiiiiig—

"This is Darron speaking."

"Yeah I know!"

"Brother John! This is a FUCKING cool surprise! You gotta explain it to me, but I'm just happy to be a part of whatever it is!"

"Good, so you read the letter?" I said.

"Yeah! Sounds real arty, but I kinda get it, even though at first I was like, 'Oh is this some art baloney?'"

"Yeah yeah, listen. Are you in front of Ma or Father John?"

"Huh-uh, I'm in my car already."

"Good! Okay, come out and get me now. I'll explain when you pick me up, but basically I'm not waitin' in these damn woods for a week, if you hear."

"I got the keys in the ignition! Where are you?"

"It's what I gave you the map for!" I grouched.

Laziness is as what fat lazy men do, or whatever saying you could say for it. It would've taken a minimum of four days for us to find each other, and what's the difference between me sleeping in bear shit four days or me sleeping in a hotel four days? The difference is bears. I'd have Darron take me back to the woods in four days and drop me closer to where Carol's drop spot was. So sue me. And send the bill to my mother—she'd be happy to pay it. Talk about a fair fare.

I went out to the road and waited. When cars passed by I dove into the bushery. You know—don't let anyone recognize

The Haircutter in case the arm of fame can reach Wyoming and point him out. I paced the road and tried playing with a stick but knew I wasn't the type, so I ditched it. I started getting choked up on "poor Carol" stuff—*was I doing the right thing?* It was hard for me—let's just leave it at that, along with leaving Carol in the woods.

The blue car in the distance. A rusty Volkswagen Golf. Coming at me like a slow unzipping. Darron's smiling face. Har-har. There's my little brother. Two chords up the back of his straight boy's neck; one missing tail. When we were little in the summer he'd have to go outside to get warm because Father John put the A/C up high and Darron didn't get fat genes like everyone else. Sitting on the sidewalk by himself tickling his eyeball with a blade of grass, moaning.

Tires crackling over chipped road. He cranks the brake. His door asks, "Huh?" then falls shut, "Oh."

"Brother John!"

He comes to hug.

And smells the same.

And says, "I just seen Carol! Hitchhiking down the road a few miles back!"

The words swarmed around my head trying to find my ear holes, but they were blind and senseless; wrought, with hands bound. (Or whatever. It just sucked, is what.)

"She's a brunette now?" he said.

I shrank in relief.

"No."

"Are you sure?" he said. "That was her."

I said, "No it wadn't, she ain't brown-headed."

He said, "But don't her legs kinda go backwards when she stands?"

Wrought. Felt like I was swallowing long, flexible needles.

I said, "What'd you just say?"

"That was her, I swear to god, I know her face. And I think she recognized me too cause she was like—," he made a surprised face and turned away to hide it.

I said, "Shit!" I said, "Really?" I said, "Christ!" I said, "She's prolly goin' to a hotel like me!"

"You're goin' to a *hotel?* Aww, you dog! Y'all are cheatin' on your thing or what?"

I said, "Hurry up, get in the car." I thought quick, "Now listen here Darron, this is what's gonna happen. I'm gonna get in the trunk, no matter how hard you gotta squeeze me, and you go pick her up, k? And try to get as much info as you can outta her. And if she asks if you recognize her from Blue Bear, you just say no. Even if she says I'm that Blue Bear waitress, you say, 'Hell, I'm usually dancin' so hard I can't capture faces, they're all a blur.' K?"

Darron nodded slow and serious. I was really grateful for how seriously he took all this, and I still am.

I said, "Now most important thing is you say you were up these ways cause you got called that your friend shot a buck up here and needed help getting it in his truck cause his saw was busted, but when you got up here, just say your friend used a hatchet instead and didn't need your help."

Darron said, "Dang! That's all real smart! Okay, git in the trunk."

I curled up like a stupid roly-poly hugging onto my backpack and Darron shut the trunk.

I heard him go, "Looks like the car's got a shit in its rear," and I chuckled at that, even though I was confused as hell, and nervous, and still felt like I was swallowing those long needles.

We rolled to a stop a few miles later. I heard the muffled voice of a female with the exact musicality of Carol's. She got in. I heard waka-waka talking between the two of them. Once we started driving, I couldn't hear a thing—only the engine and the sexual sounds that my body pushed out of my mouth when we went over bumps.

After a while, we rolled to a stop and I heard what could only have been, "Welcome to McDonald's, may I take your order?" Based on how we proceeded stop/start then for a bit made me sure that we were in a McDonald's drive-thru. *Hungry, Carol?*

Shortly after the drive-thru, we came to another stop and I heard waka-waka thank yous and goodbyes. Carol's door slammed shut.

Darron let me out of the trunk as he was saying, "She's been hitchhiking since Rock Springs, is what she said, which I'm guessing is a lie, and she told me a pervert asked her for a sexual favor, so she made him let her out. And that's where I hitched her. It's good she dudn't hunt, cause I was like, 'there's a moose up here with a saw in its rear, and my friend needed help gettin' it in his trunk.'"

"WHERE'D YOU DROP HER OFF?" I said.

"The bus station," he said.

"The BUS STATION!"

I watched Darron army crawl up a grassy hill down the block that summited to the bus station parking lot. He saw Carol waiting with her long backpack. ("Was it red?" "Yes.") He saw her with her head down and the bangs from her *wig* covering her eyes. He saw a bus pull up and watched her get on. He bolted back to the car and smacked the hood, "Duck down! We got a bus to follow!"

I said, "HONK! Go catch her!"

Darron said, "No way!"

I instinctively went to yank his tail but it was gone.

He said, "What good's that gonna do if you don't spy? Then you'll never know the real reason *why.* Where's she going? We gotta *spy*, big bro."

I said, "FUCK YOU, IS WHAT!"

Talk about hush, howler. He was right.

The day faded into night.

Keep your eyes on that bus was the theme.

"Maybe she's goin' back to New York," Darron said.

"Why would she do that?"

"Maybe she forgot somethin'," he said.

"She didn't."

The familiar square of the bus hovering mirage-like ahead of us. Fuck you, is what.

Darron said, "I'm gonna use this cell to call Ma and Father John."

Right now I should be at a motel vending machine asking what things I'm gonna get, I thought.

"Ma?" Darron said, "I just wanna let you know I decided last minute to go outta town on a Salvation shoppin' spree."

I heard my mother whine her worries.

"Actually, I found my New Year's resolution list the other day? And I was like, Oh my god, I forgot one'a my goals was to go on a Salvation spree for Imitation supplies."

Where did she get a wig? Was it made of real hair? Whose?

He hung up wincing.

"I don't like lyin'," he said very quietly under his breath.

My brother got nice genes instead of fat ones. Or maybe he got fat ones too, but kept them at bay with dancing. Maybe we got nice genes too, but we just can't tell because all that fat being there makes the heart's function penetrate through less efficiently. Darron's heart's function penetrates through like light through a window you wash. Or some math like that where I'm fat.

The night faded into day.

"What'd she get at McDonald's?"

"Chicken sandwich, a thing of chicken nuggets, two large fries, strawberry shake, and a Coke," he said.

My eyes filled with tears at the thought of her enjoying that nice meal—the bus blurred into the horizon like this was all a dream.

The three people who had just driven to Wyoming together were now driving back to New York in three separate vehicles. Charlie Quick was singing in the empty wolf job truck and feeling more protected than he'd ever felt before in his life. His task was to drive, and his doing it could not be improved upon—he was driving. He held a low note that crackled into a whinny when he realized that there is as much protection in absolute freedom as there is freedom in absolute protection. He took his right hand off the wheel and punched his window out. One hundred and fifty-three miles back, The Haircutter was telling his little brother about all that had happened to him and Carol since they'd settled in New York—Darron was so impressed, he took his right hand off his mouth and rolled his window down. Fifty-three feet in front of Darron and H.C., Carol was leaned into a bus aisle watching the road roll under the window shield—she had a hand up her shirt and she was twiddling a nipple unbeknownst to her. She only stopped that task to sleep or to shit her nerves into the little bus toilette—the other passengers thinking, *She's goin' again.* She'd crack the toilette window to watch cattle pass while she sat. When she'd flush, she'd tell the pot, "Swill that down, you're used to it," and the pot would guzzle like a lupo hick trying to make her puke.

Tinkle twinkle, little pussy little stars. Each one asking, "What the hell?" "What the hell?" "What the hell's going on?" It didn't occur to me to be bothered by the fact that Carol was so fancy-pants she kept her pajamas under her pillow, or that her skin looked like the underside of a bar table since she'd started wearing so much makeup. I had one thing in mind, and one thing only—how'd she learn how to take a bus by herself, and what did it mean about where she was going? Carol at transfers having to switch buses like a game of cups—which one has Carol? We followed the buses through Nebraska, Iowa, Illinois, wherever-the-stupid-fuck. Darron slept with his mouth open and it smelled like a soggy box of firecrackers from a garage flood. I drove like a bull on fire, snorting and making a high-pitched sound while getting burned alive wondering what the hell's going on. My mind thought, "Hey maybe this is a little cat and mouse aspect she added!" Then, my mind roared, "She's goin' back to New York and leavin' you in the woods and you know it!!!" My mind's eye showed myself sleeping in the pup tent hugging onto my bear mace being like, "Carol, I love you! Maybe tomorrow I'll find you!" I wrung the steering wheel and made that high-pitched sound. I was connected to Carol by telepathic tendons plucked by thought, and a fever ignited in them when she wouldn't respond. *Why aren't you out in the woods right now? . . . Carol? . . . Why am I not at a vending machine right now while you're out in the woods?* The fever bent down into heartache, then boiled up into rage, then bent down into heartache, then boiled back into rage, then became the fist of pain grabbing me by the heart, twisting it like a T-shirt, lifting me up off my seat and saying through gritted teeth, "*FEEL*." Darron said, "There there," which was such a strange and parental thing to say, it actually did calm me down. My high-pitched sound retarded. Rock-a-bye H.C. (Just after you kill yourself.)

Carol's buses stopped for sometimes half an hour to let passengers off, and we'd have to keep an eye on her so we could run to the john and purchase snacks. I officially found out that we were headed back to New York when we stopped in a town in Pennsylvania. We slid into a parking spot on Main Street across from the bus depot, just close enough to be able to watch Carol's little wigged head on her bus. There was an old man hobbling up the sidewalk with a flyswatter, using it, and Darron and I laughed about it until we saw him enter a Salvation Army store. I looked at Darron and he was biting his lip, wincing badly. He wanted to go buy Imitation Cowboy supplies.

I said, "You eyein' that Salvation?"

He said, "I could just duck in while those new passengers load."

I said, "Fine—you prolly got a half hour," allowing him to go.

The cornfield that the bus depot was build on stunk of grasshopper poop. The sky was the color of chicken soup. It was raining tenderlings that patted me on the hand as I reached out to Carol's bus going, "*Why, my Love?*" A car pulled up next to me at a red light and blocked my view, and the woman driving was yawning and she looked like a demon screaming. If I were a kid I would've wet myself. I scoffed at her when she looked at me.

"Close your mouth," I said, looking away to see Darron come out the doors of the Salvation with ten bursting plastic sacks strung up on his arms and a few cowboy hats stacked on his head. He heaped his loot onto the back seat of the Golf.

"Quit smilin' so hard, she's gonna sense it," I said.

"I ain't sayin' nothin'!" he said.

"So close your mouth."

Carol stepped out of her bus and walked toward a picnic bench with a cig.

"She wants a cig," I thought, happy for her somewhere beneath my fat.

Darron handed me a plastic bag, "Here, I got you this disguise."

I saw a blond wig, a white church hat . . .

I said, "Huh?"

He said, "You're gonna need a disguise so no one recognizes you. What if someone tells Carol they saw you, or what if they rat on you guys that you didn't do your project right? Why do you think she's wearin' a wig? Aren't you supposed to be out in the woods? I got you a fat lady costume, no offense."

The bag was full of cross-dressing equipment.

Once again, my little brother had proven to be worth having.

I said, "She's wearing a wig! Darron, you're right! She doesn't want anyone to recognize her! You know what that means?"

"What?"

"She's prolly goin' back to the woods after all this!"

"I always used to wish you were a detective!" Darron said.

I said, "I gotta hurry up and get into this now—who knows when the next stop's New York."

The Haircutter stood up into the street holding his shitty plastic bag tight to his breast as the small-town air held him tight to its teat so he could get milk-fed. The rain fell straight, as if suicidal. Nobody watched me hustle to the bus depot, as they were used to fat people. Everyone wore sweatshirts or jackets or T-shirts with the names of sport teams or colleges or medical centers on them; everyone was Midwestern. In the Women's Room, mosquitoes hung in the air like perfume. I went to the handicapped stall, deciding I'd come out drooling if I saw wheelchair wheels waiting under the door before I came out. The rain fell harder as I opened the sack to see what Darron had bought.

Pantyhose . . .

A floral muumuu . . .

A pair of sea-green high heels . . .

A gold bracelet—(worth something?) . . .

White plastic flower earrings . . .

A knit pocketbook with Christmas trees on it that said *Warm Greetings* . . .

"Jesus Christ, Darron," I thought.

I removed my clothes. The floor was gritty and thunder gathered in the clouds.

I sat down on the toilet and blew into the pantyhose to puff them out ready to get my legs.

Then lightning struck hot pink through the opened door—Carol had entered.

My atoms are sensitized to her. And her *Bad Influence* was so strong I could taste it. She plopped down in the stall next to mine and shat hard in an exhale. Her lighter flicked and a cloud of smoke billowed when it hit the floor. I bent over to look at her feet and saw her hiking boots that we'd paid $64.95 for. Her cig ash hissed at a drain in the floor between us.

"Surprise!" Carol said.

I gasped.

"Oh sorry, I didn't know anyone else was in here!" she said. "I'm practicing for somethin'."

I almost said, "Practicing for *WHAT?*" but quickly thought against it. Wrapped in a thin slice of time like a spring roll, I'd chosen the healthy option. "*Don't blow your cover yet no matter how bad you want it!*" I heard Darron say in my head.

Carol farted a plop of shit out.

"Sorry," she apologized for it.

Our bodies are built to shit when we're scared so that we're lighter to run. *Carol, what are you running from?*

Thunder cracked and lightning struck three seconds later—a tornado was three miles away. We could hear the bus driver's walkie-talkie through a vent high up on the wall. And then he crunched away on the soupy gravel. The bus farted and Carol called, "Don't leave without me!"

Static electricity made its too-good-for-us-all way across the cornfield and gathered in the eyelashes of a cow for sparks to blind her when she blinked. I worked the pantyhose skin up my shin until my shin burst through them as Carol pulled on her paper roll beside me. She wiped as I spat on the earrings to get crust off them, and they were white flowers as I clipped them to my lobes. Carol was sixteen when I was twenty-four and our moms got our food from the same grocery store as these years later I stood up from the toilet and slipped a muumuu over my head—it fell down floral to my ankles to whisper a soap opera theme song at them. Carol dropped her cig into the drain and it hissed when it saw how hot I looked in the dress. The bracelet popped off my wrist and hit her stall wall. I was Cinderelly as I slipped into the sea-green high heels and they fit.

"Swill that down, you're used to it," Carol whispered before she flushed.

I sucked on the hook where women hang their pocketbooks while I waited for her to finish with the sink. The cold metal satisfied the sick instinct to cut her wig with my scissor (which was in NYC).

She left the restroom saying, "Surprise!"

The rain let up like a hand relaxing after casting a curse.

The Haircutter didn't even look in the mirror. He opened the door and steam had rolled off the field to cover the lot in fog.

It looked like a nightmare.

We pulled up to New York in the golden late afternoon—the same time of day that Father John and I had pulled up eight years earlier.

Darron was driving and craning his neck around, pretending not to care.

I said, "Go ahead—holler."

Then it was all, "WHAT! THIS IS NEW YORK!!!"

I ticked my tongue. I flipped down the mirror to start putting some makeup on. I was sitting in the passenger's wearing a white church hat placed on a blond wig; there were boob indentations on the muumuu where the owner's boobs used to go; and I was applying purple shadow the way I'd seen Carol do it when she did.

"Couldn't you have gotten me a regular pocketbook instead of a Christmas tree one?" I said.

"Well I thought cause of your art guy!" Darron said, defending.

"I don't care about Christmas!" I said.

I emptied the contents of my pants pockets into the pocketbook. My green Velcro wallet, the change, the comb that I never used. The cell phone that should've been deep in my backpack in the woods. I turned the cylinder on a lipstick Darron had bought and the lipstick emerged pussy-pink and girly-smelling. I applied.

"Big bro, I'm sorry, but you look like a man," Darron said.

"No, I look like a *cross-dresser* pretending to be a fat lady," I said. "It's a perfectly normal thing to look like in New York City."

"Well you don't look like The Haircutter," he said.

"Then that's what counts."

When the bus disappeared into Port Authority Bus Terminal, we lost it.

"I'll call you on the cell," I said.

I stepped out of the car and slammed the door shut, holding my Sunday hat tight on my wig. Swooping seagulls overhead squeaked like sky mice. Passersby chatted on cells like mice. Where's a broom when you need one? I bought a paper from a newsstand and the wind snapped my floral skirt like a flag. An orange cat ran out of the newsstand with a paw lifted above its head—it struck my skirt-flag rapidly. Meowza! Excuse me! The guy who took my quarter shouted, "Get off his dress!" and came round to get the cat. I cleared my throat and walked toward the entrance of Port Authority, my heels tick-tocking the concrete.

I scuttled to the arrival door of the bus Carol had come in on. I waited behind the newspaper off to the side. The article I was hiding behind showed a guy looking out from the page like *What the hell's going on?* I tried to read the headline for a clue, but I was so nervous my vision was blurred—it said *MetgEsteOoNeyfler.*

I saw Carol come out the door.

An idiot part of me had still doubted that it was her, but there she was, rabbity as ever but in an attractive brown wig. It was all I could do not to call out, *Carol! What is goink ooon-uuuuuh?!* I'd been dipping my very dick underneath those camping clothes into her hidey-hole, and there we were hours later—not allowed to be seen by each other!

I followed her at a distance. The shouts from people saying, "Dang! That's a dude!" would've caught her attention had I been walking right behind her.

This is what she did: she hailed a cab. It took her to the grocery store by our apartment. She shopped, buying *lots* of food. I was afraid that she'd recognize my sea-green heels from below the Women's Room stall, so I hid my feet behind a tower of chips and leaned my body out to watch her. She tossed things in her cart so fast she broke a jar of pickles. "What time is it?" she asked the zit prince who cleaned it up. The store manager told me to please leave when he saw me stalking her. She hailed another cab and had the cabbie help her load her many sacks. She shouted our address.

I got out my cell and told Darron to count with the car to 37th and 6th.

I walked to my apartment and as I turned the corner Door-man Diego was helping her unload.

"Bring them upstairs!" she commanded, handing him bills of my easy-earned cash.

I stood in the parking spot directly across from my building where last May someone got hit by a bicyclist and lay with his brief-case open until the ambulance came in case his spine was broken. ("Nobody touch me!" he'd screamed into the concrete, sending shivers down the perfectly healthy spines of everyone witnessing.) When Darron slid the car into the spot, he was in a long, fancy red dress. He somehow had makeup on, jewelry, and a brown curly bangs wig.

I got in the passenger's. When he saw my face he flinched, wondering what he'd done wrong, "It dudn't look rill?"

I hissed, "Where'd you get that?"

"Same place I got yours! We don't want her to recognize me too, duh!" he said.

I said, "Now how the hell are we disguised right now?! We don't look like friends, Darron! No one would ever believe we're hanging out together!"

"Why not?" he said.

"Well look at us!" I said. "You're some prom queen? Couldn't you have been a magician or something?"

Darron bit a knuckle, "Oh no! I'm sorry! I guess I wasn't thinking."

I started crying, "It's okay!"

"Whoa, you're crying!" he said.

"My head feels weird!" I said. "What's wrong with Carol?"

"Do you want to go to the hospital?"

"Now how the FUCK'S that gonna help?! Why don't we head to the fuckin' opera, Darron? I'm sure there's a prom on the way!"

A cop came by to find a reason why we couldn't be two "women" in a car throwing a fit but he couldn't find one so he moved on.

We monitored Carol's activity, which was none. No one I recognized or didn't recognize came or went from my apartment entrance. Night seeped into the city. Streetlights made an octagonic haze around my little brother—there were diamonds glued to the tips of his eyelashes, glitter stuck in between his teeth. He was telling a story about the neighbor's dog, saying, "Their daughter's in ROTC so I always see her leave for school at 6:30."

We cranked our seats back and unzipped the backs of each other's dresses.

"I put perfume behind my ears and it stinks," Darron said.

I removed my bracelet and put it on a soda cup lid in the drink console. Darron picked the diamonds off his lashes. The Golf shook when cars passed it.

"Why'd you go so far with the dress-up?" I said.

"Cause it's fun! I never get to do stuff like that," he said, and I grunted.

"You make me look like a poor hag next to you," I said.

On the back seat, on top of the Salvation haul, a sea-green high heel sat idiot-stiff with $4.99 written on it in red crayon.

"I bet people would think you're prettier. You have them eyes that Father John has," he said.

"Quit tryin' to cover your buns," I said. "You know how good you look."

Darron had to pretend to look out the window so he could hide his smile.

We fell asleep.

In the early dawn, I opened my door and found my penis under my dress to pee with, and Darron went to a coffee shop to pee in their john instead of in the gutter like a hog. I said, "Don't stray too far!" saying "stray" on accident instead of "go."

I was slouched down grouching behind my makeup face when Darron tapped on the window—he was crouching like an action movie, pointing at my apartment. I jerked my church hat down over my eyes. I strained to look through the white weave. Carol was in her wig disguise throwing away two big bags of trash. She took her hanky from her camping shorts and blew her nose.

"Crying, Carol?" I said in my deep voice.

She went back inside. I put on the sea-greens. I got out of the car with my legs half asleep. See the fat lady have a hard time crossing the street. I opened the trashcan lid and the trash smelled really good—*huh?* I lifted a bag, but then I heard Doorman Diego singing Spanish to himself as he sauntered out to stand at the entrance! I dropped the bag and scuttled back to the Golf, my "high hills" making a racket.

Darron socked my arm, "What were you *thinking?*"

It was good that I didn't look through the trash, because Carol came back outside, this time carrying two more bags, and she had her tampon backpack on her back. She threw the trash away and went to put her finger to her lips, telling Doorman Diego, "Shh!" I started the car and pulled out as Carol got into a cab.

We followed her back to Port Authority.

Darron said, "She's goin' back to the woods."

Darron and I parked the car, then walked the guts of the massive bus station. We had to split up, what with our mismatching looks that made no sense. I walked around hunchbacked and hunting, my heart on ice. I was one big goosebump. I checked the McDonald's and gasped when I saw Carol's backpack in line. I watched her place her order and wait. I watched behind a pole. I rubbed on the pole while I watched, and forgot I was in a dress until a little boy pointed at me and said to his mom, "There's another one!" Carol was sucking on a Coke, waiting for her order number to be called. I saw she was crying. Carol! I started crying too—hiccups and blubbers—all that. I plucked some muumuu out of my stomach fat. "Ca-rooool!" I said quietly. People who saw me were moved so hard by compassion they covered their mouths from barfing, saying, "Life's weird!" or "Oh my god, did you see that? That was so depressing!" or "There's a cross-dresser over there cryiiiiink!"

Carol's number was called, and she took a big bag of McDonald's and walked toward the escalators with snot glistening on her upper lip. I followed her—we rode the same escalator—and at the bottom, Darron appeared coming at us through the crowd, his cherry-red dress falling down to expose a nipple on each side with each stride he made in his high heels. When he saw Carol, he froze.

She walked right past him and went through a doorway marked *Bus #309 Pittsburg.*

"Yep, she's goin' back," I said.

"My disguise worked!" he said.

"You don't know what it's like," I said. "When I look in her eyes, it's like looking in the mirror. I love her."

We stood breathing, having done our very best there in the city. Then it was like, "Let's go back to the woods." Darron's dress had a train that made him need to walk in a circle in order to turn around.

Why'd she have so much trash and why did it smell so good? Why'd she come back to New York, only to then go back to the woods? Why did she lie to me? Why did she want me to picture her impaled upon another man's dick? Why did she like art and people so much that it made me on some level forget that I loved her? Why did I forget how lucky I was to have her? My heart went topsy-turvy down the rabbit hole of sadness. I hunched in my seat and cried on my fingers that squirmed in the air halfway to my face—they just couldn't make it.

Carol. Mary. Mathers. Laughing without hesitating, fucking without even noticing, fucking while laughing and hesitating. I slapped the dash and roared to stop the thoughts. Headlights lit my contorted face. I would rub her hair on the contours of her face and her voice would come out of her in the sound I'm used to hearing.

I made the seatbelt cradle my head. We cut through darkness. I thought of her fuzzy rump, her fishy smell issuing up.

At some stop, Darron came back to the car with a stick. "For you to bite on when you can't no longer bear it."

"Her heart and legs open every day, Darron," I said.

"Well that sounds nice."

"Her panties like little dove skins," I said.

"Sounds fancy," he replied.

"We were livin' in a poem. How come I didn't see the rhymes?"

[.................]

"Her face in the morning!" I said to his silence.

Silence still.

I bit the stick and it cracked in half.

"Aw fuck!" I said.

An ant crawled up my cheek and I smacked it dead.

We got a motel. ("If we ain't got no bus to chase, hell.")

Darron took a bath.

The hand of pain tossed me fetal-posed on the bed, making a plume of mixed skin cells burst off it.

Darron and The Haircutter drove the freeway listening to soft country radio. It was the hardest thing Darron had ever done straining not to sing along with those songs. He wrung the steering wheel and strained so hard his left eye snapped off its chords and went lazy. He let out a sexual-sounding sigh.

H.C. lifted his head to say, "Darron, do you know what I just realized? When Carol and I get back to normal, I'm gonna get her lowered from the ceiling of Carnegie Hall during some show. Like the featured guest gets lowered from the ceiling, spinning around? Dudn't that sound pretty?"

"Yeah that sounds real nice," Darron said, and H.C. said, "I know she'd like that," and cradled his head in the Golf's seatbelt again.

Darron furrowed his brows at his brother and pursed his lips. He looked at the road, then at The Haircutter, then at the road, then at The Haircutter, then realized that with his new eye he could look at both in tandem. He got used to it, then whispered with his face pointed at the glove compartment, "It sounds like y'all are a good couple and this can just be somethin' you clear up."

At some rest stop I went to the john and there was a cigarette floating in there like Carol. I shat all over it. When I got back in the car, Darron tossed something at me—a pickle in a plastic sleeve. He said, "I always remember you like these."

I said, "Aw fuck, Darron, thanks. I can put it in my backpack for a nice treat in the woods."

He said, "Good! And I was thinkin'—we should give our disguises to Mom."

I noticed it was as if I were in a good mood.

I said, "That's a nice idea. I can see her in the dress I wore and the jewelry that you wore."

"Yeah. Mom looks like a badger in sweats. I think she'll like it. Maybe she could re-introduce usin' makeup. That purple you wore on your shadows looked good."

We passed the sign that says Wyoming Welcomes You.

Darron said, "You got a tent?"

"Yeah."

I noticed that the sky was grey to match my mind.

Ten minutes later, I said, "It ain't a Coleman's, but."

Darron let a little time pass to pretend it was nice to let a long time pass, and said, "How much they charge you for it?"

"They gave it to me for $16.99 at Kmart, but—"

Darron whistled.

"Ach, clearance," I said.

Then Carol came flapping to perch on my lips wanting to peck down my throat in search of my heart.

I dug in my backpack and got out the pickle and ate it in four bites. I drank the juice from the plastic sleeve, then I burped and the sleeve creased away from me.

Darron didn't say anything.

The traffic said, "Shhhhhhhh."

When we got into Ten Sleep we went to the bus station and asked if Carol was coming. The woman behind the logbook bobbled her head in the throws of some disease as she turned the pages and opened and closed her mouth adhesively. Her tee had a howling wolf on it to mock me with a skin-colored cigarette snap case in the breast pocket. She was proud to not say anything while she worked, and was even prouder to finally say, "You'd've had to check in New York, not here."

I said, "Take me back to the woods!"

Darron said, "Let's get you back to the woods. Carol's prolly been in there the whole time this lady's been turnin' the pages knowin' she cain't even give us an answer."

"I ain't had my coffee yet," she said.

We tried to leave in a huff, but there was a Boston Baked Beans machine so we stopped to each get a dimeful.

I sat in the little blue car as my little brother drove me through the Bighorn Mountains.

"I hope I find her," I said.

When we got to Carol's drop spot, I only had him drive a mile past it.

"What if I don't find her?" I said like a loser, and caught sight of myself in the side-view mirror as I was saying it.

Are you The Haircutter, or is The Haircutter you? I heard from the shadowy halls of my being.

"I am The Haircutter," I answered.

"Huh?" Darron said.

"Is that all you are?" the halls asked back.

"I don't get the question," I said.

"Oh I was just like *huh?* cause you said something," Darron said.

"Nevermind," the halls stubbed out their cigs and walked away.

"No don't go!" I said.

"I have to, don't I?" Darron said.

Then it was like: hush, howler—hunt.

The little blue car receded into the hazy distance. I hoisted my backpack up on my back. I roared, "CAROOOOOL!!" No birds flew out from the trees and my words didn't echo. They sounded like they were roared at a brick wall right in front of me. I got out my bear mace to hold in my hand and took off running.

Day 1

The sunny Wyo wind took the calls in every direction within a single "Carol," pointing my hair whichever way to go with. The shimmering floor of the woods made me dizzy. I had to step over streams, then up on chunks of rock, then pause to figure out where to step next so I wouldn't walk into either a spider web or a bunch of sticks hanging from a tree. It was all about figuring out where to step next. I hated it.

I did Carol calls until I sounded like an old man. I swatted at bugs and bushery. Indian Paintbrush splattered a bloody God sneeze. God shat pellets of all shapes and sizes through the bowel systems of animals of all shapes and sizes, then absorbed it all into the earth and grew trees out of it, as if to comment on some artistic idea he'd had in mind since fourth grade—*Yeah, we get it—hope you're enjoying your stage, rich boy.* He pissed waterways and whistled the other way while we had no other choice but to drink from them. It was all one big show that I wouldn't have bought a ticket to if Ronald McDonald himself had coaxed me. ("Then why doesn't he shut up and let *us* go camping and enjoy it?") Just after God shits through my bowel system and grows a tree from it for you to camp under.

I unrolled my sleeping bag, liking the factory-fresh smells. I got out a sack of burgers and ate two standing outside. Lightning bugs blinked at different depths to match the stars—white and gold. A mosquito bit my face, so I washed the burgers down with a few swigs of Coke, then took the sack to a nearby tree and reluctantly left it there like the survival book said. I set my bear mace by the zip opening of my tent next to my Coke and settled in, not bothering to change clothes. A let's-get-this-over-with kind of thing. I laid listening to nocturnal animals activate their bodies and creep around the woods, racketing between gusts of ancient wind—all that. I've just never been one for nature, or for anything else for that matter. The wind rocked the trees, making them creek like witches trying to get me to wiz myself. ("Ach— just don't break and fall on me.") It was hot, so I removed my clothes and got back into the sleeping bag naked. I waited like a piece of snail meat to fall asleep.

Day 2

I looked around for bears and didn't see any, so I dismantled my tent and got it into my backpack along with my sack of burgers which had gone untouched-by-bears throughout the night. I got my toilet paper roll and dug a hole in the earth. I squatted for a dump, the morning air shooing my balls up into my stomach fat. I refilled the hole when I was done—nighty-night Poo and Paper. I got out the map and logbook I'd been writing my tracks in like the survival book said. I used my compass to find Northwest, and made some notes using the pencil I'd been keeping behind my ear and liked having there very much. I thought about cooking rice but it was ninety degrees out—*let's just get this over with.* I ate some jerky and started on Carol calls, finding a stick that I could use as a walking stick while I called like some commercial.

The Haircutter used his size XL lungs to massage the Bighorn Mountains with Carol calls on the fifth day of *Hush, Howler—Hunt.* He didn't once think about trying to find her using only his heart. He thought little of the wolf he had dropped off those months ago in the same woods, but when he did think of it, he shouted out for it too in a howl. "I wouldn't mind seeing that thing again," he said aloud. He thought of his bear mace as a gun. He felt protected and impatient. Though, he sometimes stopped to cry, abjectly feeling like he'd never see Carol again. Once, by a stream, while his long backpack laid on the bank like a desultory turd, he closed his eyes and reached out to touch her. His fingers explored her face, then felt the length of her neck and pulled her close to him. Their hearts fused together and the stream babbled in applause. A coyote yipped nearby and they didn't even flinch.

The ever-present smell of sagebrush bragged about how stylish it was. I saw a sly fox and some sly deer. ("Hi, yeah, I get it. I see you.") The sun shown through the trees, casting skeletal shadows. My shorts bunched between my thighs, casting my thoughts towards Gold Bond. Wild flowers made a liquid scent of the heat—I drew it in through my nostrils and coughed. ("Ach—get out of my nose.") I stopped before a spider web and watched the wind bend it melodramatically. I got out a burger to eat while I watched the spider hold on. I said, "Go Sally, go," in my head, and said, "Shut up!" out loud.

Of all the sounds in the woods, the sound that wouldn't shut up most was the sound of my thoughts.

"You're disgusting."

"But only when someone's looking."

"How come you're so homely looking?"

"Ezekiel Bradscrafty wrote *To Eat His Own: The Man Who Ate His Fingers* in 1978."

"What dipping sauces did he use?"

I roared, "I'm thinking so hard!"

"Just call me Mindstein."

It was the most annoying day of my life being out in that peace and quiet.

"I'm looking forward to the Zen." Yeah, so's my grandma right before she *dies.*

At dusk, the sky looked tie-dyed and plant life held their colors till they turned to judgmental figures in the night. Mosquitoes fuzzed the air around the poor Haircutter who sat on a stump letting his mistrust in Carol take root.

I looked at the black water in front of me and thought about drinking it, drowning. I looked up at the black velvet sky and wished on a pearl of white light for Carol.

To see what the instruction booklet was talking about, I removed the "star flap" from my tent after I hitched it. I felt funny as I was reaching up to unhook it, and I realized it was because I'd lost some weight. I stuck my finger between my belt and stomach and it fit.

I got back in the tent and told my backpack, "I lost some weight." It continued on with just being a brown backpack— being stiff and not being obliged to respond. I flipped onto my back, not being obliged to grunt while doing it.

The sky was stuffed with stars. They blinked, as if to watch me. They winked, as if to tell me I was right—I *had* lost weight. They were the lights that lit the length of New York avenues, that flitted up and down dancing jewel-handed women, that were flashbulbs going off at me, that were droplets of spit shot from the millionaire mouth of one Leslie Christmas. I saw Carol's sternum pearl as the North Star and wished I'd had the sense to swallow it. I started to cry. Here's H.C. in a tent that would no doubt whip against his dense silhouette if the stakes uprooted. Here's the tree creaking above him, living its life, not giving a dead leaf about his heartache. Here's him crying. Here's him searching—Ooh!—excited as a kid remembering where candy is hidden—here's the spot on the sleeping bag where Carol blew her nose, and he his! He holds it at a distance, "Well look at you!" Smiling so hard he coughs. Brings the crusted corner in for a hug tight to his neck crook. Then says to himself, "That's damned weird and you know it." Honks a clot into the spot and rubs it in. "Quit bein' a pussy," he says a tone deeper to equal his father's voice. He settles in and shuts his eyes and rapid thoughts bat through the skies of his mind like rabid bats on drugs with their tiny pricks out.

Day 3

On that summer's day three, I rolled my sleeping bag scroll-like to shove it up the yellow-suited cowboy's metal spinning ass. The mental vision of Carol's face flashed like a guiding light, like a beating heart. I found a stream and shat in it pleasantly, peasantly, instead of a hole. "Talk about a food log," I thought as I watched it float away and get caught in an eddy. I used the water pills to get a drink of water and gagged the whole time I was drinking. And when I was done, I thought, "While you were gagging, did you hear a distant *John?*" Moths flitted lowly and sporadically rose to my height.

"Ach—get out of my face," I said.

And when I'd said that, wasn't there a distant *John?*

Branches bobbed in a breeze.

"*John!*"

"Here we go!" I screamed.

I hoisted my backpack and roared, "CAROL!"

I ran Northwest in the mudded hiking boots we'd paid $89.95 for my pair for and $64.95 for her pair for.

"Carol!" I skidded to a stop on the edge of a burnt forest. Worms wiggled below me in suspense.

"JOHN!"

I saw her blond body hopping mirage-like through the blackened trees like the Black Chicken Salad from Applebee's.

"Carol!"

" . . . JOHN!"

Yes, please.

I ran.

"JOHN!"

I ran.

"CAROL!"

Hungary.

She was less than a skyscraper's length away from me. I was on the ground floor, ascending, and she was on the twentieth, coming down.

"John!"

"Girly!"

Boots kicking up ash, making it hard to see. I was on the tenth floor and she was on the thirteenth.

"We did it!" were the last words.

The sexual swoop in the stomach that accompanies a drop from an amusement park's seagull-dotted skies accompanied as The Haircutter's body dropped to China and a gong faintly rang.

They fell into a sinkhole fourteen feet deep. Lumps of ash landed on them in splashes like ink. The mouth of the hole was muffled by a burnt, uprooted tree and a boulder balanced on its branches precariously. A ribbon of sunlight dangled down to H.C. like, "Here kitty-cat." He opened his eyes and they were upside down in their sockets. He lifted a hairy hand to play Bat The Ribbon as his eyes untwirled in spirals. The Goblin of Pain perched invisibly on Carol's protruding sternum and drew long groans out of her lungs—they made a *hi* sound.

Carol and I lay potentially paralyzed in the poses we landed in. A thought came at me on a pogo stick from a chink of light in my unconsciousness—it was this: this is *something*. I didn't know *what* exactly, but I knew I'd read it in a book somewhere. Bravery or Survival Story were words that came to mind, but they seemed too good for me. I opened my eyes to see if there were tweedle birds around my head but there were none. Just a black diamond mist in a stripe of sun. There was a half-disintegrated tree facing down on me to watch how I was going to get us out, and a big boulder was balanced on its branches.

"Carol?" Soot came out of my mouth like a mummy.

Carol's goth-noir hair was covering her face—I reached over but couldn't reach her.

I realized that I had somehow gotten the map and logbook out of my backpack to find where we were. I had gotten out my cell and was dialing Darron.

"Listen here, you hold your breath so you can listen good. We need to make sure you get these instructions in case we get disconnected," I said. "We're somewhere stuck in a sinkhole." I said, "It's about five hundred feet north of the yellow blaze trail heading west off the parking lot near Kara's Lake,'bout four miles into the trail, got it? It's a patch of burnt forest, okay?" I said, "Get your car and get some friends and come up and look for us. We've got an uprooted tree stickin' into the hole and there's a boulder on it. Everything's burnt—I'm breathin' in soot." I said,

"I'm gonna shoot a flare in exactly one hour, at one o'clock, so get out here and be lookin'. Don't worry about the pic—just find us."

"What?" Darron said.

And then the line went dead.

Just to see what it felt like, I rolled over and treated the ground like a pillow, and I fell asleep.

Half an hour later, Carol was sitting up slumped against the raw wall of the hole.

"Wake up!" she said.

I woke up and stood on my backpack and tried to reach the charred branches of the tree.

"When's he coming?" Carol said.

"I don't know if he is," I said.

"We're gonna be on the news," said Carol.

I jumped off the pack and pulled myself up by a branch, but it turned to soot in my hand—I landed *Oof* on my back—you know. My head was cricked to the side and I saw a dead bird in the darker part of the hole with flies swarming on it. I hoped Carol didn't see. She was busy with her moaning.

"Carol? Do you have a concussion?"

"Prolly," she managed to say.

"Do you wanna use my first aid kit?" I said.

After a long while I heard: "I don't think nothin's cut."

She had fallen asleep.

I said, "Okay," all gentle, and turned the page on the flare gun instruction booklet.

"What time is it?" she asked.

"Shh, it's no time. It's okay, Carol."

"No what time is it, Dummy? What time is Darron supposed to come?" she said.

I said, "I don't think he's coming."

"Well that doesn't mean he's not coming! What time is it?" she lifted her head and it slapped back to the ground, covering her head with a fresh cloud of soot.

I looked at my watch and it was three minutes till I had told Darron I'd shoot the flare off.

"It's three minutes till one," I said.

"Shoot it! Shoot the gun off!" she screamed.

"I can't jump high enough!" I said. I probably even still had traces of makeup on my face.

"You gotta try shooting it off!" she said again.

"What if he's looking down when I shoot it?"

"Well it makes a firework doesn't it?" she said.

I tried to find a picture of a firework in the instruction booklet.

"So what's your other plan then?! You just gonna eat me when you start getting hungry?" She started coughing and fell quiet. "What's gotten into you?" she said.

I realized in a buck of panic that she was right. *What had gotten into me?!* Darron seeing our flare go off was our only shot at survival! I remembered a section on Emergency Situations in the final pages of the survival book. I got it out of my backpack and read:

Adrenaline is the most conducive conductor for emergency energy when it's most needed. Suggested, is to find a source of anger from deep within, or to ask a peer to anger you if you know them well enough. This might invoke a measure of adrenaline that could save your life.

And then it talked about drinking piss and eating plants.

I put one boot up on my backpack and then the other. I braced myself with one hand out on the "wall." I had the flare gun in my other hand.

I was like, "Hey, Carol."

Carol was a crumpled body like some hag in a horror movie. She sat up and said, "I can't move."

I said, "I know. But hey, look at me."

Two white eyes showed.

"We're hurt real bad, Carol. And we're stuck in this hole unless I jump off this backpack high enough to get this gun past these tree branches so I can shoot it off, okay?"

"That's what I've been sayin'!" she said.

"So I have a question for you. I need you to tell me what you were just doin' in New York."

Her face flickered on like a fortune-teller machine. Her jaw dropped—her cheeks hollowed. A fly buzzed into her mouth and ate from one of her molars and she didn't even notice.

"Me and Darron followed you. I cross-dressed for it. What'd you do over there?" I said, "And lay it on me hard cause I need some adrenaline to get us out of this hole, Girly."

The fly flew out of her mouth well-fed off McDonald's, and she started heaving breaths like her heart was growing with each beat. She started whimpering, "Whuuuut?! Whut?!"

I said, "Carol, we got half a minute for me to shoot this flare gun off so's Darron can see it." I said, "Come on and piss me off."

She exhaled long and choppy, "I didn't go to—"

I tried once without adrenaline—I jumped off the pack and caught a branch I'd picked out and lifted my body so I could stick the gun through a gap, but I couldn't lift myself high enough. Plus, the branch broke, and I landed, "Ah! My back!"

I stood up and saw on my watch that it was time.

"Come on Carol! Come on! You can do it, come on, time's up! We need to get out of this hole—"

And she cut me off, "HE BROKE MY HEART!"

I froze.

She gulped, "He knows I'm not lovable!"

She wailed, "He's so smart!"

I dropped the gun.

I said, "Who broke your heart."

She said, "SCOTT!"

I said, "What the hell are you sayin' to me."

She crawled to the center of the sinkhole, clutched her heart, fell to her back in a fluff of ash, and screamed toward the tree, "I went back to cook for eem! I told eem I'd be there for eem when he got outta the starve box and I'd cook eem a feast! He called me Co-Co, and it was called Co-Co's Kitchen! I made each table be from another country! Chinese on one! Italian on one! Ethiopian! Southern! I cooked my ass off and I don't even know how to cook! And he never came! And when I called eem he said his art project worked! He said he didn't love me anymore cause all the heartache got out!"

I jumped my fatass off the pack and simply grabbed a branch a foot higher than I'd expected, and stuck the gun through a gap and shot it the fuck off. It shot me back down into the hole.

Commotion came off the tree. The boulder fell from its net of branches.

I looked to Carol in time to see it drop onto her head so hard her body came up off the ground and popped.

CHAPTER SIX

THE

HEADSTONE

I lived in my old room again and my brother lived below me in his, tuning his radio to all the ballad songs and looking up at the ceiling. He encouraged me to grieve. He'd walk around on his boot heels like a little kid, feeling shysies about how proud he was to be helping. In the mornings, I'd awaken my prick from its mourning slumber, and it'd lift its shrunken head to spew Carol's memory out into the dusty-pink bathroom sink. I labored at it like a panicked bird with a broken wing, until Clarity tapped that clean, naturally-filed fingernail and said, "She cheated on you. She didn't love you." The inertia of those words shook loose the romantic content of my mind, it seemed. I loved her less and less. Carol Mary Whogivesashit. Aloneness: at least I trusted it. I went to the cemetery every day to sit on Carol's headstone to crush her harder. Sun rose red on the distant mountains she had died in; I used to crush Carol in our red-curtained Chambers when I orgasmed on top of her. At five o'clock, my mother picked me up to bring me home where a neighborhood kid would coast by in a puffy coat on his bike taunting, "Where'd you go?" My childhood freezer was full of the same old foods—the little claws on chicken wings were stacked frozen in the dark with only barking dogs as their late-night company. Patty and Father John cracked peanuts with their life-stained fingers in front of another new TV. Pictures of my art pieces framed it in frames. Darron had recently gotten a tail approved at a faculty meeting. Our house continued to not give a shit about the people inside of it, as our hearts and brains continued to rot as we minusculey aged.

—

Carol's long backpack was blood-crusted and still stuffed with her bloody camping equipment. I kept it under my bed, and every night I dreamt it was her dead body wrapped in a sheet. I dreamt that there was a devil in the closet reading and pretending not to be interested in the delectable dead body under my bed. I saw his legs sticking out of the closet wearing pants that looked like he'd gotten them from a church donation box. I lay listening to him softly turn the pages of his book. He cared as much about messing with me as he cared about Carol's body. I'll never know what he was reading.

One morning, I woke up to see maple leaves falling through the bland view of brain-dead sky out my bedroom window. Darron's downstairs radio was saying that Fall's officially begun. As if the time were right, I got the bloody backpack out from under my bed and took it to the cemetery.

Carol's grave was on a hill under an apple tree. The wind made the leaves shimmy, which sounded like the sound toilet paper made on her pubic hairs when she scruffed them dry in the hollow bowl of a john.

Under the apple tree, I scalped the grass, creating a hole in which I put a pair of her panties, then I covered it with my hands and patted the mound nice and foo-foo. I did this for each item in the pack. I talked to myself as I buried her things, doing a fake conversation between me and someone really nice who didn't know the whole story.

"A boulder fell on her head," I said.

"Oh you poor thing! Are you serious?!" I did a high voice for the woman.

"Yes. Her body popped and there were holes in her legs with steam coming out of them."

"*Steam?*"

"I know—nature, right? Her blood splashed under my hiking boots when I stood up and went to her. How could I have known that Carol's blood would be splashing one day? It's lucky I haven't lost my mind."

"Well you must be a genius."

"Ach. That's what they all say."

I buried Carol's clothes, toiletries, and camping things until I buried the backpack skin itself. A lot of people had to be buried standing up in their coffins with pools of skin around their feet because the cemetery was so hilly. Apples scattered drunk on the ground around me in Fall fermentation. They stunk and lured a groundhog over to eat. He looked like me, so I ignored him, not letting nature have its way with my psyche.

At the funeral, Carol's mom Trish had stood staring at me like Old Auntie. I was wearing a black veil on my forehead, cooperating with how serious I was supposed to be.

Spiders flitted like froth on a headstone close to Carol's in a fast-forward funeral.

"We are gathered here this morning to put to rest Carol Mary Mathers," some pastor said.

Jesus Christ, I thought.

I thought, *Let's just get this over with.*

A female gravedigger spun a crank that lowered Carol into the ground instead of lowering her from the ceiling of Carnegie Hall. The gravedigger had a bucktoothed overbite and was seven feet tall.

At sandwiches time after the funeral, it was only my family and Christmas and Charlie Quick in my shitty childhood home. Father John was on the couch sitting up straighter than I'd ever seen him sit before. He held a bottle of beer on his knee like it was his country's flag.

"His work is very well-received," Christmas said, passing around glossy pics of my pieces.

"I could do that," Father John said to almost every picture in the stack.

Darron was leaning against the wall near his senior high school portrait, and he looked exactly the same as it, and was wearing the same shirt.

I said, "You shoulda seen it."

I got down on the brown carpet and asked my mother to hold my legs up in the air.

"Imagine if my mom weren't holding my legs," I said. "This is what she looked like after the rock dropped on her head. But with her arms up too, like this—everything shot up and stayed. And a honk shot out of her cooter."

My mother let go of my legs in disgust, and when they hit the floor a honk shot out of my mouth like Carol's banshee cooter. I could see through the glass coffee table Father John looking down on me like he'd looked down on us in the hole—he was revolted.

Christmas waved from the passenger's seat of a red rental car when Quick drove him away toward the airport. *Who was this well-mannered man?*, I thought. Standing and sitting quietly abiding in his role as Funeral Guest? He'd even brought a Western-themed hanky to wipe his head with instead of a Christmas one. The only sign left of the real him were some microscopic snowflakes on Charlie Quick's shoulders.

"Or were they dandruff?" Darron asked, lifting his chin like a teacher encouraging me to consider the right answer.

On my apple tree hill, I saw the gravedigger come out the mouth of her machine shed on her CAT backhoe, so I dug up Carol's binoculars to watch her dig a grave. From that day on, I unburied the binoculars whenever I wanted to watch her work, because I deserved to be entertained.

She had headphones and a Walkman, and she never looked at me. She mowed a circle around me on her riding mower. Her overbite was so extreme she only closed her mouth against grass clippings. I saw her drool when she walked past me with a weed whacker once and it blew in the wind like a spider's web before disconnecting from her mouth and slapping to the grass. She touched her teeth and blushed, and then whacked the grass with the weed whacker where the drool had landed as if she knew a pro tip about spit, grass, and weed whackers going together like bacon, lettuce, and tomato.

One day, a series of waves of wind blew through the cemetery. They rolled ribbons and flowers and teddy bears across the lawn and made tornados out of leaves. I looked at my groundhog and he was holding onto the grass with his translucent fists like it was the mane of a horse he was riding. My grass scalps started blowing off, revealing Carol's things, so I rushed around reburying. Then I found the gravedigger in the binoculars and grabbed an apple to eat.

A wave of wind lifted a bouquet of flowers off a grave and hit her in the head with them. She screamed and spun around to fight. She bent out of my circular sight and cranked back up holding the flower bouquet—colorful petals blew off it toward me. She stiffly walked to her little stone office hut in the middle of the cemetery and I watched her through a window. I saw her put the flowers into a bronze vase on the wall, then she stood staring at the floor with her eyes bugged. Then she did a routine of reenacting how she'd spun when the flowers hit her head—she did four reenactments until she nailed it and sighed in self-disgust. I lowered the binoculars knowing that she knew I'd seen her get hit in the head with a stupid bouquet of flowers, so I thought I should go talk to her in case she was going to try to kick me out now like ripping the bird pages out of her encyclopedias if she were a hermit embarrassed about being caught looking out the window by a bird who accidentally flew into it.

I chucked my apple at the groundhog and he took the blow. I walked the hills of my cemetery. The gravedigger came out of the stone hut to trim rose bushes that grew against it. The wind died into a breeze and the sun shined violently.

I approached her with a finger pointed at her and asked, "Why's there a female gravedigger?"

She spun around and her face went rose-red.

She said, "What's wrong with that?"

Her voice was deep and clean like a cello. She looked the same age as me.

I said, "I'm surprised your arms aren't more muscular if you're doing all that work. Wouldn't it go faster with a man?"

She did an athletic flinch and a tissue ball shot out one of her sweatshirt sleeves and landed in her hand. She used it to pat her dry forehead.

"I use a CAT for excavation," she said.

Her eyes were enormous and had a lot of white space below the blue irises, making her look dumb. Her lips were enormous and seemed useless. The top lip flipped up on her buckteeth and almost hid the tip of her nose.

She said, "I think the old man who hired me thought I was a man. He can't see or hear well."

I said, "Oh? Well, what's your name?"

"Wendy," she said, but with her overbite it sounded like she said, "Randy."

I said, "It sounded like you just said Randy. And you're seven feet tall. He does think you're a man."

She said, "I know. He calls me Randy, but I pretend he's saying Wendy."

A bee swarmed around her sheers and she caught it between her pointer and thumb and squeezed it till it popped. She wiped it on her turquoise sweat suit. She had the Walkman clipped to the waistband of her sweatpants and it caught my eye. I saw through the little plastic window that she doesn't have a tape in there.

Oh my god!, I thought. My bowels started rumbling.

"Are you okay?" she asked.

I said, "I'm mourning," and walked back to my apple tree hill.

The groundhog was in the depths of a bush, but he puckered his eyes when he saw me, like a karate teacher.

"Hi," I said to it for the first time, so grateful for its company.

"Why's she not have a tape in there?" I asked.

His eyes puckered harder, telling me *you know why.* I remembered a show on ghosts I'd seen in a TV megastore on 34th Street. Twenty different-sized screens told me about how ghosts can't hear music. So when you think you're hanging out at home listening to Toby Keith, they think you're just snapping and doing mouth exercises. I'd never been one to fool around with people not-of-this-world, but I wasn't going to let "the gravedigger" run me out of my graveyard with whatever trick she was trying to pull with that Walkman.

A final wave of wind blew through slow and retarded, like a caboose full of ghosts having a party. It went, *WooooOOOOoooo!*

Every day, she would leave the cemetery when she felt like she was done, and she'd walk the broken sidewalk chunks to the bus stop on the highway that I could see from my hill. So, that day, I followed her.

I buried the binocs in their spot when I saw her lock up the stone hut. I looked back at my groundhog and said, "Wish me luck, sensei."

He screamed, "HEI!" and it pushed him further into the bush. I never saw him again after that.

I hustled over the hills, my butt seeming like a rump for the first time ever because I'd never had to hustle before.

The street that led to the highway was under an oak tree canopy. The gravedigger's stride was so long, she could've been floating off the ground. She passed a house where there was a little kid jumping on a couch in his front yard and he said hi to her because everyone knows that kids see dead people.

When I passed the house, I put my finger to my lips to shush the kid, and he yelled, "Hey lady watch out!"

Wendy spun around and saw me.

"Oh, hello," she said.

"Are you walking to the bus stop?" I said.

"Yes?" she said, pausing.

"How's it feel?" I said.

She said, "What?"

Her buckteeth looked like tombstones as if it weren't obvious.

I said, "You can cut the crap. You a ghost?"

"A ghost? No, I'm not," she said. "There's no such thing as ghosts."

Her hair was brown and thin against her skull, like she just got out of the hospital. Her ears stuck out of her hair like making a part in the curtains to wave with embarrassingly large hands.

"Is everything okay?" we heard.

We looked and saw the little boy standing on the sidewalk with his chest puffed out, faking the extreme concern he assumed someone older than him would show. He was standing on his boot heels like Darron.

"Yes, I think so," Wendy said.

"Okay," he reported. "Just checking," he said and ran at the couch and started bouncing again.

"I seen that you don't have a tape in your Walkman and I got spooked," I said to Wendy.

She exhaled in relief and kept walking.

"I found that Walkman in the office, but there aren't any tapes. I still have to buy one."

"So why do you wear it?" I said.

"Because you sit over there quiet and never say anything. I wanted to give you privacy."

"Psh!" I said. "I don't care about you."

A couple cars clapped past on the highway. She put her purse down on the bus stop bench and leaned into the road to see if the bus was coming.

"I've been caretaker here for ten years. You're not the first person I've used my Walkman on," she said, and crossed her arms to make a shelf for her turquoise breasts. The sky behind her set like it had makeup on.

"Why don't you quit?" I said.

"Why would I quit? Tending land is my passion. Besides, none of the bars would hire me."

I said, "Why wouldn't they hire you? You're not *that* tall."

She looked down and said, "Never mind," embarrassed of some secret I didn't care about.

"Have you always lived in Ten Sleep?" I said. "I used to work at Brother and Son's and I've never seen you."

She uncrossed her arms and her breasts relaxed into their skin sacks—she had a nipple poking out on one of them as if to say *I see you lookin'.*

"I've lived here for fifteen years, but I wash my truck myself," she said.

"Where's your truck?" I said.

"I like taking the bus better. It's just me, I don't need a big truck."

"Psh. What, do you not have a husband?" I said.

"No," she said.

I looked at her empty wedding finger and the crushed bee was beside it on her sweatpants looking equally kindergarten.

"Where'd you live before fifteen years?" I said.

"In the country at my farmhouse. It's where I grew up, but it fell apart so I can't live there now."

"So fix it up," I said.

She said, "That's my dream in life. It's on good land, but I don't want to live there alone."

"So get a boyfriend to fix it up," I said.

"I don't have any of that, it's just me," she said.

We stuck our necks out to look for the bus and saw my mother driving towards us, her Fair Fare van sliding across the highway in the wind.

"Do you mind giving me a ride home? It's right at the start of town," she said.

I said, "Sure, okay."

"My name's H.C.," I said, and we shook hands.

Patty crackled to a stop and rolled her window down, "Hello?"

"You got a client here. But don't charge her, it's a favor," I said as we got in.

Patty bleated like an accordion she was testing. "How tall are you?" she said.

"I'm six six," Wendy said.

"Good *lord*," Patty said.

We rode in silence.

Wendy clutched her pocketbook and sniffed without taking her buckteeth into her mouth. I saw her face turn red.

"What address you at?" Patty said.

"Oh sorry—it's the Rodeo Inn. 335 West."

"The Rodeo Inn?" I said.

"Yes."

"*You live at the Rodeo Inn?*" I asked.

"Yes," Wendy said.

I rode like a derailed train paused midair between a bridge and a frozen lake so someone could run to the bathroom and then they died on the toilet and someone important kept ringing the bell on the porch again and again and again . . .

The Rodeo Inn. Room 104. How in the HELL could I not have recognized her? That overbite? That unnecessary extra foot of height? How do you forget a seven-foot-tall woman?!

When we got to her "home" she said, "Thank you very much for the ride," and got out.

"Wait till she gets her door open," I said to my mom.

She went to Room 104.

She opened the door and I saw it had pink carpet with vacuum lines. She shut the door before I could make out anything else.

We drove through the streets that led to our house.

Patty said, "She had a cute unit."

....*Wendy!*...

Five minutes later, I said, "What—the pink carpet? MAN, women are suckers for pink! You couldn't even see inside it!"

She said, "What?"

I said, "You think her unit's cutesy?"

She said, "No, it's that store with matching sweat tops and bottoms that are all really cute. It's called Units. She had a good one. Was that jade-colored, or . . ."

I said, "Oh, that turquoise thing she's wearing? Psh. Had a bee on it."

Oh my god! Wendy! ....

A newspaper blew across an intersection, unfolding itself again and again to reveal the news!

Back at home, I turned down honey mustard chicken wings to pace my room. Darron came up with a drumstick in his hand, making his lips shiny while he stood in the doorframe and I sat on the bed.

"Mom said you wanted to pace?" he said.

"Why're you always so nosy?" I said. "I just gave a ride home to the gravedigger woman from the cemetery."

"Oh, you made a friend?" he said. "You sure do hang out there a lot."

I said, "Ach."

I didn't want to tell him the rest about Wendy, because then he'd get all these ideas in his head. He looked around my room as he snarfled on the chicken, trying to find something to comment to me about.

He said, "How are you doin'?"

I said, "Why're you always asking that?"

"Well, because now you don't have Carol," he said.

"Thanks for pointing that out!" I said.

He pulled on a tendon from the chicken's leg and realized he couldn't bite it off unless he gnashed his teeth together, so he did, and then swallowed the tendon whole in a slurp.

"Are you gonna go back to New York?" he asked.

"Psh!" I said.

He said, "Yeah. You don't give a rodent's derriere. You don't care about nothin'."

"You're the one wearin' lip sheen," I said, snuggling up protected to my headboard with a paper pad ready to make some lists.

He swiped at his lips with his forearm and kept eating.

"You don't wanna make any more art?" he said.

"I never wanted to make art!" I said. "I made a friend, didn't I?"

"Is she a potential romantic partner, do you think?" he said.

"Crimeny, Darron!"

"I'm just sayin'," he said, "I think Carol would want you to keep goin' in life."

"The gravedigger's ten feet tall!" I said.

He nodded and hung his chicken arm down in an exasperated swing, then swung it up cause he missed it and kept eating.

"Then you should just go back to Brother and Son's and start makin' your lists again like you're back at square one," he said. "And I'll stop sellin' Imitation Cowboys and go back in the closet. And we'll both turn ten again for our next birthdays and get matchin' cowboy boots, which you'll never wear cause you like your tennis shoes."

I spat on the ground and it landed between us as an ocean of divide.

"I'll do whatever The Haircutter pleases" was the closing remark to our conversation. The closing action was Darron inserting the chicken's bone into his mouth and then pulling it out sucked clean while he looked at me.

As soon as he left, I looked at my blank piece of paper and wrote *Wendy!* Then I pointed at it so hard my fingertip glowed.

The phone started ringing. The familiar sound of a deranged woman gargling electronics.

"Junior!" my mom called.

My hand twitched like a hunk of heart on the exclamation mark in *Wendy!*

I went downstairs and passed Father John in his TV spot with his dinner plate on his lap.

My mother was holding the phone to her milk jugs in the kitchen.

"It's someone named Finn," she said.

"Finn?" I said.

"H.C.! Oh my god, it's so nice to hear your voice!" he said as I was putting the phone to my ear.

"What're you callin' me for?!" I said.

"Sorry! I just thought I should tell you—something's been happening. I went to a party at PS1 last night, and I saw something that I thought I saw once before, but I wasn't sure, but this time I saw it clearly and I'm sure. It's Scott Harp?"

My puffy white sneakers creaked from my toes fanning out.

"What're you weird or somethin'?! I don't care about this stuff!" I said.

"I saw him cut someone's hair. He's totally copying you," he said.

I saw the reflection of fat H.C. in the kitchen window holding an avocado-green childhood phone to his ear.

"I don't care!" I said. "Aw FUCK—yes I do! Fuck you! How'd you get this number?"

"I work for Christmas! He hired me to look after your apartment. But wait—the worst part," he said. "I had a party when I first moved in—I'm so sorry—your scissors are missing from their plush pillow in your sock drawer."

[.................]

"Didn't you know I was staying in your apartment?" he said.

"No I didn't!" I said, and ripped the phone out of the wall and threw it through the kitchen window. The glass shattered three times louder than I'd ever bet it would. I heard my mom scream for the first time in my life. Father John's boots walked toward the kitchen. And down the block, the yellow-suited cowboy spun with his bird shit-eating grin.

"Oh whoa!" I said. "I'm sorry. Hey Mom! I'm sorry! I'll pay for it. I don't know what just got into me."

I remembered Harp and started shaking.

"Look at cher hands shaking," Father John said, pointing at them.

"I'll get out of your hair soon. I just need time to make a plan."

"Better tape that window up," he said.

"Tape's my middle name," I managed.

I got tape out of the utility cupboard and a cardboard box from the recycling. Father John hovered around me because I was doing a project. He took a new toothpick out of the toothpick holder, which was a pewter fish standing on its tail, and he widened his stance like the fish to watch me work. He came out back to see how I was doing it when I went out back to do it.

"John Tape Reilly Junior," he said.

Neither of us laughed—we were busy with our project. We discovered a way to make a nice seal happen by inserting a stick into a gap and taping it in, and we walked away from the project when it was done. Father John put the tape away in the utility cupboard, wanting to have played a part. He checked his cell phone for the tenth time that day to see if any hired jobs had come through.

"Sorry, Ma," I said.

"I just hope everything's alright, Junior! I know you got a big life over in New York!"

I walked up the stairs and Darron was in his doorway seeing if I'd tell him what the crash was about.

"I'm going back to New York," I said.

"YES!" he went.

That night, I lay in bed shaking so hard the bed skidded across the room. I wanted to walk to New York in a straight line, upturning every card table I saw on my way there. But I couldn't go yet, because—*Wendy!* When I remembered Wendy, I'd smile with a paralyzed face and the skidding would stop and I'd sink into the mattress. When I remembered Harp, the skidding would start as my eyeballs shook within their paralyzed frames. The bed touched the closet wall and came back to where it's supposed to go as I spiked and stopped between Harp and Wendy thoughts. I got up and checked the little window that showed out onto the street—there was that same newspaper unfolding more fucking news!!! Harp and Wendy, Wendy and Harp! I fell asleep in an armchair with half of me a woman and half of me a man, like a Halloween costume.

The next morning, I woke Patty up at five and had her drive me to McDonald's where we did the drive-thru for some hashbrowns and breakfast sandwiches. The Fair Fare headlights licked the highway toward the Rodeo Inn.

Room 104.

"Bye, Mom," I said.

Knock-knock. The cold tightened the skin on my face like a serial killer.

Wendy answered the door wearing a long floral nighty gown. The room was flashing blue from the end of a late-night Western on her TV.

I switched the McDonald's sack to my other hand and then back again as I said, "What are those, Oleanders? Lilies?" looking at her dress.

"What are you doing here?" she asked.

I said, "I'd like to continue our conversation."

She overbitically said, "Is that McDonald's breakfast?"

I realized I was holding my breath, so I exhaled and it blew her hair back.

I walked onto the pink vacuum lines and looked around the room. There was a kitchenette area in back with floor-to-ceiling windows that showed a foggy ditch where there were mule deer grazing. Everyone was getting shot on TV. There was a framed picture of galloping horses above the bed. Cigarette smoke seeped through the walls on both ends. I heard a man cough next door.

Heard his news reporter squawk when Wendy put her sound on mute.

"Let me change," she said, and went into the bathroom. And as she was shutting the door, I saw a white sheet taped up to cover the mirror.

"Huh?" I said under my breath.

I started putting our sandwiches and hash browns on the kitchenette table using the flickering light from the TV. There were globs of purple jelly, but I put the sandwiches on them, pretending I didn't care or didn't see. One of the windows wasn't closed and a crack of cold came through. I heard Wendy peeing, which sounded like hissing cats, so I gave her privacy by looking around the room. There was a small crystal wolf figurine beside her bed!, along with a Holy Bible open face-down so as not to lose her place. There was a bag of chewy peppermints and wrappers on the nightstand and floor. There was a laundry basket next to the front door full to the heap with muddy laundry. There was a *Better Homes and Gardens* magazine on her desk with a scissor that she apparently used to cut out pics of her favorite floral ideas— there was a notebook with some clippings glued in it. There were reading glasses and a half-drunk glass of milk like she was watching a Western and gluing flowers into her notebook at five in the morning before I came. There was a basket of colorful yarn on the banquet next to the TV. And when I checked the ceiling, I saw the glow-in-the-dark stars. I remembered wishing upon one of those stars. "Please let me know what to do," was the wish, which hadn't come true.

She came out of the bathroom wearing a Unit—this one had red and grey. I scurried to the kitchenette table and started shaking our orange juices.

"You like wolves?" I said.

"Oh, my crystal coyote? No that's a coyote. Up at my farm-house you hear a lot of them, so I ended up liking them a lot."

She turned on a floor lamp behind the mini fridge and we sat down at the table. The mule deer looked up at us and waited. Wendy waited for me to pick up my sandwich so she could pick hers up too. Instead, I took a deep breath and pointed a finger at her and said, "You know what? You look familiar, but I didn't recognize you at first. I think you hit on me in a bar once when I was twenty-five, do you remember that?"

She said, "I think so, yes."

"You had short blond hair back then?"

"Oh, that's right."

"Willie's Bar."

"Yes."

I said, "And then we . . ."

She said, "Yes."

"Right there on that bed," I pointed at the bed.

She wrapped her teeth in her lips and nodded.

I said, "Cool. I just wanted to point that out."

It was a hot and rainy night in May. I was picking up Father John from Willie's. He wanted to have one more drink, so I played pinball while I waited. A seven-foot-tall woman approached.

She said, "I have to tell you this straight, I'm attracted to you."

I said, "Whoa."

Wendy had short blond hair curled under her chin at twenty-five. She had a short purple skirt on. She hunched to talk to me.

"Is that okay with you? If I'm attracted to you?" she said.

I said, "Hell, *what?* Who *are* you?"

She said, "I saw you walk in and you made me do a double-take. I've been watching you play pinball—you know you kind of hump the machine?"

"I do?!"

"Yeah, and it's not sitting well with me—I'm about to get my period so my boobs are all full and heavy—it makes my nipples hard constantly and they rub on my shirt when I move, and it turns me on. It's the worst time of month to be teased by someone like you. I love big men. Do you want to come back to my motel room with me? To be honest I'm tired, but I'm not ready to fall asleep for at least another thirty minutes."

I was very taken aback and all that, but I was also nearly blind with lust at her perverted description of what her nipples were doing to her coital drive. My mouth watered.

She said, "I have a truck."

I said, "I'll meet you outside."

I thought it would be the normal thing to do, and I wanted to do it.

I went up to Father John and handed him the keys to the car that Darron and I shared at the time. "Drive yourself home, I'm gonna walk—it's a nice night out."

"*WALK?*" he squawked.

We went to her motel room—104—and like I said, I was blind with lust. Literally—I could barely see. I definitely don't remember her body. Don't remember her being so tall. I remember her hair covering her face as she drove to the motel shifting gears. I remember her thigh muscles lifting when she went to brake or clutch. I remember her turning on lamps in Room 104 to show how lived-in it was. I remember knocking my hand on the TV screen when I spread my shirt open. I remember lying on the bed and wishing upon one of those stars—it wasn't even glowing yet because it was only six o'clock—*Please let me know what to do.*

Four blocks from Brother and Son's, ten blocks from Blue Bear, and twelve blocks from my childhood home, I lost my virginity. So what!

She squinted in the crack of cold that smelled like deer dander. She looked away from it and her profile shimmered in the lamp's light. She had goose bumps on her arms as she lifted her triangular hashbrown and took a bite. I tried to remember the color of her triangular bush hairs, but couldn't remember because I'd been blind.

She said, "I've found God since then."

She put the hashbrown down and it went "Shht" on its paper sleeve.

I said, "That's always sounded boring."

The sound of the cute little hashbrown sleeve made me come-to and dig in.

"Maybe it's boring if you have other stuff to do, but I don't," she said. "I had to brainwash myself into trusting it and then it took over. Like chasing God until he starts chasing you back. And then you don't have to do anything but run to the scriptures. It feels good to read them. Probably feels like love, but I wouldn't know."

I saw Carol smiling at me, saying, "Ooooh, I love you," cooing like a dove. I saw her littlest, pinkest heart get smashed by a rock by a little boy playing Dissect-the-Dove under a pine tree on Christmas.

"Well you seem completely different than the girl from that night," I said. "Sorry if I didn't act like a gentleman, I remember being pretty much blind."

"That's more than fine," she said.

"I remember when I was walking home I was flinching at every car that passed me on the road."

"I'm sorry," she said. She closed her mouth and looked down.

"Hell no, Girly!" I said. "I'm the one who didn't leave my number and what. I was just scared of you, kind of."

She parted her lips and her teeth sprung out of her mouth to cut into her breakfast sandwich. "So what's life been like for you since then?" she said.

I said, "Well, they think I'm an artist."

She said, "Oh? What kind of artist?"

"Just pieces and paintings," I said. "When I was thirty I stabbed my dad's dog in order to save my girlfriend's leg from being chewed in half, so my father took me out to New York and left me there to become a man. But that's not really my thing, so in my free time I would cut little locks of people's hair on the street when they weren't looking."

She held up a tip of her hair and stopped chewing.

"Yeah, I cut off their hair."

She swallowed a hunk.

"I was all alone. So it felt like we were makin' that board together, like I'd always want to show a person their hair lock after I cut it off. Like, 'Look what we did! You didn't even notice!' Some sort of cat-and-mouse aspect where the cat actually *liked* the mouse? Hell, I'm not even gonna guess. But it was the happiest I've ever been."

Wendy shook her head and sincerely said, "I entirely understand."

"Okay? Well, it gets better. So I made a big board of these hair locks and called it my Hairboard. It's still my Hairboard, but these old people have it. I had around three thousand locks on there dated and noted, and it was just *my* thing, but then this gallery owner got wind of it and ended up telling me it was a piece of art."

I saw Christmas shooting a contract with his pistol on the dotted line. I saw myself signing it "The Haircutter" and then crossing it out when Christmas said, "We need your legal name there."

"He sold it for $XXX,XXX.XX dollars. Then he made me make other art pieces after that, and now all I want is to have my scissor back so I can go back to being happy."

"Did he take your scissors?" Wendy asked.

"No, they turned my apartment over to this fanboy Finn, and I'd completely forgotten about my scissor till he called me last night to say that my rival *stole* them and he's cutting hair with them."

"Ooh!" Wendy said, sympathetic.

I told her more—all of it. The wolf job. I told her about Carol as my gimmick and girlfriend, I told her about *Private Particulars,* which sounded really dumb. I told her about *Hush, Howler—Hunt.* About Carol's hog trough she cooked for Harp and then her violent death. Wendy gasped.

"So that's what you're mourning about," she said.

I said, "Ach. She probably thought it was artistic to die."

A house on TV exploded with the sound on mute. I saw the reflection of it burn in the galloping horses print above the bed that I lost my virginity in.

"I've never met an artist," Wendy said.

"Well, I'm a fake one," I said. "And no one knows. Christmas would just tell me it's time to make another piece and I'd make one."

"So why do you have to get *those* scissors back? Why not just buy another pair?" she said.

I farted hard and it made her jump.

"I don't want another pair."

"Okay, I can understand," she said.

"I'm not giving him my scissor like they're some *wolf*," I said. "Plus, I should do another art piece and get a bunch of money while I'm there. Then I won't have to work again for years and I could start a new life somewhere cutting hair."

"Well, it sounds to me like you're going back to New York," she said.

"Well, what kind of piece should I make though?"

She said, "Say! I am not helping you with that."

I said, "Huh?"

She said, "You haven't come up with an art piece on your own yet without help or without being told to."

I said, "That's not the way it works! You have to force me to make something! What do you think I'm here for, to see your flower scrapbook?"

She said, "Hey, what's wrong with you?" standing up for herself.

I felt guilty, so I shot another fart out of me so hard it made me have to catch my breath. She looked like I'd thrown a drink in her face. A bug fluttered inside the lampshade behind her like her mind trying to decide what to do. She simply opened the window crack wider to let more wind in. A man walked past smoking on the lawn and she said, "Hey Duane."

I thought, "Who's Duane?! Stay away from my gravedigger!"

I looked back to the bed that I'd lost my virginity in and wondered if there was a word for someone who took your virginity. I wanted to ask her if I was that word for her too, but I knew that I probably wasn't, and the thought of her humping on someone else made me jealous. I looked back to her and she was looking at the clock on her VCR, with her overbite sticking out of her face the length of a canned green bean.

"It's time to catch the bus to work," she said. "But why don't we drive my truck there? I haven't driven it since last April."

"Dang, Girly!" I said. "Why not?"

"Because, I told you—it's just me. I don't need a big truck. And there are other people on the bus, so," she said.

"Hmm," I grunted. "Lonely," I said, pointing at her.

Wendy's truck was parked by the dumpsters and had morning glories covering it. It was a tan pickup with a blue stripe. The morning glory blew like hair as we drove toward the cemetery. I bounced and held onto the roof while Wendy steered the self-possessed wheel, her skeleton bouncing beneath her Unit in her blood, her head floating in time with us. I noticed that her hands were tan and her fingers were elegant. She had long nails off the ends of her long fingers like ten ellipses pointing toward . . .

"Why are your nails so long?" I asked.

"Oh!" Wendy looked at them. "They grow like wildfire."

Carol's hands were chapped and narrow like a rabbit and her fingernails were chewed with stress. I smiled, glad that she was dead.

We drove a pleasant road of trees with butterflies and Wyo wildlife hopping out of our way. When we arrived at the cemetery, Wendy got out to unlock the gate and I saw how tall and pretty she was and it put me in a good mood knowing she was attracted to me.

I said, "Do you know anything about Lit?" when she got back in the truck.

"Is that a drug?" she asked.

I said, "For some people, yeah. I'm talking Literature. I used to think it was interesting, but now I'm not sure. I think it's just listing who wrote what and when they wrote it that attracts me."

Wendy drove her old truck ruts to the little stone office hut, not caring about my special talent.

"I *love Better Homes and Gardens*," she said as if I'd told her she didn't.

We parked and I smiled like, "Hey, this ain't bad."

Instead of going to Carol's grave I followed Wendy around on her daily routines. The first thing she did was use a key to open the little stone office shack. There was a desk and two chairs and a woodstove. She threw some logs in and started a fire.

"Where's the old man who hired you?" I asked.

"He lives up the road."

A cloud of smoke obstructed her body like back when I thought she was a ghost.

She sat down at the desk and opened a logbook, "This is where I schedule digs."

She pressed a blinking red light on the telephone and picked up a pencil.

Hello this is Stan from Bauman Funeral Home and Crematory calling to confirm a hole for a funeral on Wednesdee at 1:00 p.m., please call me back at your earliest.

"So now I call him back to confirm."

I watched Wendy talk to Stan and noticed how her overbite works attractively with talking. Her lips bob on her teeth, cleaning them, making them gleam. A pulse on her neck creaturely ticked while she penciled-in the dig, erased something, swept the eraser crumbs off the page, said, "Okay."

We walked the hills with garbage bags picking up trash that had blown in. Breeze lifted her hair off her neck as I walked behind her. "After I use the riding mower, my body vibrates for almost the whole day afterward," she said, and my loins awoke to take note of it. We warmed our hands periodically back in the stone hut to check new messages. A pimply sounding kid said his family has a plot there and does it have room for his mom. Wendy checked a registry and called him back to say yes. There wasn't a single task left undone, unless left undone intentionally. Yellow leaves covered half the cemetery and we raked them up. Wendy shared her lunch with me. We ate on a bench by a cedar tree. Dried apricots, sardines and buttered bread, half a store brand Twinkie for dessert.

"Is this store brand?" I said.

"They taste the same," she said.

They did, and people at the store saw her pick them out and pay for them and didn't know her like I did. Smoke was stretching out of the stone hut's chimney like twisted pantyhose taking off into a hard blue sky.

After lunch we went to the machine shed and she mounted her backhoe.

"How'd you learn how to drive that thing?" I shouted as I walked beside it over the storybook hills.

"I just played with it till I figured it out," she answered down.

I watched her dig the grave Stan ordered. The CAT tucked the earth under its chin to carry it from the hole to the pile of dirt. She used a ladder to get down into the grave to clean it tidy with a shovel. Then she removed the ladder and draped sod over the mound of dirt to make it look nice. Her face flushed as she took off her upper Unit to show a yellow T-shirt wet in the pits. I stood squinting in the wind that whipped my hair around idiotically.

"How deep can that thing dig?" I said, pointing at the CAT.

"There are all kinds of sizes. Some have longer arms to dig deeper. This one is set at six."

Wendy was sexually panting when she came to stand beside me, taking a tissue ball from her pocket and sopping her nose with it.

"Now we distribute the extra dirt around the property in any place that needs it," she said.

"No, save it!" I said. "We're gonna need all the dirt we can get."

"Why?" she asked.

"Just how dumb *is* that old man?" I said.

See a freight train split through Ten Sleep screaming. See the neon flashing sign for the Rodeo Inn. See how the Boston Baked Beans are all stuck together in a gumball machine beside the 24-hour tenant in the lobby. See the peephole on the weather-warped door to Room 104. Hear the words "Yes! Yes!" coming from the other side of it. Move to the mustard curtains and put an eye up to a moth hole to peep H.C. pacing in the blood-orange lamplight, talking out his plan. Wendy sits on her bed, hands in her lap, saying, "Yes! Yes!" H.C. bites at McDonald's sandwiches and tosses them at their wrappings on the bed—he's got four going at the same time. Gripping his hair and leaving it standing out on end, he says to Wendy, "And someone will paint a vagina on the twat of the mannequin. Will you do that?"

"I will not do that," Wendy says, boundaried in her support of him.

That night, I went to Father John's La-Z-Boy and found him kicked back watching football on a tiny portable TV set on his belly. Since his thing was to wait for calls about hired jobs, I walked past him and into the kitchen and dialed his cell phone number, which was on a chalkboard. He made a happy grunt when it started ringing.

"This is John Reilly," he answered.

"So's this. Can I hire you and your hired-work friends to build my next art project?" I said.

" . . . " he said, angry.

I poked my head around the corner, "Tell you the truth, I'd be shocked if you're able to pull it off."

"Psh! The hell is it?" he said, and then swallowed like a pussy accidentally.

I'd said the magic words.

I pulled out $X,XXX.XX dollars cash. "Here's what it pays," I said.

"Where the fuck'd you get that?!" he said.

"I didn't make art for free."

He put his footrest down. The TV toppled to the ground.

"You gonna let me sell a wolf this time? I still got that guy in Rainer."

We hung up our phones and did our first meeting.

And so it came to be: I knocked on the country door of one Heath Millcrawford one Ten Sleep afternoon with a clipboard in my hand.

Heath Millcrawford opened his door, making a sound like an old man grunting a shit out, which he very well could've been. I'd borrowed my dad's windbreaker for a professional feel. Heath looked like a turtle crawled out of its shell and into a white T-shirt and briefs.

"Hey Randy," he said to Wendy.

"Hi," she said. "This is John Reilly, the man I told you about."

Heath stepped onto his porch and held out a hand that looked like a bunch of carrots he'd found forgotten in the back of his fridge.

"What's the weather doin'?" he asked as I was squeezing his carrots.

"It's nice out," Wendy said as Heath stood in her shadow.

I said, "I'd like to use a corner of your property and one of your CATs to build an art piece that will be transported to New York City on a flatbed once it's done."

I showed him my clipboard and the drawings I had drawn up on what I planned to do.

There was a drawing of a steel ramp that Father John would haul in for the CAT to climb.

There was a picture of a sixteen-foot-by-sixteen-foot-by-sixteen-foot wooden box stained dark to resemble casket mahogany. The box was on a flatbed truck, with nearby chains ready to strap it down.

There was a picture of the CAT on the ramp puking dirt into the box.

There was a picture of the box brimful.

There was a picture of a team of men stomping the dirt to pack it in.

There was a picture of a fourteen-foot-by-ten-foot hole dug into the box of dirt, with the CAT behind it with some dirt on its mouth to suggest it dug it.

There was a picture of myself inserting a ladder down into the hole.

There was a picture of a team of men rolling a boulder up the ramp and then a picture of it in the bottom of the hole on the head of a mannequin. The mannequin's arms and legs were up in the air and it was wearing Carol's lace duster dress.

I said, "It's called *The Headstone.* I've been hired by an art guy in New York to create this, but trust me the money is right here—"

I turned the page on the clipboard and showed the check for $X,XXX.XX that I'd clipped to it as the final page.

"—And we'll be out of your hair in less than two weeks, hopefully. And no funny business," I said.

Heath stood panting on his age. Cotton drifted past. He looked up from the clipboard and said, "Randy, what's this?"

"He" said, "Yes sir, I'll make sure they stick to their agreements."

"Okay. Now get a haircut," Heath said.

"You have been telling me that for ten years, and I'm sick of it. I'm a woman," my brave gravedigger said.

Heath must've thought we were talking about women, because he said, "My wife is dead, otherwise I'd be porkin' her right now."

"Thank you," we said.

One week later, at our family dinner table, Father John and I sat covered in dirt. Patty and Darron were clean. Father John and I hogged on spaghetti and drank milk and left streaks of mud on our glasses. I'd watched Father John and his team of men crest a cemetery hill on the first day of *The Headstone* construction—I was on my apple tree hill looking through Carol's binoculars— and I'd inhaled a pansy little breath and held it. Father John used to go off on mysterious hired jobs and I'd pick him up at Willie's after a long day's work, and for all I knew he had just gone behind the bar and rolled around in the dirt. But here he was with six men I'd never seen before, all in their jeans and dungarees with tool belts on and flannel sleeves rolled up. Cigarette butts behind their ears, pine trees balanced on their erect dicks. Father John took my clipboard and hid it from his friends as soon as he saw my childish drawings. They didn't ask *why* they were building, they just asked *what*. They had their meetings around a cooler of beer; they had their names on their belt buckles. Father John used fresh sheets of paper to draw up plans. They somehow got the flatbed semi I'd demanded. They somehow got the mannequin, too. Every single permit I would need to drive cross-country with a sixteen-foot cube. I'd never been as impressed by anyone before, and it was my own father. I didn't know how to feel about that, so I just joined in, standing around as The Art*eest*, saying "that's what I had in mind" when they showed up with six sixteen-foot squares of wood and pointed at their craftsmanship with sharpened pencils.

"High-quality cuts . . ."

" . . . stained mahogany like you wanted," they said.

Wendy sat in the cab of the flatbed truck and taught me how to play with it until we figured out how to drive. The owner of the truck refused to teach me, saying he "didn't want anything to do with this"—he just wanted the money I gave him. Wendy and I drove around the block and drove around the block, making a joke twice about *Should we see if this fits through the McDonald's drive-thru?* After the driving lesson, we pulled back into the cemetery, where the men were ready to nail the box together on the flatbed.

Wendy said, "I've got to hurry up and decalcify the sprinklers," and walked away in the other direction of the men, hiding from them. "I want them to focus," she said. "I care about your piece," she said, reminding me of Carol. For the time it took to build *The Headstone,* she worked in the office hut or at the opposite end of the cemetery. She stood facing the fence holding her weed whacker. In the binoculars I could see her ears wiggling while she talked to herself.

Father John crossed paths with her one day when he needed to use the phone in the office. He walked up to me under my apple tree after.

"Why's she so familiar?" he said.

I said, "Cause she's lived here all her life."

"Then what's her name?!" he shouted.

"Wendy," I said.

"Don't recognize it. I never forget a name. There's no way she's lived here all her life."

"Pretty sure she has," I said when he was a hundred feet away.

I went back to painting the twat on the mannequin's vagina with the little paint kit I'd demanded and a porn picture for reference.

For dinner, we drove Wendy's truck to McDonald's or to the Taco Bell that Carol and I first made out in the parking lot of. Once, we picked up Darron and went to the sub shop for a three-some dinner. Darron was the happiest I've ever seen him.

He said, "You must feel so alive!"

I said, "Ach."

Wendy said, "I know I do!"

"It's that New York state of mind!" Darron said. "I could never live there, but it's got that energy! John's always had that."

"John! That's your real name?" Wendy said.

"Oh, you know him as H.C.?" Darron said while lightly smiling like it was a nerdy fan club meeting.

We ate on our subs and chips while our lower bodies shifted when they had to.

"So you don't have kids, or?" Darron asked Wendy.

"No, I don't," she said.

"You ever had much boyfriends, or?" he asked.

"No, never. I'm not opposed to it though, there just isn't a great pick in this area."

"Tell me about it," he said. "I think I've thought about teaching in Texas maybe this year or next year. Once school gets out I'll apply. I need to stir things up," he said, and I grunted, proud of him.

"And there are a hell of a lot more people giving their hats and jean jackets away to thrift stores down there," I said.

"You're right!" Darron said.

I looked at Wendy to tell her about Imitation Cowboys, but she was staring sad-eyed at a mother breastfeeding her infant lump at the table next to us. I squirmed in my seat and squeezed my sub harder between my hands. I gestured toward the mother, "The baby eats milk from the breast, and the adult eats ham from the sandwich," I said.

Wendy huffed a little laugh.

Darron wiped his mouth and tossed a ball of napkin on his tray, "It's a what-you-eat world," he said, sighing.

I bit in.

Patty had her hands in the sink with bubbles up to her elbows when I told her and Darron about the piece. (Patty loved the white plastic flower earrings that Darron had picked out from the Salvation Army for my cross-dressing, and when I walked in the kitchen she yanked them off her lobes and hid them in the dishwater. She got compliments from the mailman, her van folk, and even from Father John, but did her best to remove them when I happened by. To remind me again and again of the fact that I was wearing them optimistically outside my apartment as Carol cooked turducken for Scott Harp.) Darron was doing pull-ups on the pull-up bar he'd screwed to the kitchen/den doorframe.

"Isn't that grotesque or somethin'?" Patty said when I described the part of *The Headstone* where there's the boulder on Carol's head.

"What's grotesque is what Carol did to him," Darron said, and she nodded like *he's right.*

Father John came in from the TV room to get a toothpick, and he handed one to me—the equivalent of handing me a cigar.

"So the, ah—the loose ends? They all been thought of?" he said.

"That's what I hired you for," I said.

He nodded, accepting my answer.

"I just wonder if the hole is gonna hold up on the road or crumble in a little," he said. "Them dirt walls could collapse. We could put a sealant down, but that's not the look you're goin' for, I'd assume."

"Well, stick a couple shovels in the cab of the flatbed so Christmas and Charlie Quick can clean out any crumbles once I get to New York," I said.

He whistled with a smile.

"You sure got 'em wrapped around your finger," he said, and star lines shot out from his eyes—the same ones he had with Jenny.

And that's when I knew: I had succeeded in becoming a man to him.

And it didn't feel like anything.

I lifted the smoky phone receiver to call Christmas to tell him the plan. Darron came down off a rep to put a hand on my shoulder as the line was ringing, "I'm so proud of you! This is inspiring! I knew you'd grown."

I shook him off—"Quit bein' so close," I said.

Charlie Quick answered the line.

"Thank You," he said.

"You're welcome," I said. "This is The Haircutter."

"Is it?" he said in his accent, pleasantly surprised. "You alright?"

"Where's Christmas?" I said. "I got a new project."

Charlie Quick put the phone down and I heard him say, "Haircutter."

"HAIRCUTTER!" Christmas shouted and came on the line. "What is it?!" he said.

"You'll see it," I said. "But I don't think it'll fit in the gallery, so what do we do?"

"Is it a *large work?!*" he squealed like an XL sow fitting into an L dress.

"It's a sixteen-foot cube," I said.

"I'll rent a space!" he said.

"And I need two sets of stairs built that can go up each side of it sixteen feet high and then a scaffolding platform thing up there sixteen feet long for viewers to stand on so they can look down into the piece," I said.

"Yes, we'll take care of that. And I'll send out a crating team—what's the location?"

"Leave me alone!" I said. "I've got everything taken care of. I'm showin' up with it, okay? And I want the opening the night I get there. Okay, so just get it set up so we can sell this thing. We need another half week and then I'll drive the piece out in two days. So the seventeenth."

"Why don't we get a two-prop helicopter to fly it here?" he said, like I was a little toddler he'd just found playing with its wiener in a sandbox.

I said, "I'm sick of your funny business! I'm doin' this right and then I'm gettin' the hell out of that flim-flap crap! You dang ruined my life with all this bullshit! And I want my hairboard back—how much is it?"

Christmas hysterically laughed.

"Shut up!" I said.

"Oh, oh, oh," he said like the backwards of *Ho, ho, ho*. "My apologies!" he said. "*The Hairboard*, privately, would sell for roughly $X,XXX,XXX.XX."

"$X,XXX,XXX.XX!" I said. "How's that?! I thought it was $XXX,XXX.XX!"

"Yes, it *was*. I purchased it for as much to set a price for your future works. Now—the open market value would probably be much more, which is why *The Hairboard* isn't for sale yet. Any time your works reappear on the market the value will jump significantly. Do you want a lesson?"

"You! I thought the Weinsteins bought it!" I said.

"I traded a house with them to pretend they did."

Charlie Quick came on the line and said, "Don't tell anyone he told you that."

I said, "Ach! See this is what I mean! I don't get you fancy people! Keep *The Hairboard!* I'll make a new one! Just get my party ready!"

Christmas said, "This is what I live for! All I need is your artist's statement and a description of the piece."

I said, "My statement *is* the piece. It's called *The Headstone*. It's a coffin thingy."

"Tell him what's inside," Darron said.

"It's a cube. Open at the top. Stained mahogany. Something's inside," I said.

"Fantastic, Haircutter," Christmas said.

He gave me the address of the space he'd rent in case we didn't speak again. Darron wrote it down for me.

"Tell him the concept!" Darron said and I stomped on his foot, "That's enough!"

Christmas said, "How are you holding up?"

I said, "Shut up!" and hung up.

You've got your hillyass cemetery. You've got a fake mahogany box big enough to look like it's up to no good. It's as tall as the trees around it and as tall as the hill it's snug under. You've got a large steel ramp with a CAT backhoe on it; you've got the head of the CAT filling the box with dirt. The sun beat down on Father John's team of six hired men. Meadowlarks met in the sky above them to shoot the breeze about why this was the first real art piece I had ever done. Crows walked into the dank depths of bushery to smoke cigarettes talking about how they wish they could be inspired to do something so artistic. The hired-men's machinery whirred. I paced the cemetery, held to it by gravity. I saw myself pass through a puddle in which the heavens were reflected. The fibrous cosmos existed behind that shield of sky like the depths of the tar-sticky soul that say, "This isn't that good of an art piece and you know it."

Once the box was brimful and tightly packed with dirt, the CAT excavated a clean hole—fourteen-feet-by-ten. The sinkhole

Carol and I got stuck in. The men dangled in rest, and their belt buckle names burned to the sun's promiscuous touch as I inserted a ladder into the hole like Darron did when he rescued us. In order to lid the box for transport, I wanted the men to cut a hole in the lid around the ladder so it could stick out like a straw.

One of the men (Bob) said, "Why don't we just put the ladder on the flatbed and you can put it in once you get there?"

"Because I want to sleep in the box at truck stops on my way out to New York," I said.

Another man (Kurt) said, "So why don't you just put the ladder in yourself when you get to the rest stops?"

"How am I even gonna do that without a hole in the lid of the box, Kurt?" I said.

Father John had his arms crossed listening like a gorilla judging his band.

"Men!" I shouted. I pulled a ruler out of my back pocket and used it to talk with, "I want any of you to tell me the last time you tried to put a ladder into a box twenty feet off the ground at a fuckin' truck stop. Now listen up—I will need a sixteen-foot ladder to even get on top of this box. Then I will walk across the lid and pull back a tarp that covers the ladder hole. Then I will climb down the ladder into the hole and I'll sleep in there for my artistic shit. Okay?"

"Should the ladder hole be round or rectangular or square?" someone (Dale) asked.

"That's a great question," I said. "Let's go with square. A metric system square."

The more complicated it was, the better it felt for them.

I turned to Father John, "Also, someone get me a dead bird with flies swarming on it."

—

The final step was to put Carol's "body" in there and then drop a boulder on her head. At the family dinner table we all decided to do it as a ceremony, which I said was going to be called The Mannequin Ceremony. The mannequin lay on the floor by the front door, overhearing us. *So let it hear.* We would do it the day before I left for New York, and after the ceremony we'd lid the box and chain it to the truck, then we'd all go out to the Blue Bear to dance. The Mannequin Ceremony was our first family plans since Darron and I were children and we went to the zoo where I rode a tortoise like a fat kid on the best day of his childhood. I would've been uncomfortable with having plans again, but things were different ever since Carol and I fell in that hole, and I wasn't going to argue with Difference anymore. It was smarter than me. It was gonna do what it was gonna do. It knew.

"Now listen here I don't want y'all to yap at Wendy about Carol. She knows she's dead and that's all she needs to know. Don't mention one word of it," I said.

My family all bobbed their Adam's apples swallowing and giving each other glances.

"You don't wanna tell her the truth?" my mom said, and Darron stomped on her foot under the table.

Darron said, "We'll do whatever you want us to, big bro. No talkin' Carol, we got it."

That night, I brought the mannequin to bed with me and called it Girly. I didn't kiss it, I just laid in bed with it, seeing if it could make me love Carol. It fell off the bed in the middle of the night, waking me up. I looked over the edge of the bed and it was facedown smiling at the floor. I saw the rear end of its painted twat and I jacked one to Wendy.

The day of The Mannequin Ceremony, I had on my good forest green belt and my collared shirt with the ducks flying on it. Wendy honked outside my house in the afternoon, earlier than she was expected.

I went out to her like, "What's this all about?"

She was wearing blue jeans and a grey T-shirt. She leaned over to roll down the window, "I'm taking the day off."

"Okay?"

There was a plastic Hy-Vee bag on the truck bench. I spied some makeup and a brand new curling iron in it. Under the plastic bag was a purple dress spread out to not get wrinkled.

"I was wondering if you might want to run out to my farmhouse with me," she said.

I imagined there being a dead mule deer in the living room that would make Wendy scream and clutch onto me like Carol, so I said, "That sounds so fun."

She said, "I've always wanted to show it to someone. And since you're leaving in the morning—who knows if you're coming back."

I knew sure as hell that I was coming back so we could F and make L, but I didn't tell her, so I could come back knocking on the door to Room 104 like Jesus in a crack of thunder.

"Yeah, who knows," I said.

We took the freeway out to Rasmuss Pass and followed some off-the-beaten-paths to a shitty dirt road that pointed at the house like a witch's finger. The house had colorless shutters and sat mute like it had Alzheimer's.

Wendy said, "This was all crop," talking about the fifty-acre front yard we were driving up.

"How 'bout them woods?" I said.

To the left of the house began (or ended) a heavy wood.

"I never walked far into them," she said. "But I always wanted to."

Wendy killed the engine near the side door off the kitchen.

She said, "The chicken coop," and pointed at a decayed chicken coop in front of the truck.

We slammed the doors and field birds rose up off the yard like dust.

"We never used the front door, it was always this yard door," she said. "This house was built in 1886."

The kitchen had stone walls and a woodstove, and a couple of Amish-looking instruments to make god knows.

"My parents were so religious they went to church every day, so we lived off the land," she said.

Standing in the kitchen you could shoot the fireplace in the sitting room on the other side of the house.

"Back there is the sitting room," she said and walked toward it. "My mother would sit in her orange chair and my father would sit in his green one."

There were dead rodents in the fireplace and dead birds on the floor. Wendy didn't scream and clutch on to me—she didn't hold her hands up like a tour guide—she went around checking things like a criminal checking a safe-house while she talked.

"They watched this show called *Miracles Found* that had a number on the bottom of the screen for you to call if you had a miracle. I was always outside doing stuff, or up in my room listening to the radio, but sometimes it was so cold I'd sit by the fire to knit. 'Today, on *Miracles Found . . .*' This was all before they lost their minds, after that it was different."

My eyes sprung out of my head and into the asylum she'd brought me to.

"Lost their minds?" I said.

She pointed at the ceiling and there was a big hole in it.

"Then they left when I was twenty-four," she said.

She guided me upstairs and the steps creaked like they were breaking.

"Today, on *Miracles Found*," she said again, under her breath.

The hallway was short with a steep wooden staircase at the end.

"My mom had short hair like a ball around her head," she said. "She was short and fat but same lips as me. And my dad was tall like me. He had my teeth. This was my room."

There was a cold white room with dead birds in it. Three windows looked out on the front yard slope. There was a rocking chair facing them.

"I sit here when I visit," Wendy said about the rocking chair. "My mother watched my father and me tend land in this."

"Where are they?" I asked.

"My mother lives in Reno and my father died. She sent me a letter years ago saying he died like one of those oversized dogs with short life spans. She said the same thing will probably happen to me."

"Do you ever see her?" I said.

"No, I don't care about seeing her, and she doesn't either. They were weird folks," she said.

She brought me across the hall, "This was their room."

There was an iron bedframe with no mattress.

"The wind sleds down that back hill and freezes you out. I spent half my life under covers." She pointed to the bed. "For a period of time, my dad was so scared of standing up that he only crawled around like a seal. I remember the sound of him getting out of bed in the morning."

"What'd it sound like?!" I said.

"Like a bag of bones falling on the floor."

"Why the hell was he scared of standing up?!" I said. "Now what's all this?! Why'd they go crazy?!"

She took me down the hall to the steep wooden stairs that she said went up to a watch room. There was a big hole in the floor at the foot of them.

"Be careful," she said.

We looked through the hole and saw the sitting room downstairs.

"For home repairs we just couldn't do some. This spot here was rotted from the rain that came down these stairs from the watch room windows. One day, my mom fell through it and landed on my dad who was down there sitting in his chair watching *Miracles Found.* They were both knocked unconscious and I was out in the yard at the time tilling, so I don't know how long they were lying there—it could've been two hours or two minutes. When I came in, I woke them up and then they started laughing really hard." Wendy put a hand up, "I'd never seen them *laughing,* let alone *hard.* My mother was holding a cup of tea when she fell and it burned her face so she looked like half a gargoyle and never went to the hospital for it. They stopped going to the church or leaving the house altogether. My father took the underwire from my mom's bra and stuck it up his nose to scramble his brain, and my mom was cheering him on. And they started having sex a lot, which they never had done much of. My father hee-hawed like a donkey when they were doing it."

"Eew! Dang, Girly, this is yuck!" I said.

She stepped over the hole and ascended the steep little stairs that lead to the watch room.

"Come up," she said.

I thought, *Hell, why not.*

There were two chairs up there.

"I've always wanted to show this place to someone and I never have," she said, sitting down.

There were six little windows in a circle around the watch room that saw out over the treetops and over the land to the far-off mountains.

"Isn't this beautiful?" she said.

"This is my kind of watch room," I said. "Am I gonna fall through the floor if I sit in that chair?"

We sat there shivering. The sky was bloodless and the windows rattled in their rotted frames. We could hear coyotes yipping. Like a pack of sixty-year-old women getting tickled by Brad Pitt.

She sniffed, "They just went nuts, is what. My father smashed a lot of the windows saying nothing matters. But smiling while he did it, you know? I saw him in a corner licking the wall talking about *Charlie and The Chocolate Factory.* If they saw me crying they'd say they never wanted kids so it's not their fault. The deal was, it was always my father who had all the hobbies and interests and ideas, and my mother adopted each one of his and pretended they just happened to be her interests too because she didn't have any and desperately wanted some. I think he got brain damage from when she fell on him, and my mother just went along with it as her new thing. For a period of time, he said that he felt suicidal, and so, low and behold, she goes suicidal too. She always climbed up on the roof in the middle of the night and she'd get down on her stomach to tap on my bedroom window with a stick to wake me up just so I could get scared watching her threaten to jump. She spoke in a Lucifer voice I'd never heard her use. God, I love the sound of coyotes. I was too naïve to know to go get help or call *Miracles Found.* Anyway, I couldn't tend the land by myself and without supplies, so the crops dried up. I ate the chickens. My parents didn't eat unless I tricked them. I had to pretend I wanted to put on a play for them and part of the performance was audience participation where they ate a bunch of corn. They went along with it. Called it 'my performance.' They talked a lot about my performance if they hadn't eaten in a couple days."

I huffed and said, "Eccentrics."

"I'm lucky I stayed sane. My mom would trance-up all the time and say the roof just blew off before I walked in the room. She said she saw Hell where Heaven should be. My father nailed live animals to the ceiling to keep the lid on. I slept in the woodshed, it smelled so bad in the house. They would fight all the time over nothing, and smile while they did. As if it was glamorous to fight."

"Psh!" I said. "Idiots," I said, lifting my nose at the landscape before me.

"Well, yeah!" she said. "You get the gist. And then one day they left on foot and never came back. And I remember I petted a yard cat so hard its body touched the floor with each stroke. I was almost horny about eating it. I was so hungry I thought its purrs were loosening leaves from trees so I went out and ate leaves off the ground to spite my mother thinking they were dropping down from Hell. I finally got the clarity to walk myself into town. Went to the old church and they let me get fed and showered. Thawed out. I puked up all these leaves. Got my first waitressing job."

"Man alive," I said. "I hate eccentrics."

"Me too," she said.

"Just don't get 'em!" I said.

"Same here."

"My gallery owner is like that," I said.

"Is he? Well I'm glad you're getting out of that racket."

This was the first and best conversation I'd ever had. Wendy was the first person I ever never disliked. This was my farmhouse moment, and I'll never forget it.

"But I still like this house," Wendy said.

"It's a great house!" I told her.

"All I need is a family for it," she said.

I coughed like a dog. It made me hiccup and push a long burp out. The burp's terrain had boulders and streams on it, which The Haircutter traversed.

...............*Alls I need is a family for it, she'd said*...............

We sat uncomfortable.

I noticed my teeth were chattering.

I noticed that steel butterfly was awakened somewhere in the sticky abused piping of my stomach.

I noticed: *Wendy.*

I smiled.

"Dang, Girly," I thought, jiggling my legs.

"It's cold up here," she said.

We went back down the little stairs and stepped around The Hole That Changed Everything.

"Oh, the bathroom," she said and we walked in. I immediately went to the tub to see if there were any dead animals, and saw a rat's nest cuddled up cozy at the drain. When I turned around to show Wendy, she was staring at the mirror in shock.

An owl hooted on the roof like her mother trying to get her attention.

I said to her reflection, "I, ah—I seen that sheet taped up over your mirror at the motel."

She gasped and snapped-to. She pointed at the toilet, "That's where I was when I first learned about Toxic Shock Syndrome if you leave a tampon in too long. It's my biggest fear."

"Not a bad face, if you ask me." I pointed at her reflection. "I don't get about why you wouldn't want to see it. Your overbite's pretty, I swear." I raised a brow and put my hands in my pockets.

"They were *rags,* not tampons, let alone maxis," she said.

I sniffled and looked at my shoes, letting her have her way.

"Now that I've looked in the mirror I might as well use it to put my makeup on. I'm going to get it from the truck," she said.

I waited downstairs while Wendy put her makeup on in the mirror by her old period. I heard the little compacts snapping shut through the ceiling hole and it reminded me of Carol. Thoughts of Carol—like walking room-to-room in a dilapidated house with a bucktoothed gravedigger, saying what used to be here. I tried to imagine Wendy's parents going nuts, but instead I thought about what a nice house it would be if it were fixed up. You could put in a fire pole down from the ceiling hole, or a spiral staircase. Curtains with frying pans and chickens printed on them for the kitchen. A painting of a sea storm beside the front door. Anchored land under your feet, wildflowers in your fist. *Better Homes and Gardens* in the mailbox on the road. A telescope for wolf packs in the watch room. Rugs that Wendy could beat with a wooden spoon, or that John Junior could beat with a base-ball bat. Whoa—*what?!* Wink, wink. Talk about a stiffy for the gravedigger.

I opened a door off the sitting room and saw it was a little mudroom with a door to the yard.

"I'm going outside for a bit," I tried.

" . . . Okay," I heard.

I thought about getting up on the roof with a stick and tapping on the bathroom window as a joke, but thought against it.

Behind a pine tree, I found the woodshed. I opened the rickety door. It was a small, perfect room that smelled like the periodic table. *A desk would fit perfectly in here for a summer office*, I thought.

I left the woodshed and walked toward the land in front of the house, inhaling hard on the cold bright air. Crunching on the crystalized straw underfoot. Wild turkeys ran across the field fog garbling like computer geeks. Crows cawed like they didn't know anything about technology.

I was standing in the threshold to the kitchen imagining a mushroom pie steaming on the woodstove when I noticed the height marks on the wall. Starting at my knees and reaching all the way to the ceiling were notches carved into the stone. They said *Anna-Patrick* next to them. There was one near my shoulders that said *Donna* and one all the way up that said *Silas.* All the rest of them said Anna-Patrick. Not one said Wendy. My legs shot straight erect, making me grow notches taller as a jolt ran through me when I thought, "This isn't her house."

The world tightened in on me and seeped into my pores to squeeze my heart. A dead bird had its neck broken near me and was looking at me like *That's Right!*

I heard Wendy coming down the stairs.

"I'm done, we should go, I want you to curl my hair in the cemetery office," she said.

"Aaaaah!" I shrieked.

She was in a long purple dress with long sleeves—*and her face!*

I said, "Who are you?!"

"What's going on?!" she said.

I remembered a broom in the mudroom and hustled to get it.

"If you don't tell me what's goin' on, I'm gonna make this hole bigger!" I said, putting the broom handle through the ceiling hole.

"What's wrong?!" she screamed.

"Why's all those height marks say Anna-Patrick?" I said, and when I had to look at her to ask the question, I felt puke rise up my neck. *She's so beautiful!,* I thought.

"I'm gonna vom," I said.

If someone in the field had been watching with binoculars, they would've seen me open the front door with a broom and projectile puke like I'd been slapped on the back.

Blaaaaarg!

"You're vomiting!" Wendy said.

I once saw a Golden Retriever gag when his owner hit a high note on the subway.

"You look different!" I said.

She gave me her grey T-shirt to wipe my mouth with instead of licking the puke off my lips like a dog—"Gimme that!" I said, and snatched it.

"My name is Anna-Patrick," she said.

"No, it's Wendy!" I shouted, and threw her T-shirt at the ceiling hole and it went through.

A rat ran down from upstairs, interested in that pile of puke.

"Get me outta this freak storm!" I said.

"Wait!" she said.

A vein came out on her forehead.

Her facial features relate to each other like beautiful people selected from each continent getting along better than anyone would've imagined on such close quarters as a face.

"I didn't want anyone to know my real name. I wanted a fresh start," she said.

I said, "Okay? What, are you supposed to be interesting or something?"

"I'm sorry?" she said.

"I don't really do *fancy*," I said.

"What's wrong with you!" she said.

I farted to put a cloud of distance between us (it rattled like thunder).

"Excuse me! That smells awful!" She pinched her nose and moved to leave, her dress flowing out behind her like exotic fins. "What's with all the toilet humor?" she said.

"What toilet humor?" I shouted after her, abusive.

She slammed her truck door and honked for me to get in.

I blushed until blood came out of my pores.

I went to the truck and got in, being careful not to grunt. The golden light lay over the land and lay in our laps like our future children. She started the engine, and I said, "Wait, stop."

She shut it off and we sat there silent. She reached forward to coochy-coo some dead flies on the dash with her tan, elegant fingers. I noticed that I missed her.

"Your name's Anna-Patrick?" I said.

"Yes. Sorry I didn't tell you, I sort of forgot."

"I don't wanna fight," I said.

"Well it looks like you do!" she said.

"I don't care about your name. I'm just like, 'Where'd that face full of makeup come from?'"

She sniffed and wrapped her teeth in her lips.

I was vulnerable as a schoolboy with lice crawling on his forehead as I said, "You look SO pretty."

A blond butterfly fluttered into the cab like it was Carol being jealous. I clapped my hands on it, then wiped it on my penis. I saw a bucktoothed smile in my periphery. I slowly looked into her eyes.

Christ! I bit my hand white.

She laughed and it sounded like geese.

She started up the truck and we drove toward our cemetery.

I saw a man walking the hills holding a dead bird by its foot for the dead bird I'd ordered. From the little stone hut's window, I watched him toss it into my sinkhole. Dale and Kurt were polishing the mahogany to make it gleam for The Mannequin Ceremony.

"It's ready," Anna-Patrick said.

I turned around and she had the curling iron in her hands. She set it on her desk and sat in a chair facing the open door. The crickets were doing a call-and-response from one side of the cemetery to the other. I lifted a chunk of her hair and it immediately felt like I was going to cut it. I picked up the curling iron instead.

I said, "Carol used to do this."

Carol curled her hair before going out for a romp with Harp. Came home late with an upper lip raw from his midnight shadow. Her hair was cold and smelled like smoke. The Haircutter literally turned the other way—he rolled over in bed and let fire truck sirens redden him back to sleep. A swine's smile on his lips for a happy little pig in a blanket. Carol smoked a cigarette, ashing in her bedside fern, thinking, "Oh my gosh, *Scott*. Oh my gosh I can't wait to *see him again*."

Each chunk of hair that I wrapped around the iron sprung down as a curl. I heard the distant men calling each other pussies. I peeked at the side of Anna-Patrick's face and saw her eyelashes blink.

"Look," she said, pointing out the door.

Patty was walking up the truck ruts toward us from the cemetery gates, and three men were rolling a lumpy boulder up the lawn toward my work of art.

"They're ruining the grass," Anna-Patrick said.

"Oh, sorry!" I said.

"No," she said, "It'll give me something to do while you're away."

I said, "You're sure laying it on thick, Girly!"

She said, "I don't care."

I licked on my bottom lip, smiling.

"Knock, knock!" Patty shouted from one hundred feet out. She had her keys in her hand and they jangled as if by our ears.

"Hi," we said.

"Gol! Do you ever look pretty!" Patty shouted, astonished at Anna-Patrick and forcing her legs forward to get a closer look.

"Thank you," Anna-Patrick shouted.

"I wish I cleaned up that nice!" Patty said, now fifty feet away.

I released the final curl from the iron-hot rod.

"Did you bring it?" I asked my mom.

She held out a trash bag and kept walking towards us, panting.

"I like your Unit," Anna-Patrick said about a new maroon sweat suit Patty was wearing beneath a yellow blanket shawl.

"Thank you!" she said, twenty feet away. "I liked yours, so I thought it was inspiring. What can I say?"

"Is Darron here?" I said.

"Yep. We're ready when you are," she said, and finally arrived at the door of the stone hut and handed me the trash bag.

"Why don't you put your earrings on to top that outfit off?" I said.

She blinked and said, "Well good idea, son," and took them out of her pocket and clipped them on.

"Go and get everyone ready and gathered round," I said.

"Alrighty," she said and went away up the hill. I saw she had a Romance with her to read while she waits because she doesn't do nature, like me.

Me and my gorgeous giant alone in our stone hut. I opened the trash bag and pulled out Carol's lace duster dress.

"This is what she used to wear all the time," I said.

"Was she wearing it when she died?" Anna-Patrick asked.

"No, she was wearing camping clothes, but this was in her long backpack and everything in there got bloody. So it's bloody—look out. But the point is, everyone in the art world knows this dress. They know it represents Carol."

The lace duster was sewn to the stomach of the dress in a C. I thought, *Creative, Carol.*

I looked at Anna-Patrick's beautiful face, now framed by curls. I bit my hand again. Anna-Patrick was Miss Universe, and Carol was Little Miss Basement Bathroom of The Shopping Mall Where There's No Toilet Paper And Somehow Diarrhea On The Wall.

I put the dress down on Anna-Patrick's desk and said, "Stand up."

She stood up and flipped her head upside down and ran her fingers through the curls.

"You're ruining it!" I shrieked.

"No, this is what you're supposed to do."

Her fingers separated the curls and made hundreds of smaller curls, making her hair bigger than it usually is.

"Watch," she said upside down.

Then she flipped her head back and her hair flew up and landed behind her in a bounce.

I grabbed her rump and yanked her close.

"Ah!" she screamed.

Our eyes locked clean, and in three deep breaths, Anna-Patrick's rib basket was rested on my stomach. She lowered her face and we kissed. I put my hands in her hair. Felt the hot melonic ripeness of her head. Felt the warmth of her inner mouth with my tongue. Felt her rump again. When we pulled away, she was smiling, her teeth and gums protruding from her face. It made me squeal and honk a titty.

"Aah!" she screamed and clutched at it. "Let's take it slower than that!" she said, smiling.

"Let's get this over with," I said, grabbing Carol's dress.

There's H.C. in slow motion walking toward his mammoth art piece with his mammoth girlfriend. A trophy was growing inside of his chest ready to burst through it. There's six hired men gathered funeraly around the base of the sixteen-foot cubular coffin. There's Darron and Father John soldier-straight by the boulder at the ramp. Watch "Wendy" descend a steep hill to stand by Patty Reilly and the hired men. See The Haircutter walk up the ramp and move down the ladder into the sinkhole, the famous dress draped over his shoulder. There's the mannequin waiting in the bottom of the hole like Carol Mathers. H.C. dresses it swift and quick. Doesn't put panties on it so the viewer can see her cooter twat. He spies a strand of Carol's hair caught in the string of lace like wolf saliva. He leaves it there. He positions the body on its back in the center of the sinkhole. Then climbs the ladder. A nod to Darron sets his voice box off, "We are gathered here today to put to rest one Carol Mary Mathers."

Darron had memorized the script, "She died in the Bighorns during an art project called *Hush, Howler—Hunt.* All the men present have helped to construct this life-sized re-creation of the sinkhole that she died in."

"Some women helped too!" Patty shouted, pointing at Anna-Patrick.

"The glossy outer walls represent her coffin. *The Headstone*'s title represents the stone that dropped on her head. Her brain was smashed completely, along with her mind? One would wonder, and never get anywhere with it. Her lower body came up off the ground and seemed to pop. Steam came out of holes in her legs. Our goal today is to re-create her death and hopefully get her legs to stay up in the air off the ground. The Haircutter, whenever you're ready."

Father John was looking at me with a look like you'd give someone who was telling a really great story. He shook it off when he saw me see him.

"I'm ready," I said.

Darron and Father John came to get their hands on the boulder and their feet gripped to the earth. Patty rattled her keys and knitted her brow in the shrieking pink sunset, and Anna-Patrick sopped a tear duct with a tissue ball. The team of six hired men hung their mouths in disbelief and hung their calloused hands around their belt buckle names for handy frames. Some pee-crusted white-trash children hung on the fence in the background.

"Go!" I shouted.

We roared and pushed the boulder up the ramp. It went faster than expected. It dropped suddenly off the edge and fell into the hole. We almost fell in with it.

The boulder landed on Mannequin Carol's head. Her legs shot up and stayed aloft.

Everyone cheered enormous hoots and emotional laughter.

"So long, Girly," I said under my breath.

We put the lid on, then we had to chain the whole thing to the truck, even though it was so heavy a tornado couldn't lift it off. The chains left scratches on the varnish and Father John ruined the mood of the ceremony by yelling at the men who'd voted chains instead of cloth straps, and then Anna-Patrick fixed the mood by saying that whoever buys *The Headstone* won't mind the scratches because "coffins are usually scratched." We put a tarp over the hole where I'd climb down the ladder at truck stops to sleep, and my mother screamed, "Anyone could get in there! Don't let no knife murderers see you climb down in there!"

I said, "Shut up, Ma!" fourteen in front of my new girlfriend.

We affixed red flags and flashing lights to the chains and then panted on the ruined grass in front of *The Headstone*'s square and military mass, like eleven morsels of humanity having completed a Mannequin Ceremony.

Anna-Patrick and I got in her truck and followed the Fair Fare van to the Blue Bear Saloon.

"That was emotional," she said.

"Psh," I said. "I'm just ready to cash the money in. Perhaps use it to fix up your house."

Her chin started quivering and her eyes welled hard.

"Don't look so scared," I said. "Or hell, I can just move to Miami Beach with it and never see you again!"

She laughed and shook her head like she couldn't believe her luck.

"Believe it, Bucky," I said, which I wish I hadn't.

In the Blue Bear parking lot, all the hired men joined us with their wives and denim families to whoop and shout and show how their cowboy-dressed little sons could stick their tongues out of their mouths while doing fancy footwork. A smug little wifemom walking adroitly in high heels as though they were her hooves asked me about art and I announced to the parking lot that I don't talk about art anymore. We flooded in, and I saw Carol Couch from when I'd come in looking for Carol. I said, "The Blue Bear," aloud for some reason instead of nodding hi to her. It smelled like sawdust and cigarettes. I saw the waitresses pump their fists when Darron ran toward the dance floor and slid on his knees across it. Carol Couch went and lowered the lights, making the Christmas lights shine brighter. Gravely voices cut through uppity country music with opinions they just *had* to express to each other. Anna-Patrick, quiet as a church mouse, taller than the doorway to a house, held my fat hand in her tan elegant.

"This is great!" she said.

"Well this is Darron's place," I told her.

Patty set an armful of Imitation Cowboys on a table that the Blue Bear had made especially for Darron with a sign that explains what the Imitations are. Customers went over to buy them.

"Would you like a drink?" I asked Anna-Patrick.

"Sure! Coke please!"

We sat at a table with Patty and some of the hired men's families watching everyone dance and get drunk. I saw Patty watching us, and she leaned forward and smacked Anna-Patrick hard on the shoulder. She screamed over the Toby Keith, "Junior's quiet and ornery but he's got a heart! This time he nicked himself with a pencil and came to me screamin' about Let's get to the hospital before the lead poisonin' starts!" She pinched her straw and sipped on it coy and fast. (She really did look good in those earrings.)

"He is very smart," Anna-Patrick said.

Patty said, "I never went to college."

I said, "Neither did she!" happy for the coincidence.

Anna-Patrick smiled at me and bobbed her shoulders in time with the beat.

"You wanna go dance? Darron would like it," I said.

"I wanna see *you* dance!" she said.

"Aw hell, it's been a while," I said.

"GO! DO it!" Patty shouted.

I was in a good mood, I guess. The happiest ever.

"Darron!" I shouted over the music, "Hey, Darron!"

Darron spun around quick in his black clothes, his tail flying out from his neck, "Yeah?"

"You still remember that Scissor Step?" I said.

He bent his legs and screamed, "GET YOUR ASS UP HERE!!!"

I took a big gulp of Coke. I stood up and yanked my belt up around my fat and stepped forward on the damp carpet until my sneakers were catching drag on the shiny wood dance floor. Darron joined me at my side and we waited for the right part of the song. Darron wagged his finger to count with, and when I looked up, everyone was watching us.

"GO!" Darron screamed, and we crisscrossed our feet sideways down the dance floor. I knew right away that I wouldn't be able to do the whole length of it, so I roared hard, thinking it would help, until I tripped on my legs and fell to my hands and knees.

"Dang it!" I said.

Darron tripped over me and did a somersault, then sprung up like a Halloween cat. Anna-Patrick was pulling me up, laughing like a flock of seagulls just got tossed a net of shrimp scampi. She screamed, "My turn!"

Carol always blushed while she danced, doing these little movements that looked like she had to pee. Anna-Patrick circled me like a predator, her right hand flicking on its wrist in time with the drums. Elvis's voice came on and she turned away from me and spelled each word he said with her hips. She did it in a circle and then did a move where she fell to her knees and popped up again, fell to her knees and popped up again, with her lips closed tight over her overbite. Hoots and whistles came from every patron in the room. I swear it was like she was moving *inside* of the song. She was like an added instrument.

I said, "Goodness gracious, Anna-Patrick!"

I backed up to sit with Patty to watch Anna-Patrick and Darron dance. Her head laughed back and her mass of curls rippled like a flag. Darron was in the presence of someone as good as he was at dancing. He was smiling so hard he kept choking, and soon he was crying. He pulled out all his best moves—ones he hadn't done in ages because there had been no one to appreciate them. His face was neon red. He did a spin that seemed to last a half minute, where he nearly disappeared. Then he stuck his landing, and Anna-Patrick took the challenge to do a spin of her own—she spun so fast that she disappeared, making it look like Darron was standing alone. When she landed, they both bent their legs and moved in a circle enthused with each other, snapping like orphans in a musical.

I decided to get some water to make sure my gravedigger was hydrated when she was ready for a rest, so I moved my way to the bar. Father John was sitting there so he could get his glass filled without waiting. I pressed my stomach into the bar and shouted, "Waters please!" to the waitress.

Father John was looking at Anna-Patrick. His eyes had those star lines shooting out of them again, like God trying to scratch them open.

Anna-Patrick was doing leg kicks in consecutive moments where her knee touched her buckteeth.

"Oh! Her name is *Anna-Patrick*," I told Father John, happy to report.

"Here you go!" the waitress said and handed me the waters.

Father John said, "HEY!"

I flinched and water dripped to my shoes like a bubble had burst.

He was squinting at Anna-Patrick.

Then he was howling.

"I said I know names, didn't I! That's the whore I paid to take your virginity!"

I walked back to the table with the waters spilling in my flapping hands. I set them on the table and went out onto the dance floor.

I said to Anna-Patrick, "I didn't know. I'm dumb."

She shouted, "What?!"

Darron said, "Whoa, big bro, what's wrong? Your face is all white."

I shouted into Anna-Patrick's ear, "I'm goin' to the john, and then I want you gone. I don't need a girlfriend."

I walked off the dance floor and looked back at her once. She was standing there doing a *hoo* sound with her overbite, crying.

I went into the john and tossed the trashcan at the wall.

I'll admit I cried. So what.

Then I peaked my head out the door and Anna-Patrick was there.

"Hi!" she said cheerfully. Trying things.

"Go away!"

I shut the door and she came to shout on the other side of it. Someone was pooping loud farts into the toilet as she said, "Did someone tell you? I didn't know if you knew or not! It doesn't mean I can't love! It was the only thing that made me feel! I was all alone!"

"*Feel?!* Yuck!"

"No, not like that! I can't explain it, H! These men they'd get all inflated as they were coming back to the room, and then they'd be deflated when they left, and it was interesting! I don't know why! They were coming in like flashcards or something—I mean, fat ones, skinny ones, old ones, young muscly ones—just go to the grocery store and see how wide of a variety there is! Bless, I guess it's weird now that I think about it, but at the time—bless, H! Honestly, I didn't even enjoy the sex part, and that's something I'd still like to discover in myself and I look forward to your help! H.C., please understand me! That's why when you said about your haircutting I understood!"

"I know how fat I am, okay?" I said. "Quit pretending and scram!"

"Hoooooo," she cried. "You're not fat!" she blubbered.

"It makes sense why you're a prostitute, you're gorgeous. Who wouldn't want to sleep with you," I said to the sink.

"I'm not!" she shrieked. "I only did that for a couple years, and then I got the graveyard job and that replaced my need to feel something because I LOVE tending land, I told you! It was so long ago, I was just a dumb person all alone! I didn't have anyone, H! That's why I've been hiding all these years and why I changed my name! I can't even look at myself because it reminds me of what people would think if they knew my history! Tonight I thought, 'I'm just going to show my face!' Because it's time to grow up and move on and I finally found a man I love."

More *hoo*'s as she cried harder.

The pooper came out of the toilet and I saw he was a scared little kid in cowboy clothes.

"Does your tummy hurt?" I snarled at him, and he ran out of the john without washing his hands, and I saw Anna-Patrick there with all her makeup smeared looking hopeful like, 'Ooh is this an opportunity where he's going to catch the door and talk to me now?' I let it swing shut.

"Make sure them cemetery gates are open tomorrow at 4:00 a.m.," I said. "Now go and leave my family alone. I don't even know you. Scram."

When I finally came out of the john it was time to go, and everyone was asking me what the hell went on that made the tall girl cry and run out. Father John was laughing and Darron helped him get in the van. "That's a prostitute," he said, hiccupping all the way home and trying to spell "prostitute." My mother said under her breath, "And a very nice one at that." My brother mouthed to me, "Screw him." I rolled my eyes and took out a toothpick.

Darron and I hugged goodbye at the stairs to my attic.

"I'm gonna come visit you wherever you go next," he said.

"Yeah," I said.

"I think you should give Wendy a second chance," he said.

"She only had sex with me cause she got paid," I said. "By *Father John.*"

"It's pretty cool he never told you that, though. To make you think you lost your virginity on your own?" he said.

"Darron! Quit bein' so dumb!" I said.

Darron shook his head and sighed long and heavy. "People grow. I can tell she really really likes you now."

"You smell like B.O.," I said.

"Well, I've been dancing for the past five hours," he said.

"It smells like you're cookin' somethin' in your pits," I said. "Damn it, Darron, I'm gonna cry tonight. That woman was somethin' else."

He put a hand on my shoulder, "You and her go together. You can just *tell.*"

I saw Father John's dusty workboot tracks pointing into his room from when he came home from being a man.

"I spent all my money," I said.

"You did? I thought you were rich!" Darron said.

"I was," I said.

"Is your art not that good?" he said.

I said, "Ach! That's enough with being around people! Get The Haircutter out of here!"

I woke up at four in the morning and Patty was downstairs with two coffee mugs. We left the house and a wolf ran out of our bushes and into the streetlights, where it looked back at me before getting hit by a bus. We got in the Fair Fare van and it still smelled like Father John's alcohol from before. We wove through the streets toward the highway that lead to the cemetery. I sipped on my coffee, but stopped when I realized it only made me more nervous. I was so nervous to see Anna-Patrick again, I almost farted the shit out of my ass. My mother rolled my window down and I saw myself in the side mirror reflection.

I don't need a girlfriend! I'd said. *Scram!*

Anna-Patrick had opened the cemetery gates like I'd commanded.

And she was nowhere in sight. She didn't want to say goodbye.

"Good," I said aloud. "That's right," I said. "It's me and the road, me and the opening, then me and my scissor," I said.

"Yeah, so what's your plan, Junior?" my mother settled in snug thinking I was opening up.

I walked toward my flatbed truck with my stupid art project on its back. The headlights gleamed in the dark as I crested a hill and saw it there. It radiated like an unchained bull waiting complacently for me to ride it.

I climbed up into the cab, sat on the blankets that padded the bench. I started the engine and pulled out of the cemetery, my mother honking goodbye. I was ten feet off the ground. I spread my legs wider to grip the floor mat. Checked my mirrors to make sure all's alright. Resisted the urge to drive past the Rodeo Inn. Made that now-familiar turn onto I-80 East.

The truck slid onto the open road, undulating like a puppy with a long tail. The cab was cold and smelled like piss. I put the heat on and it smelled like carpet. The sunrise looked like my wolf had clawed at the foot of the earth trying to escape. I don't blame him. Even if he did find his pact, how the hell could he relate after all that? After being put on a pedestal as an art piece in New York City? Eating Cocker Spaniel pellets the whole time—how embarrassing! He was a wolf, folks. Fangs and a built-in charm. No one should treat a wolf like that; abuse is what humans are for. I went from the cover of the *New York Post* to the cover I've slept under since my ninth birthday, and I handled it fine. Nobody even came to see me in the hospital, let alone an entire pack of people with antiseptic tongues ready to lick my wounds. When my family came, they were there to see Carol. I slept on a purple plastic couch beside her beeping bed. In a turquoise hospital room by a balloon that said *Hope you feel better soon.* Why did I stay? The doctors had said I could go. Nurse Haircutter, at your service, dumber than a two-dollar can of pop. Morphine Carol, pooping herself, waking up into a nightmare where her leg is backwards and I'm above her holding a jar of green salve. I put salve on her squashed thigh and lifted my shirt to put salve on my heart. *Boo-hoo!* We were both recouping from getting crushed.

We never turned the TV off—we were afraid of being alone together in the dark.

Small-town hospitals are in-patient sparse, yet there was a 24-hour priest snoring on a grade-school chair down the hall.

In the middle of a 3:00 a.m. movie about chimpanzees, she said, "I'm ugly!"

Her saliva connecting her lips together like spider webs over a hole, "I'm butt ugly!"

Her chin a walnut, "You think I'm ugly?! Why didn't you disagree?"

As the chimp was shrieking, about to be slaughtered—"CUT IT OFF!!! Cut this leg off! It's staring at me!"

She smelled putrid.

She was visited by her dad Rev and her mom Trish and Trish's husband Ricky. They all smelled like cigarettes and they all wore jeans and belts and boots. Trish brought us a paper plate of cookies that had a pubey underneath one of the cookies as a remember-me-by. I wanted to point it out to Carol but we were doing the Silent Treatment so we ate around the pubey until it was the only thing left on the plate. We couldn't look at each other, so the pubey became something to focus on, or something to blame for our problems?, or something to fake-smile at during commercial breaks, and it was our main focus for about half the week. We shouted, "NO!" at a nurse who offered to throw the plate away. It made me feel dumb, so I blew the pubey to the floor, really pissing Carol off.

Her cross-armed declaration, "I needed spice besides just salt and pepper."

I pissed in her bedpan any opportunity I could get to remind her of how she once loved my dick.

She became tender as a drugged sloth, "I can't believe he put a spell on me."

Her voice so high it went silent, "It was a mistake!"

I discovered "Fiestatas" from the cafeteria—a Mexican pizza shaped like a stop sign covered in Ranch.

"I can't believe I hurt you," she whispered before she fell asleep snot-clogged from crying.

Patty came in with Romances and sat by the bed while Carol read lines aloud from them.

"These people don't know how to F," Carol said.

And through the plots of those dramas, story streams glistened like young teachers, telling The Haircutter more about how women think. Carol noticed him halt his pencil in his spot on the plastic couch as he seemed to strain to hear her read a particular scene, teach a particular lesson.

"Dang, see Lance is bein' too possessive, huh Patty?" Carol would say, and H.C. would grouch, "Bein' too what?"

"Possessive," Carol taught. "He's treatin' her like she ain't her own person. Like she's just Mrs. Lance Quest instead of a woman with a whole set of needs and feelings."

H.C. would respond in a grunt that packed the lesson firm into his being. So Patty came in cross-eyed with happiness holding her old wedding dress, "Carol I wonder if you'd fit in this! I used to be thinner, but I was still fat according to magazine standards."

And I snapped at her, "She can't wear dresses anymore, Ma! Or it'll look like she has a boner!"

From the knee to the foot, Carol's right leg would forever be sticking upwards at an eighty-degree angle, because the boulder had landed on her thigh. When she was to sit in a wheelchair from now on, her right foot would be eye-level with her.

But the mention of marriage made us blush and hold eyes longer than we had since the accident. Cupid bullshit passed like gas through the turquoise room. So—finally, we were about to kiss. I'd forgiven her enough, or she'd manipulated me into thinking as much. Our faces were close together as I adjusted her pillow, and the moment felt right. But then a beep in the hallway started beeping and I didn't want it to make our kiss feel dumb. So I said to myself, *I'll wait for later,* and I told her, "I'm goin' to get more food from the cafeteria."

I picked up our tray and said, "See you in a bit, little lady."

She said, "Get more Mountain Dew."

I selected new foods and a few Fiestatas five floors down in the cafeteria. While Scott Harp walked the tungsten-lighted hall toward Carol's healing room.

When I came back, I heard curious voices at Carol's bed. I tiptoed in on my puffy white sneakers and stood on the other side of the dividing curtain.

"I can't believe this. I'm literally in shock," Carol said.

Scott Harp said, "I'm taking you back with me."

Carol said, "Who says I wanna go? What happened to your heartache gettin' out?"

Scott Harp said, "It got out, like I said, but definitely not all the way, because the minute I heard about your accident . . . it came back. We're going to be together now. That's enough now, Carol."

H.C. silently put his tray down on a chair and got under the bedskins of the neighboring bed for the story.

Carol wept quietly.

The Haircutter's mind's eye saw Harp's hairy hand stroking narrow Carol's.

"Aw dang it, I must look like a hag," she said.

"I love you with you hair curled and your makeup on," he said. "You look best like that."

"Shit! If I'd known you were coming I would've found a way to curl my hair and put makeup on," she said.

"Well, you're in the hospital," he said. "Jesus, I wish I could bring you to a *good* hospital in Jersey. You could meet my parents. Come watch my dad and I play squash."

"Don't say squash. I think my leg's gonna be stuck up like this forever," she said.

"I'll wheel you around then," he said.

"Seriously though?" she said.

"Yes," he had thought about it.

She heated up, "I can put a fancy shoe on it? Always have a different fancy shoe?"

"You're so creative, Carol! I love it!" he said.

"I love art!" she said. "Will you salve my thigh?"

The Haircutter had *just* salved it.

"Like this?" Harp said.

"Yeah, in circles like that," said Carol.

"Does that feel good?" Harp said.

"Yeah, you do it way better than him."

The Haircutter burst into flames.

"It's squishy," Harp said.

"It's gonna harden up," said Carol.

"I love you so much, Co-Co," Harp said.

"This must be a dream," she said.

"Don't cry. Where's The Haircutter?" Harp said.

"He went to go get more food on his tray."

Scott Harp snickered and Carol swatted him, "Stop!"

Then they giggled hard together like *he's fat!*

"Your, uh . . . your vaginal area? Does everything still work?" he said.

"Hee-hee-hee," as she said it does.

"YES!" as he was relieved he could still fuck her.

"What are we doing, he's gonna come back any second. Are you ready for this?" Carol said.

"Yes," he was ready for it.

Carol whispered, "I love you."

Scott said, "*God,* I love you."

"Shh!" Carol said.

Then H.C. heard kissing.

"No, stop, he's gonna come back any minute!" Carol said.

They waited. Two patient motherfuckers waiting for the fat Haircutter.

"It smells like mashed potatoes and gravy," Scott Harp said.

"Maybe you should go wait in the hall. He's gonna drop the food when he sees you," was a suggestion.

Scott Harp came around the dividing curtain and saw one walrus-fat H.C. under a hhhhwhite bedskin that went up to his chin. His eyes were fixed wide at the ceiling. His instinct was to play dead.

Scott Harp said, "JEsus."

Silence.

"Are you alright, man?"

Silence, still.

The Haircutter remained "dead."

Scott looked back to Carol, "Uhh, Carol?"

He walked forward like an eraser deleting the divider curtain.

"AAAAAAH!!!!" she screamed.

I snapped to.

"Now what the hell's this?" I croaked out of my throat.

"I'm going to wait outside," said Scott as he walked away.

"Oh my GOD!!!!!!" Carol said.

She covered her mouth, "Oh my god!" she said through her fingers.

"Now see I'm gonna grunt and stand up. And I'm gonna come over to you and ask you what you expect me to say," is what I said.

I did as intuited—I grunted as much as my body was damn well requiring, and when I went to her bedside she said, "I can't believe you were just spyin' on me!"

"Wake up, Carol," I said.

She looked appalled and then started crying.

Scott Harp came back with two cups of water, whispering, "The Haircutter, I'd like to say a few things."

And The Haircutter fast as a bat knocked the water cups flying.

"It's John to you," I said.

"Assault me!" Harp challenged, spreading his arms, then immediately cowering behind them.

I tried to fart but couldn't. I walked out the door. That's the last time I saw her.

Now here I come.

CHAPTER SEVEN

A LADY
SCREAMED

Carol isn't dead, sorry. Fuck you. There was no funeral, I'm so sorry.

I left the hospital in my fat body and didn't call Patty for a ride home because I didn't want her to see me cry. I started walking the highway, and after a while I came upon a cemetery. I knew what to do as soon as I saw it. I entered the gates and walked the sloping grounds until I found the most condolence-card spot— under an apple tree on a hill. I sat on the wrong side of a headstone and pretended I was sitting at Carol's grave and they just hadn't been over yet to etch her inscription in:

Carol Mary Mathers
1969-2001
"It was a whirlwind-type dil."

I pretended that the boulder had fallen on her head and that she was dead. It worked. I imagined the funeral she would've had. I buried all of Carol's things. Said aloud, "Oh you poor man, that's the worst thing anyone can endure!" "Yes, a boulder fell on her head." My family caught on and played along with my therapy. They didn't say anything about the hour-long sessions where I punched the living room couch repeatedly. Father John said, "Just grabbin' my glasses," quietly when he came into the room as I was bellowing, "You do it way better than him!" and giving the couch its blows. Patty and Darron drank milk and whispered about the signs they saw in Carol's darting eyes and whistling

S's. They pretended she was dead, solemnly dropping me off at the cemetery. Patty borrowed a book about grief for me from the library. It was the nicest thing they've ever done for me.

When the boulder landed on Carol's leg, it made her calf point up in the air with her camping boot pointing at me like, "*You* did this!" Darron puked into the hole when he found us. Father John held the rescue ladder to the top of the car with his arm out the window as we sped to the hospital that we were all born in. I put pressure on Carol's squashed thigh. She screamed like someone burning in hell, her boot ripping up the fabric roof, her finger-nails tearing bloody rivulets into her face until she blacked out.

After a week in the sunny turquoise hospital room The Hair-cutter was ready to kiss, but there was a pussy ass beep in the hall that made him go get more food . . .

I was slicing down the road toward Carol Mary Harp. To show her where that rock should've landed and to get a million dol-lars for the statement. The route was familiar now. I remembered almost everything on the road. ("Oh, there's that sex bookstore Kitty Poos-Poos." "Oh weird, I remember that tree.") But I didn't stop at that rest stop with the bronze eagle, I didn't stop to buy cherries from Genderless-stuck-in-its-chair, I didn't stop at the gas station where the attendant stole my per diem when a thousand dollars was a fortune to me. My adrenaline was pumped to the maximum and I drove twenty hours straight. I didn't even listen to the radio. I only stopped for gas and snacks, but I don't remember eating the snacks at all. The edges of my vision were black with late-night landscape and regret. *I don't need a girlfriend!*

I don't even know you!, I'd said. I cared less and less about having Carol see me show up with *The Headstone* (I actually didn't care at all) and more and more about Anna-Patrick. Anna-Patrick! I should've been riding my flatbed like a lardy little boy riding a tortoise on the best day of his childhood, but all I could think of was tall Anna-Patrick squatting over a dick that looked like a witch's finger. *She was all alone. She wanted connection with people. Like haircutting. They entered the room inflated and left deflated like a stupid balloon.* A fever throbbed in my heart, eradicating the beat. Playing it like my head landed on a bongo drum for a while during a seizure on my way to the floor: *Aaaa-na Pat-rick, Anna-Patrickkkk, ANNNNNNa-patriiiick, Anna-Patrick . . .*

I finally said, "Sleep!" and it woke me up and I saw a sign for a truck stop. I pulled in and parked like dying after slipping on a banana peel but before hitting the ground. There were a few other trucks around, and some booze bottles tumbling through oil puddles like stepping on a banana peel but not slipping because you're a cool alcoholic.

I started getting my sleeping stuff gathered to take to the hole and I felt sad about "*Scram! I don't need a girlfriend!*"

"Ah, fuck," I said. "All I care about is Anna-Patrick now," I said, and started to cry.

And just then, a hooker walked by.

She was short and old with short maroon hair.

"Hey!" I said.

She heard me through the truck windows and squinted until she found me.

"Hi!" she smiled, and came around to the passenger's door.

I unlocked it and she got right in, hoisting herself up by the truck step and landing on the seat like a trick.

"How are you?" she said.

She looked around fifty.

"I'm tired," I said.

"What do you want?" she asked.

"I got a hole in back and I want you to go down into it with me, and then leave when I'm ready to go to sleep," I said.

"Okay, and where are we going to do this?" she said.

"In the hole," I said.

"*Where* though? We're not doing anything here," she said.

"We gotta climb back there."

She craned back to look at my box.

"It's an art project," I said.

"*What's* an art project?" she said, snarling.

"The whole thing is. It's a sinkhole in a coffin," I said.

"You have a coffin in there?" she said.

"No the box is the coffin. That's why it's mahogany. There's a life-sized sinkhole inside. What happened to your ear?" I said.

The prostitute had a ripped earring hole, so her earlobe was split like tiny vagina flaps as her cutesy advertisement.

"My daughter hugged me and my earring got caught in her jacket zipper. How does a person get a sinkhole inside a box and what the hell does a person use a sinkhole for?"

"I filled it with dirt and scooped a hole out. It has my ex-girlfriend in the bottom, but her head is smashed by a boulder, that's why it's called *The Headstone*. NO—not smashed. Ah fuck, never mind," I said. "You know what? Never mind."

"I'm leaving," she said.

"She's just a mannequin!" I said. "Quit askin' me about art! I'll get in my sleeping bag and you can sit on the ladder rungs. I just wanna ask you questions."

"I'm not getting in your fuckin' box," she said.

"I know it!" I said. "Dang, Woman! I just wanted to ask you questions in privacy with a flashlight."

She said, "Why can't you ask them in here? I don't see anyone else sitting in this truck."

"MAYBE I HAVE INTIMACY ISSUES! YOU'VE GOT THE MOON ALL BRIGHT! BOTTLES ROLLIN' ON THE FUCKIN' GROUND!"

I took out a toothpick, irritated by the loud man in the truck until I realized he was me.

She put a hand on his thigh.

I said, "Don't touch my thigh! Is that normal?"

I started to cry again.

"I have exhaustion," I said. "I've been driving for twenty hours straight and I don't remember it. I could be dead on the side of the road right now for all I know. I just wanna sit here and ask you questions about what it's like being a prostitute so I can understand my girlfriend."

"You're falling asleep," she said, and opened her door to get out.

"Don't leave. I'll pay you two hundred dollars," I said. "If I fall asleep I'll pay you fifty dollars for every hour I was asleep."

"A hundred," she said.

"Okay," I said.

"Okay," she said and took off her shoes and put her legs up on the bench. She opened her pocketbook and got out a cigarette. I saw she had a nice gold tooth when she sucked in the cig smoke with that teeth-baring inhale people do like a leaf blower has quickly passed over their face. I thought really hard about something to ask about Anna-Patrick having sex, but kept forgetting what I was asking it for. I slapped myself.

"Can I call you Red?" I said.

"Sure."

"Dear Red, I was wondering . . . hold on," I said.

I thought of a question mark and I captured it, but it evaporated like trying to hug a ghost. I opened my mouth and a moan came out—I fell asleep.

I dreamt that Scott Harp trained the wolf to let him pee into its mouth. The wolf was trained to guzzle fast enough that not a drop dripped out.

I woke up with the prostitute poking my shoulder.

"Hun," she said.

It made me wince and want to cry, but I didn't want to scare her.

"You've been sleeping two hours, are you gonna pay me?" she said.

I pulled out some cash with my eyes still closed and opened them slits to count out for her.

"Don't go away," I said as I handed it to her.

I fell back fast to sleep.

"My gravedigger love interest," I managed. "I just found out she was a prostitute."

The prostitute said, "Wake up, you're dreaming."

I opened my eyes and looked at her and she was still smoking, but it was bright out now. I looked in the rearview hoping to see that someone had stolen *The Headstone,* but there it was—chained down.

"The opening's tonight," I said.

"Are you gonna pay me? I've been sitting in this cab all night knowing you're gonna pay me and I better not be wrong," the prostitute said.

I pulled out the cash and counted out for her.

She took it with her maroon nails and put it in her purse.

"Thanks! Do you want a cigarette?" she said.

"Okay," I said.

The cigarette smelled like Red's spicy perfume where she'd pinched it out of the pack.

"Do you mind driving me to the next exit? There's a diner there," she said.

I lit the cigarette and in one drag the ash was hooked toward the floor. I rolled my window down and wide-loaded our way out of the truck stop.

We drove a short distance and then exited into a parking lot the size of two football fields. We parked the truck and got out and walked the sunny concrete as it was starting to snow.

"I lost Anna-Patrick, I lost all my money cause I keep spendin' it, he stole my scissor, and I'm showin' up with my next piece," I said. "Sounds like a bad country song."

Red ignored me, which was interesting, so I took a good look at her for the first time. She was in tennis shoes and a little white cotton dress with a red parka over it where the fur collar looked wet but wasn't. She had gold jewelry and brown lipstick on. I thought she probably has old pics of her daughter in her wallet before her earlobe was split like a vaginette.

She saw me looking at her and said, "Listen, I don't mean to be rude, but it's a real treat for me to be able to have a nice quiet meal at a diner, and I'm really hungry, so do you mind if I eat alone?"

"I'll pay you the rest of my money to let me eat with you," I said.

"Okay," Red said.

The diner was part of a gas station/restroom/souvenirs/food-court complex. Truckers and bladderful families entered and exited the complex like ants. Red and I sat in a gold-speckled booth on yellow padded benches. Snow fell diagonally out the window that said *!raeY fO emiT tahT* in frosty green cursive. We ordered the Gimmie-It-All special and I smiled at her when the waitress left, like *We got the same thing*, but she didn't smile back.

"You seem really nice," I said to her.

"And married," she said, holding up her wedding finger.

"Oh?" I said, "And how's your husband think of you bein' a lady of the night?"

She lightly snarled and said, "He thinks it's just fine. It pays the bills and I only have to work when I want."

"Huh? But what does he think about you havin' sex with other men?"

"Me and my husband have a good relationship. He knows it's just sex and it's no big deal. The dick goes in and the dick goes out. It's just an action. I tell my clients exactly what they can't do with me. No talking. No calling me slut or whatever. No kissing me on the neck like you're my lover. No sucking my tits unless they pay extra. I only do blow jobs to healthy dicks—and I'm the judge of it. Always use condoms, duh." She opened her purse to show a gun, "And I think they can sense it. No one's ever really crossed my borders."

My face hung on its skull frame.

She cleared her throat and lit a cigarette.

"You really did just find out your woman did sex work," she said.

The waitress came back with our specials.

"Yeah, I did," I said.

As we ate, I started to feel better, like my mother always said I would if I ate. I replayed my kiss with Anna-Patrick. *Had she meant it?*—you know. I found myself smirking, and thought— her parents were crazy! Makes sense she'd go off and do whatever!

"You know what?" I said.

"What?" Red said, very comfortable with me.

"Nothing. I can't wait to see her," I said.

She picked up her cig and sucked it, squinting at me through the smoke.

"Good for you, grown-up," she said. "If I saw your ball sack I could tell you exactly how old you are. That's how old you should be acting."

I grunted.

"She loves you and only you, I promise," she said, smashing out her cig and then biting into her toast.

"Psh!" I said, pretending I thought Red was overdoing it so she'd be uncomfortable instead of me, which she wasn't. She was swishing her fingers together on her toast-eating hand to get invisible crumbs off while looking around.

"What's your name?" I said.

"Bobby Jo."

While we were waiting for the waitress to clear our plates, Red showed me pictures of her family because I asked.

"There's X, there's X and X, and my daughter's kids"—you know.

"Well they all look pretty normal," I said.

She said, "That was a lovely breakfast, thank you very much. I'm just going to sit here and nurse my coffee and buy a paper now."

I said, "Thank you for your help, Ma'am, I really appreciate you opening up," and I got out my wad of cash and gave it to her. Then I grabbed the check and took it to the register and paid with a charge card. I took a peppermint, then pulled my jean jacket close and waved at Red when I walked by the booth outside and her face was next to the exclamation point in *That Time Of Year!*

When I pulled up to New York City, I fished the address of the Opening out of my jean jacket. I talked to cops and showed them paperwork and wide-loaded through special entrances that made me beyond impressed with Father John's capabilities. I knew from those moments on that I'd forever be interested in him and I couldn't wait to tell him about all that. I drove the entire borough of Brooklyn looking for the address. I had to do a corn maze of pulling into streets and backing up when I realized I wouldn't fit through. ("Hey buddy, fuck you!") After two hours of that, I finally arrived at a warehouse on Butler Street in the stench of the Gowanus Canal.

I honked my flatbed at the closed garage door and waited. In five seconds, the door started rolling up. I saw two pairs of shiny dress shoes and knew—there's Christmas and Quick. The door revealed one Christmas-colored suit and one blue, and the endless depth and height of a black room behind them. Christmas saw me give a functional wave at the wheel of my flatbed truck and he yowled with laughter, clutching onto Charlie Quick so hard Charlie's suit sleeve tore off. Christmas yanked it off his arm and bit it like a dog, stomping around in a circle. "YES!" he said. "YES!"

Charlie came around to my side of the truck and had surprisingly large muscles on his exposed arm.

"Pull in!" he shouted.

I turned the headlights on to illuminate the room and fifteen white cats scampered to hiding spots like cockroaches.

Christmas's team had built the scaffolding frame like I'd asked: two sets of wooden stairs to go up each side of *The Headstone* and a platform on top to connect them so that viewers could look into the sinkhole. It was monumentally still as the only thing in the room. A spotlight hung from above it. The ceiling was so high I couldn't see it.

A pack of art handlers appeared in the rearview to close in on my cargo. I got out of the truck and Christmas had Siedle the elf on his hip like a toddler. My heart doubled in beat. *Oh my god!*, I thought. Someone in the darkness flashed our pic.

Christmas said, "Haircutter! I believe this!"

The elf blinked like a real person. He had real-person teeth.

"Hi, how are you?" it said.

"I'm fine, thank you," I said, and my vision began to blur.

"Just fine?" it questioned.

I started shaking. "Christmas can I talk to you in private?"

"Sure! Let's go to my office and sign the contract."

Siedle ran to Charlie Quick on his curly shoes and Quick held out his unsheathed arm and the elf swung around on it like a gymnast on bars. Charlie's facial expression labeled that the contents of his brain were used to this—he was patient as the elf grunted and swung.

"Disgusting!" I said under my breath.

I followed the old familiar sight of Christmas's bald head moving forward as if on a conveyer belt while his lower body did all the work as if on a unicycle. He pulled aside a thick black curtain to reveal a little office he'd fashioned. It had the furniture transported from his Thank You office, so I sat uncomfortably down.

"I don't want Siedle at the opening. He intimidates me," I said.

"You?" Christmas said. "Intimidated by something?"

"Huh?" I said. I thought of Harp and said, "Oh right, I mean interested. I want a lot of elves at the party. I'm interested in them."

He sat on his desk, "So, we have forty-four minutes to get the piece set up, isn't that sexy? We have three potential buyers coming, and there's usually one or two others hidden in the crowd. I'm going to introduce you to Valter Konig, he's the really tan one, and Laaren Ray, she's the hippie heiress who's secretly a murderer, and The Jewells, a young couple who love folk art. Okay? So make sure you tell them about how much the piece means to you, okay?"

"Well it ain't a molehill, but okay," I said. Then I thought of Harp again and said, "I mean a mountain. I'm interested in the piece I made."

Was I drooling? You can add all that. It had been a while since I'd been in the spotlight, and I remembered that same old feel of wondering *Is this how?!*

Christmas put his hand down his pants to rub his candy-cane little excuse for a penis, "This is what I live for—look at this fuckin' place. I'm sorry about what happened with Harp. I dropped him from the gallery. He was too trained anyway, I never really liked him. But Carol's leg is a work of art! I've never seen anything like it!"

"Ach. I just want my scissor back, and let's get this thing sold. Now where's the contract, then let's have Charlie Quick hose me off—I'm smelly."

In a single motion, Christmas whipped out a contract with his left hand and whipped out a gun with his right and shot the contract with his pearl-handled pistol on his dotted line.

I waited for his hole to cool, then signed it *John Reilly Junior.*

"I'd like an extra request," I said. "I'm done with that apartment I lived at, so tell your Finn to throw my stuff away. I wanna sleep in a side room here before heading out in the morning."

Christmas said, "I knew you'd be tired!"

He peeled back another black curtain and we went through into a room of pitch black, then he peeled back another black curtain and we went through into a room that had a blue globe light on the floor with electricity moving in it. There was black bedding beside it that I could barely see. I noticed a melody song coming from the light.

"I'll hear the full song later, but wow, this is perfect," I said, yanking up my pants. "Hell."

"I'm so glad you like it," Christmas said. "I hope you get a good night's sleep tonight."

The light cast blue and lit pockmarks on his face and head like craters on a friendly moon.

"Do I smell food?" I said.

Christmas smiled and stepped to a corner where he peeled back another black curtain.

"*Après vous!*" he said.

We walked down a dark black-curtained hall and Siedle ran past us. He peeled back another black curtain up ahead.

"Thank you, Siedle," Christmas said.

"*Je vous en prie!*" it said and held the curtain spread for us as we walked into another black room.

There was a turkey and a goblet filled with Coke.

"That's my old writing desk!" I said.

"You recognized it! And that's your chair. And a feast fit for a king by Mario Battistel at Jean-Quatre."

I felt the turkey like it had braille on it.

"So, *The Headstone!*" he said, lighting candles with a long matchstick. "Where'd the idea come from?"

"Go see it," I said, ripping off one of the turkey's legs. "Have them put it in the slot between the stairs and take the lid off. It represents a coffin, so have them polish the mahogany to make the varnish gleam—the scratches are intentional. Then walk up the stairs and see what's inside."

Christmas wheezed at me through a smile like a party balloon with a pinprick in it.

"Would you like some entertainment while you eat?" he said.

I said, "What—Siedle?"

He peeled back another black curtain to show two actors waiting in a black side room with a vial of poison in the mouth of a pheasant on the girl's head.

I said, "Ach! Get outta my face! No thanks. Get outta here."

My temper became short, like Siedle. Christmas walked away laughing.

I took a closer look at the food. I thought of saying, "Well well, what do we have here?" but all I cared about was Anna-Patrick. I thought, "This is my girlfriend Anna-Patrick. She's a gravedigger." A mosquito hovered around a candle flame like Cupid was playing it like a marionette—he had it enter the flame and get burned alive by its passion. Anna-Patrick What? Anna-Patrick Wythe? Anna-Patrick Hoolihan? Anna-Patrick Forth?

"You're in love with this girl," I heard an old black man say in my head.

"I hope she loves me!" I said, and he simply nodded.

I loaded up my copper plate with oysters, ribs, carrots, grey jelly . . .

"I hope I'm not too lovesick to eat," I said.

I heard Siedle snickering.

"Ahh!" I screamed. "GO AWAY! I DON'T WANT YOU!"

I heard him pitter-patter away down the hall.

"FUCK YOU!" I screamed.

The art handlers had used their machinery to insert the mahogany *Headstone* into the square slot between the scaffolding stairs, and they'd polished the smashed bugs off by the time I came out of the black folds with my pants unbuttoned. Christmas was on the ground conducting the men to take the lid off.

"Can I get a shot real quick?" a photographer asked.

The photog had to back up halfway across the room in order to get the whole thing in the pic. Christmas and I stood in front of the piece and Christmas kept looking up at it. Then the photog came in close to do a portrait of us against the mahogany and I tried leaning my head back on it with my hands in my pockets because I was lounging on my art piece with my pic being taken.

"Good, and Haircutter, can I get one last one with your chin down, please?" the photographer asked.

Christmas sniffed the varnish.

"It smells like the West," he said.

Charlie Quick said, "You guys look great," then motioned to me, saying, "We can hose you down out back. The guests are about to start trickling in."

Siedle opened an EXIT that shot streetlights through the room.

"Shall I wait for you or can I see it now?" Christmas asked, pointing up toward the sinkhole.

"No—I've seen it," I said, unbuttoning my shirt.

He put his hands in his soft suit pants and walked up the wooden stairs that framed the box. He walked forward on the platform and stopped. He turned on his dress shoes to look down into the piece.

Charlie Quick hosed me off behind the warehouse in a cold alley. I rotated in the spray he made by holding his thumb over the hose.

"Just hold it still," I said. "Let's hurry up, it's cold out."

I lifted my penis and moved my hips around on the rod of water to gently direct it where I wanted it to go.

"It's so nice to have you back," Quick said.

"Why?" I asked.

"Because you don't talk much, you just deliver the work and we make loads of money," he said.

"Ha!" I liked his honesty very much. "Spray it in my mouth, I'm thirsty."

I had to walk back through the warehouse in order to get to the street exit where my truck was parked, so I wrapped my shirt around my crotch like a diaper. Tiers of oysters and tables of champagne were set out around *The Headstone*. Caterers walked crisscross getting things done. Another photographer took my picture, and when the camera lowered off his face he was already looking away from me like it was nothing personal. I heard a moan.

Christmas was pacing in the dark with his head hanging.

"Do you like it?" I asked when I passed him.

He looked up at me like he didn't know who I was.

"Hurry up and answer, I gained weight," I said, and he didn't answer, so I scuttled to the truck with my breath puffing out in a smelly cloud before me.

I changed into a plain white T-shirt and combed my part in the extra-large rearview mirror. I scraped the plaque off my teeth with my fingernails and wiped it on the seat—you know. It was my first opening without a woman, but I wasn't going to show up looking like I played the banjo.

A laughing couple walking toward the warehouse caught my eye and made me lose myself in a memory of Carol and I looking the exact same—with our eyes as wide, with our hearts as beating, with our arms entwined like the roots of two plants planted near each other—"Oh *shut up!*" I said to myself. I was lucky to not love her anymore.

I went back to the warehouse and there were early-comers viewing the piece.

"This is dumb," I heard their voices echo.

"Or is it?" they said.

"Yes it is," they decided.

I gasped and put a gained-weight hand over my mouth.

"I'm artsy fartsy, and this is even too artsy fartsy for me. Is there more or is it just this?" they said.

"I thought his stuff was supposed to be fun."

"TURN THE MUSIC ON!" Charlie Quick shouted and charged toward an orchestra that flinched and picked up their bows in one motion and started to play. They were hooked to speakers around the room. They didn't sound classical, they sounded like a human body full of nerves. I lowered my gained-weight hand and shook it near my pocket. I thought about wishing I had a gun to draw, then I imagined getting shot and didn't care. My shaking hand retarded.

Then the elf was sprinkling catnip around for the white cats; he had a terrifying little pouch. My shaking hand restarted. Christmas approached me frowning.

"Haircutter!" he said, spreading his arms and stopping on thousand-dollar soles.

"What?" I said.

"Have you been going to museums?" he said.

I said, "No?"

"HAVE YOU BEEN GOING TO MUSEUMS OR LOOK-ING AT ART BOOKS?" he said.

"No," I said. "Why?"

Charlie Quick went to whisper in Christmas's ear.

The early-comers multiplied and multiplied again and made a din that multiplied in the same pompous fashion.

Christmas said, louder, "I don't *understand*, Haircutter! There's something *queer* going on here! I almost don't believe that that work is yours!"

Now the elf was standing at the edge of the spotlight's glow, *staring at me.*

"*He intimidates me,*" I had said. "*I don't need a girlfriend. Scram!*"

My teeth started chattering.

"You don't like the piece?" I said.

"Noooooo!" Mr. Christmas stated.

"Oh wow," I said with farts suddenly puttering out of me. "Hell, I'm sorry. Do you think it'll sell?"

"My buyers want The Haircutter! This work looks like you're taking the piss out of them! We want a *Haircutter* piece!" he started pacing. "You were the real thing! You were an *original!* And now you've ruined it!"

"Well boo fuckin' hoo, Santy Clause!" I said.

Christmas held out a hand as if to show me to Charlie Quick, "I can't even laugh at him anymore. I used to think he was so funny."

"Get that fuckin' elf outta here!" I shouted.

"Get the hell out!" I pointed at Siedle and he ran to Charlie Quick and hugged onto his leg. Charlie whispered in Christmas's ear again.

Christmas said, "My lawyer is telling me to stop talking. Siedle, go home."

A set of elevator doors opened up that I didn't know were there and a group of people blinked into the room.

"How was the ride?!" Christmas said, walking toward them.

He was doing helicopter rides to and from the Thank You Gallery for the elitest of the elite. A woman riding a dying alligator came out of the elevator last. Quick gave me an apologetic frown as Siedle took off his curly shoes and had normal feet. He put on kids' tennis shoes and took off his jingle bell hat and got into a cab. And just like that he proved that there is no such thing as elves. I snarled and took out a toothpick and crossed my arms to rest them on my stomach while The Haircutter looked around.

There were school buses backed up unloading jacketed people for the party. There were candles on ten-foot-tall sticks; there were camera flashes; there were gleams on the golden ashtrays standing around the black room; gleams on eyeglasses; gleams on diamonds when they tossed the seas within them as ladies laughed. Party-comers had come to see The Haircutter's latest. The light of their cell phones lit their ho-hum faces as they descended the platform stairs after looking down on my failed piece of shit. *Anna-Patrick!* Charlie Quick stood at the bottom of the stairs passing out invitation cards for the next Thank You Gallery opening: it said LOXER VEER presents LOXER'S GRANDMOTHER and had a picture of a naked old woman vomiting into a potted plant while keeping a lit cigarette going in the corner of her mouth. A SERIES OF PORTRAITS AND VIDEOS, it said.

"Ooh, Loxer Veer's the best!" they said.

There were opinions held and opinions given, there were tampons held inside of women, there were dead foxes, dead rabbits, dead minks, the alligator died, there were people who were dead inside, people living-the-life, people who'd grabbed their keys off their living room mantels before coming out tonight, there were professions of every enviable type—all there to get a load of the genius Haircutter because everyone knows they need artists in order to have something on the wall above their beds. It was a nightmare I had no choice but to wait to wake up from. Frankincense and myrrh burned thick atop the top hats of failed-actor caterers: nightmare. The mouth of the borderless black room swallowed tuxes and dresses and con men and princesses, who greeted each other like "*Que the hell pasa!*" or "*Say, Mama!*" or "*I didn't catch the name!*": nightmare. Some of them were the type to not mind a cold ocean, and some were the type who'd rather not get in. Some had made money at desks for so long that they knew how to flip a pen in the space above their hand and catch it. Women walked into the warehouse wearing gowns that rushed against their legs like night rain on curbs. They gently took cigs out of their mouths to say, "Pretty kitties," on clouds of smoke. My testicles hid fearfully in my stomach fat near the one dollar in my pocket: nightmare.

Nightmare: maybe Scott Harp was off climbing Mount Everest somewhere? With Carol riding on his head? And my scissor in his back pocket? And panty-free Carol had her skirt over his eyes with holes cut in it so he could see? So she came and came on his head again and again as he ascended?

In between flashes of people walking by and brushing past me, and in between moths from people's attics that they got their fur coats out of brushing past me, I looked for a wheelchair—*where was she?!* I got faked-out by a wheelchair with that guy in it who has his wrists up by his head like gnats on a peach—"Ach, get out of here!" I said. I even saw Planet Head from my first train ride in New York City—"How *New York*—now get out of my face!"

Christmas was petting his white cats so hard their fur was coming off completely. He stripped each cat down to a pink excuse for an animal, then tossed it and grabbed another one. People inhaled cat hair and coughed it out or swigged it down with champagne.

"I never knew I liked lutefisk pâté!" I said, walking up to him. "Now where the hell are Carol and Harp?"

He said, "Come meet Laaren Ray."

Laaren Ray looked like a cat that stretched and got stuck. She walked like a ladybug over to us. Her eyes stuck out of their sockets like golf balls. She had an entire bouquet of flowers behind one of her ears and she held a knife in her hand.

"Hello!" she said to Christmas. "Hello!" she said to me, holding out her knifeless hand.

"Why do you have a *knife?*" I said.

She looked offended.

"He's kidding!" Christmas said.

"The work isn't like your others," she said. "What's the genesis for this one?"

I remembered the gist of the answers that Christmas had printed out for me on a sheet once.

"For this piece, I wanted to focus on more of an underlying sense of what I thought was a trajectory that made more sense to me in terms of speaking to what I originally felt compelled to make at the start of my experimenting with installation works, so for here I was processing more about dancing upon the line between obvious and more subtle. Including a Freudian slip toward my grandfather," I said.

"Hmm," said Laaren Ray, and then she took up a boring conversation with Christmas about someone else's piece they'd recently seen, and they said all the same things that I'd just said but in a different order.

"Did you catch that Freudian slip toward her relative?" Christmas said.

"I sure did," said Laaren Ray. "She *must* be a genius."

We did the same thing with Valter Konig.

"This work speaks to consumerism," I added.

He checked his watch and barely looked at me.

I looked back at the scaffolding—people were walking up and down the stairs and not stopping long to view the piece. And no one was climbing down into the sinkhole to catch the vagina twat.

I interrupted Christmas to say, "Tell people they can climb down into the piece. It's what the ladder's for."

Christmas laughed a fake laugh for the first time ever.

"I've gotta run," said Valter Konig. "But good luck."

He shook our hands and Christmas said, "Fuck," under his breath.

Then we talked to The Jewells. James Jewell had a red beard that reached the floor. Kara Jewell had E-cup breasts and a hooked nose with a small witch's cauldron pierced to the tip of it—there was a boiling brew and the green fumes went up her nose and came out of her mouth when she spoke.

"The scale is definitely titanic," she said.

"Kara, you flatter me," Christmas said, braiding James's beard casually.

"Don't make me laugh, my potion will spill," she said. "So why is it called *The Headstone?*"

"Do you know my old girlfriend Carol Mary Mathers?" I said.

"Yes, of course!" Kara said. "I love Carol! Is she here?"

"Let me ask Quick," Christmas said and blew on a whistle from his pocket.

Charlie Quick appeared, "Yes?"

"Where are Carol and Harp?"

"In the chopper," Quick said. "Should be here any minute."

"Have The Jewells gotten an invitation for the Loxer Veer show?" Christmas asked.

I charged toward the elevator and stared at the unlit red light above it.

"That sculpture's bullshit," I heard people say.

"I could do that," some people said.

"I'm sick of when people suck," I heard.

"Let's either go, or get drunk," they decided.

"He's nothing without Carol."

The red light dinged red and the elevator doors opened up.

And there she was.

In a braided-handled nineteenth-century wheelchair.

She was bickering with Harp.

Then she saw me.

Her lipstick looked like she'd just eaten someone.

My heart beat in my head, my hands, my legs, my chest, the air around my fat mass. She was in a blue dress—with a kneehole cut for her boner calf. Light winked off a crystal shoe; pearls were tied around the ankle in a bow; the leg was swathed in fishnet hose. She swiped it side-to-side like a windshield wiper and then stopped it with the crystal shoe covering her face so I couldn't look at her.

Upon seeing Carol dressed like everyone else: the shattering of a spell I'd been in.

"Carol, shut cher mouth before yer guts spill out," I said.

"I didn't even say anything!" she shouted.

"Harp. You know what I came here for," I said.

"I ain't going back with you, psycho!" Carol said.

"Good! Cause I don't like short girls!"

Scott Harp came around Carol to stand between us—he yanked on his lapels as if it would hurt me that his suit fit so well.

I said, "How's Harpy? You got a surprise for me in your pants?"

"Huh?" he said.

"He knows! I saw you!" we heard.

We looked, and Finn was charging towards us, pointing at Harp, wearing a collared shirt with rubber duckies on it.

"You saw me what?" Harp said.

"Ladies and Gentlemen!" we heard.

We looked and Christmas was holding a microphone over by *The Headstone*—the mic was the kind like a stick with a ball on the tip.

"I'm Mr. Christmas."

Everyone cheered till their voice boxes popped and confetti shot out of their mouths.

"Welcome to the unveiling of The Haircutter's *The Headstone.*"

Not as many people cheered.

Christmas walked up the wooden stairs to speak from the platform—his dress shoes scuffed the wood and sparks came off.

Half the heads in the room rotated toward me, shining the light of their diamonds.

Seconds dripped like diamonds onto The Haircutter's head.

Finn whispered, "You should go up there. I don't think people like your piece. Try to show them the way."

I walked through the crowd and it parted like Josiah's sea, or whatever the Bible saw fit.

"Excuse me," I said.

People smiled at me like flowers that look alive but are dead.

"It's toast time," Christmas said.

I climbed the stairs toward him, and people followed up to gather around and drape on the stairs like orphans cause we're gonna tell a story. The party looked floating on a black sea of tar—the candles were torches, the eyes were unextinguished souls. The red dots were recording me. Nightmare. Christmas placed a hand on my shoulder like an unexploded bomb. He handed the mic to me as cameras begun to flash.

"Hello."

The Haircutter didn't belong. His voice was a western river in a hailstorm, a mosquito hovering over it. A battered pastoral flow beneath a buzzing. His river boomed. Seven echoes. His eyes were like bright bird eggs found in tufts of twilit grass, dewed.

"Thank you for coming," I said, and handed the mic back to Christmas. I looked to Carol and Harp and saw them watching me smugly because they could tell something was off—*Why don't people like my piece?* I thought.

I turned around to see it.

"Hey!" I said.

Christmas stopped talking.

"It broke!"

It was a stupid box filled with dirt!!!

"What?" he whispered.

The hole had collapsed completely and covered Carol. The box was filled with dirt. There was a ladder sticking out of it.

"That's not the piece," I said.

The tip of a ladder sticking out of a box of dirt!

Christmas put his hands on his knees and screamed, "WHAT?!" It bursted every speaker in the room. Women flinched in slow motion as their diamond earrings burst.

"It collapsed!" I told them.

A lady screamed.

She was sitting on the stairs, pointing at the piece.

The orchestra throbbed a ten-part harmony as the center of *The Headstone* started to sink.

An elegant, tan hand burst through the dirt.

Photographers lit it with flashes.

The hand extended a long arm like a graveyard movie.

A second hand emerged—

two elbows bent to pull out a brown-haired head.

An overbite cracked open, gasping—

it was Anna-Patrick.

"WHAT?!" I shouted.

She labored hard, going, "GUUUUUUH!!!!" and pulled her long body out.

She rose to seven feet of height, unfurling upwards.

Her face was covered in blood, her breath was heaving, her hair was slop.

She was wearing Carol's lace duster dress—it went to her mid-thighs and had a *C* on the chest.

[..................]

Like a thunderclap—the house showered her with rain; they deleted her with flash pics.

She scratched at the dress and reached back to unzip it; it slipped to the earth like a wisp of hair and revealed her naked body like a camera pop. Her pubic hair was a mass of black bigger and wilder than I ever knew pubes could be—they used her legs as a trellis to display their humbling beauty. I got down on my knees. Carol's pubes were downy and barely there—Anna-Patrick's were an ode to Women.

I looked to Carol: "That's my dress!" she was screaming.

I looked to Christmas: he was pressed back against the wood railing with tears streaming. "Oh god!" he said, orgasming at the sight of such art.

"Anna-Patrick!" I said and held out my hand and she saw me and remembered: that's Him.

She stepped forward and climbed the short rungs of ladder and collapsed into my fat arms. The photographers closed in to shoot Carol's blood-crusted dress on the sunken center of the sixteen-foot box of dirt. Everyone applauded so hard their hands started bleeding and splattering their faces with blood.

"What in the dang hell, Girly?" I said.

"You were supposed to sleep in there," she said in my ear. "I was going to surprise you for a talk. It collapsed on the road. I woke up a little bit ago. I found a slice of air to breathe in. I waited until your toast. I love you," she said.

"I love you!" I said.

We kissed. They deleted us with flash pics.

"Carol, no!" Charlie Quick screamed as Carol was pulling herself up the stairs by her arms like a piece of snail meat.

"That's MY dress and MY Haircutter!" she screamed.

Charlie Quick picked her up and passed her to Scott Harp, "Do NOT let her vandalize the art," he said.

When Harp turned around, I saw my scissor sticking out of his back pocket.

"HEY!" I bellowed.

Christmas was pouring champagne down Anna-Patrick's throat.

"Come on!" I yelled and took her hand and she choked.

We ran down the stairs and I leapt forward and snatched my scissor out of Harp's back pocket and landed on my stomach for the most pleasant honk to shoot out of my mouth.

"Your scissors!" Anna-Patrick said.

Photographers flew over us on pulley harnesses like Peter Pan.

I stood up and shouted, "This is my future wife! And the woman I lost my virginity to! Look how tall she is!"

I cut off a lock of her bloody hair and threw it up into the air.

"Yes!" she said.

"Do me!" someone screamed. I ran and cut that woman's hair too.

"Mine! Mine!" I heard.

"I want a haircut!" I heard.

"The Haircutter—over here! Cut my wife's hair!"

"I'm coming!" I screamed. I ran through the crowd cutting hair and throwing locks up into the air.

"Do yours!" they told me.

I cut my own hair and threw the lock up into the air where it separated like a firework.

AND THEN